GABO DJARA

Also by B. Wongar

Walg
Karan

GABO DJARA

A NOVEL OF AUSTRALIA

B. WONGAR

GEORGE BRAZILLER

NEW YORK

The author acknowledges receiving a Senior Writer's Fellowship grant from the Literature Board of the Australia Council, which made this book possible.

For information, write to the publisher:
George Braziller, Inc.
60 Madison Avenue
New York, New York 10010

Library of Congress Cataloging-in-Publication Data

Wongar, B.
Gabo Djara.

1. Australian aborigines—Fiction. I. Title.
PR9619.3.W62G3   1987   823   87-9055
ISBN: 0-8076-1243-X

First paperback printing 1991
Designed by Claire Counihan
Manufactured in the United States of America

At Namanama
country of Gabo Djara
monster gulps boulders
        quicker he eats
        sooner he dies.

—Tribal chant
from Arnhem Land

THIS book is fiction. However, according to Aboriginal mythology, Gabo Djara, an immense green ant and the spiritual ancestor of local tribes, created the natural environment of West Arnhem Land and set the pattern of human life. He retired to the Dreaming, the spirit world, with the prophecy that should his sacred totemic site be disturbed, he would rise again, monstrous, to harass the intruders. At that tribal land the white man found a uranium deposit, believed to be one of the richest on this earth.

The traditional Aboriginal drawings of plants in this volume are by Yumayna Burarwana from Arnhem Land.

To
Prue Grieve

Introduction

SOME years before I began to write this book I met a man who was related to trees. He told me that the plants were his tribal family and would turn up with help when needed. When out to cure a tribal soul a tree could walk from one country to another and sneak inside a jail compound. "With trees about, no *yuln* suffers pain," he claimed. The whites called him *galwiri*, nut; but that might not have been his real name—perhaps they thought it was.

I had perpetual diarrhea and wished the plants could help me, though none was in sight. Our cell had a small window which, being high up, looked into the sky and gave no view of the bush. Lack of a view hardly mattered to Galwiri, though; he woke me one night to say that the plants were on the way, led by a dingo—his tribal ancestor. "They will be here in no time," he whispered, and named a number of plants which have *dal*, magic to heal diarrhea. I went to sleep thinking that if I were in the bush the plants would indeed cure me, for I had learned before that, in the hands of a good tribal healer, man is seldom left to suffer.

When I woke the following morning, Galwiri was drawing on the concrete floor the hollowed-out trunk of a large stringybark tree. I was told that in the bush dingoes suffer from pain in their belly just as often as humans, and howl for help. A hollow stringybark will answer the call and tell the distressed animal where to go and chew its bark. When seeking a cure, humans have to crush the bark between stones in order to break it down, for no man has teeth as powerful as the dingo's. While he drew with a small stone, Galwiri kept his eyes closed and hummed the words of a chant. Later on that day I watched him looking at an ant which was crawling across the drawing. I was told that to reach us the dingo had to assume a new shape, and even if anyone noticed it, the whites would take no notice of an ant. In the bush Galwiri was brought up to be a tribal healer; he knew not only about plants, but about the way his spiritual ancestors moved about.

With no apparent relief to my troubled stomach that day, Galwiri assumed that I might not be related to the Stringybark clan. The following day he drew a pandanus and, while humming a new chant, pretended that he was chopping down the tree and removing leaves and bark, and then handing to me the inner core of the trunk to chew. It was about dusk when we finished with the healing ritual; I could not see the ant on the floor, but on the wall opposite the small window there fluttered a shadow, and looking at it for a while I thought I saw a pair of pricked dingo ears. That night Galwiri admitted that the plants are not so fast in healing a man they do not know well. He drew a Medicine Bean next and tried Wild Asparagus, Emu Berry, and scores of others. I heard him often at night whispering an old tribal chant to praise the plant for its sweet nectar, good crop of fruit, and the deep shade provided on hot sunny days. He pleaded with them to accept me as their skin relative: "Poor stricken fellow, he will be good to you." The trees must have answered his plea, for I woke the following morning feeling cured.

I might never see Galwiri again; before I met him in the jail a government medical officer had certified him, allegedly for some strange mental behavior but, as at that time there were no appropriate psychiatric institutions in the Northern Territory to hold him, he was placed in jail. From the day I parted from him I have looked on the plants as my skin relatives and call on them whether I suffer from toothache or a dislocated toe, just as the wise old healer had taught me.

Dingoes Den, 1980

PART ONE

Chapter 1

IT was neither the best time nor the best place to be reborn. When Gabo Djara, the green ant, broke out from his cocoon, the world around had no time for welcome. The Speaker of the House terminated the morning prayers with "Amen," and as he led the parliamentarians into debate, the House assumed an air of business. There was no one to hold his cocoon so Gabo Djara must struggle, alone, to crawl out into the world: he clung to the concrete surface with his front legs, but whenever he plunged forward, making a final effort to free himself, the cover followed. He had no trouble thrusting out his head and thorax, but his abdomen stuck fast behind. Gabo Djara stumbled across the floor of the public gallery so it was lucky for him that Parliament sat in camera and no member of the public was present to step upon him. Presently he came to a marble bust of Queen Victoria and struggled up the cold figure of the Monarch and along the neck. By squeezing under an ear and wedging the cocoon against the edge of the lobe,

Gabo Djara pushed himself free and forced his body out of captivity.

Through the windows of the Parliament House gallery the distant hills could be seen covered in fleecy snow under a stony sky, and though Gabo Djara did not object to being reborn, he would have preferred tropical bush and warm ground to frosty hills and a concrete floor. It was the will of mighty *jingana*, the spiritual mother, that he had been brought into the world again, however, and if it was not as a human, then it must be in whatever shape she wished.

Gabo Djara rested for a little, passing his feelers up and down the bristled upper part of his legs to furbish them and contemplated the world around—so uncertain, strange, and incomprehensible. He climbed, then, and walked along the balustrade, stopping now and then to rear up and stare about him; below, in the main chamber, the white men were so busy with their rituals it seemed inconceivable that they would let themselves be disturbed by the likes of Gabo Djara, so unobtrusive and possessed of no voice at all. Gabo Djara crawled along the green wall of the chamber and down onto the Royal Arms, above the Speaker's chair—attracted to the carved and cracked old wood as a promising hunting ground. He paused for a while, feelers swaying, hoping to detect the presence of food—a borer possibly, or a dead moth—but the wood had a strange acid smell which irritated his antenna and made him feel quite dizzy.

Some of the parliamentarians must finally have noticed Gabo Djara, for a few back-benchers began to giggle, and to glance in his direction in an amused way which angered the Speaker. He slammed his gavel so hard on the bench, calling the House to order, that the echoing blows within such thick walls terrified Gabo Djara and he dashed back behind the Royal Arms to hide in the shadows. Through a crack in the wood the ant's bulging eyes peeped to spy on what game the humans played.

One of the ministers was presenting a bill; and on the volume he held, the title Uranium could be clearly seen. Next he placed a large grayish rock on the folded file and took it around the chamber, stopping for each member to clasp his hand upon the stone and to whisper passionately, "Aye."

The whites were giving their allegiance to the rock, which Gabo Djara assumed must be their god. The rock, however, looked much the same as that he had seen at Namanama, his tribal country, and filled with nostalgia, the ant craned his head unwisely from the sheltering wood, trying to see more clearly. As soon as he appeared in the light, however, the sergeant-at-arms rushed forward with a tin of insecticide emitting a jet of misty chemical which forced Gabo Djara back to shelter. For a moment or two he crouched motionless, the tip of one feeler stinging from the burning touch of acid, then, not pausing to brush this off, he looked around for a way out. Why are they hunting me? I have bitten no man.

Gabo Djara could hardly have wished for a better place to hide than in the Speaker's wig, and hoping to reach this he jumped to the floor and paused a while in the shadow of the seat, the Speaker's chair, where he felt safe, if only for a short time. The sergeant-at-arms was still blowing chemicals from his tin, directing the spray into all the furthest cracks and corners of the Royal Coat of Arms and whispering, "Come out, Oecophylla smaragdina—I'll get you yet." That must be how balanda, whites, call the green ant. Gabo Djara halted with his antenna feelers swaying slowly while trying to memorize the words which sounded unfamiliar. Though he had been in the bush ever since rocks and trees came to be about, and he had been hailed and ceremonially sung to by every tribal soul, none had ever addressed him as Oecophylla smaragdina; the words sounded hard even for a spirit to remember. Above him blasted the misty jet of insecticide directed by the white hand and partly coating him with a strange fluid. Gabo Djara had no time to clean his feelers, though the top of one was painfully burned, so he swung this behind his head to protect it as he crawled up the chair.

The ant was only halfway up, however, when the House rose for recess and the Speaker walked solemnly out, followed by the rest of the parliamentarians. Gabo Djara crept under a flap on one arm of the chair and peeped out. From this vantage point, he could see the sergeant-at-arms busily searching through papers on the table and peering into every corner of a pair of dispatch boxes, squirting gusts of chemical vapor as he probed. Instead of the small tin of insecticide the man now used a knapsack pump slung on his back, and wielded the attached nozzle on a long rod with great dexterity as he moved about the chamber.

The exit door was open, and Gabo Djara was deciding whether it would be safer to make a dash for it or to tiptoe slowly over the green-tiled floor, when he sighted the silhouette of the Usher of the Black Rod waiting in the corridor. The man dressed in ceremonial finery stood stiffly, his beady eyes riveted to the floor, hardly blinked—as a hawk waiting for prey. The rod in the human's hand rose ready to strike. Gabo Djara warned himself to tread carefully. The whites can set more traps than a tribal soul could ever envisage.

When the parliamentary sitting resumed, Gabo Djara again headed toward the Speaker's wig. First he made his way along the man's sleeve, keeping to the shady side, until he could reach the shoulder. Once, as the Speaker's arm waved in the air, the ant was forced to cling to the garment with all his six legs and to flatten his body so that he would not be blown off into space. When he had reached the shoulder at last and was about to climb into the Speaker's wig, the man's head moved unexpectedly. Gabo Djara lost his hard-won seat on a hair, slid helplessly downward, and landed on the bare skin of the Speaker's neck from where he would have passed unnoticed if the foolish man had not immediately slapped his neck. The ant, suddenly finding himself squashed between skin and wig, injected a sting from his abdomen without even knowing that he had released it.

The incident was probably not recorded in Hansard, but it certainly caused a furor as the Speaker threw down his wig and danced upon it while Gabo Djara made a rapid escape and took a shortcut across the floor to the nearest bookcase. As he climbed, his bulging eyes glanced back to see if he was being followed. The House was in uproar and members crossed the floor in droves to watch the sergeant-at-arms stamping on the Speaker's wig and then plunge it into a bucket full of insecticide. He watched the whites raising their fists and shouting, "Get the bloody assassin." The alarm bell rang persistently, metallically frightening. Both of Gabo Djara's feelers grew stiff for a while then quivered. Will I ever find my way out of here? He felt somehow that if he did not end in the bucket of insecticide the road out would be painful and long, perhaps more strenuous than any soul or tree had ever gone through in his tribal country. The bell still rang but weakened for a while to let a husky voice be heard: "Sergeant, have the House searched." The voice sounded calm as though it belonged to someone from outside the chamber—a man above the humans.

Searching through the bookcase for a place to hide, the ant came across the face of a man printed on the jacket of one of the volumes—a face scarcely different in color from the whites but it had a pair of penetrating eyes, though the dreamlike expression reminded Gabo Djara of a child who has ventured into a world far beyond the time it lives in. The ant paused—had he met anyone whom he should know? The man on the book cover did not look immortal, yet Gabo Djara felt sure he was facing someone whose mind could reach out to a world where no balanda had been before. Below him the large lettering, Healing the Nuclear Rot, smelled of fresh print. The book, partly open, showed some of the pages as well. With bulging eyes the ant peeped inside to the photograph of a woman. The whites have always appeared to Gabo Djara like reptile eggs from a single clutch, but the woman had a serene face. Her eyes glowed as though she was searching for something a world away from hers. No tribe had a woman for a healer, but if the one he was looking at now had been born black she could have been the first one. Have I seen her before? In his life, descended from the time when the first boulders came about, he had seen but few whites, whom he was now in no state to remember, for both of his feelers had been drooped by the persistent sound of the bell. The husky voice called out again, then a squad of security men, headed by the Usher of the Black Rod, rushed into the parliamentary chamber to search the place. As they peeped into every crack and borer hole, Gabo Djara chose a large volume, The Abolition of Slavery Act, 1833, as his hiding place. A layer of dust covered the book as if it had never been opened; silverfish had found their way inside the volume and had chewed away the pages to form a hollow most suitable for a fugitive ant. Gabo Djara crawled in, thinking as he did so that in the whole of Parliament House there could not be a safer place for him to hide. But as he lay hidden there, his fear began to grow, for perhaps the book was a trap, set to catch him just as its subject had snared so many of his tribesmen.

Outside the alarm bell still rang. Now it reminded him of a desperate insect trapped in a web.

Chapter 2

I T was not, at first, obvious to Gabo Djara that he had trodden upon the sacred ground of the white man. The place was a ghostly dim hall, and the acrid smell of stale tobacco lingered in the stagnant air, but the ant had learned not to be choosy about the place in which he must live. There was no tree to climb; there were no leaves to mold and sew together with larval silk into a cozy bivouac. Luck came Gabo Djara's way, however, in the shape of scraps of discarded paper—parts of Stock Exchange reports, terms, and figures—and these he carried high up to the topmost ledge of a blackboard. It was not difficult to join the paper fragments to make a cone-shaped shelter, but much silken thread was needed to bind the pieces and to reinforce the structure, and there is a limit to what a lone worker-ant can achieve, unaided.

The top of the bidding board proved to be an excellent vantage point. The hall below was not open for trading, but a bunch of computers hummed, warming themselves up for a hectic time ahead. The public gallery above them looked empty and silent, reminding Gabo Djara so much of *marain*, the sacred cave at the foot of Mount Mogo, that he felt eerily disturbed. Thoughts of the cave, the place where Marngit kept his *murga*, dilly bag, and other ritual objects full of *dal*, magic power, which breathed life into all beings and could heal withering humans, brought a moment of silent respect upon the ant's mind. It was only a moment, however, for his empty crop craved food and sent both feelers again searching in space. Far below, between the chalkboards and the gallery, lay the trading hall, and in this chasm stood a battery of dormant computers. The machines were undoubtedly of use to *balandas*, but their shape, color, and smell meant little to the ant, for chewing steel or plastic promised no comfort for an empty belly. Gabo Djara considered the computer machines grown-up beings but capable of doing only what they were told by their white masters. He crawled across the board still searching for food, passing over numerous figures which had been written in chalk during the previous day's trading and which, although they had aroused many emotions in the breasts of the whites, were of little moment to the ant. In a wastepaper basket on the floor, Gabo Djara found the remains of a peppery sandwich, but the crumbs exuded such a peculiar odor that the ant suspected the whites of having set a trap to poison him. There was something else, though . . . Gabo Djara's twitching feelers detected a strong acrid smell which he finally traced to the butt of a cigar.

The place felt eerie in the persistent silence. A picture of the man the ant had seen earlier on the cover of the book hung on the wall with large gilded lettering: P. RECLUSE— HE MADE THE MIRACLE POSSIBLE. *Balanda* had a dark bushy beard and had it not been for his penetrating gaze, Gabo Djara would have mistaken him for a white missionary he met in the bush some years ago. At Namanama the recluse had a hut. It was made of saplings leaning against a boulder covered with branches to keep the sun out. Gabo Djara had peeped inside the shelter once to find out what the white stranger was up to. The man slept on an armful of straw and had a tree stump to sit on. He had a picture of that serene white woman whom the ant had seen lately in the book drawn on the surface of the rock with a piece of charcoal. Skin different, though, the woman reminded Gabo Djara of Wawalag Sister painted on the wall of the *marain* cave at the foot of Mount Mogo. The resemblance made Gabo Djara think that the serene woman must be his foremother. No man should be prevented from worshiping an ancestor from whom his clan must have descended; this was held strongly in the mind of every Green Ant soul as well as in the neighboring Dingo people country, for both of the tribes had descended from a single mother— Wawalag. As a maiden, Wawalag traveled through the land with *waran*, a dingo. That happened not long after the boulders were made, and trees and animals came to life, but tribal man was not thereabout yet. While camping at a water hole Wawalag made a hut and gave birth to a boy, hoping to begin a new tribe. She failed to clean the afterbirth blood from the ground, though; rain came on later that night and washed the stain down into the water hole that was the home of Jingana serpent. In the bush dingoes are more wary than humans; *waran* howled trying to warn of the danger, but by the time Wawalag woke up, the serpent, lured by the smell of human blood, had coiled around the hut and it soon swallowed the newly born child and the mother—it gulped *waran* as well.

While in the bush Gabo Djara grew fond of Recluse; the man worshiping a woman who looked much like Wawalag was welcome to make hut and stay at Namanama forever. Why did the whites hang him? asked the ant, now looking at the wall of the trading hall, but soon realized he was facing a life-size picture, not a human.

The ant, strolling around in search of food, reared up to glance at the wall later on again. Am I trespassing? He assumed that Recluse might have been made guardian of the place and had wandered off, leaving behind his picture to remind intruders to stay away from the sacred ground. Would he mind seeing an old friend from the bush scavenging around? The man looked well fed and healthy, and the ant expected him to show some gratitude to people from the bush who helped him heal his wounds, though it had happened monsoons ago.

When the floor was opened for trading, four Stock Exchange clerks wheeled in a trolley and placed it opposite the bidding boards. On royal blue velvet, upon the trolley, reposed a small boulder, its raw surfaces fresh with the bloom of rock lately blasted from a larger mass, but one side . . . one side . . . Gabo Djara grew dizzy, for the marks that he could see on the stone showed that it must have come from Namanama, his tribal country. Though the hand-drawn lines were faint and some of the *malnor*, red ocher, had been worn away until they looked like faded bloodstains, the details were familiar. The rock had come from a sacred cave at Mount Ngaliur and had been a part of Gabo Djara's existence since the beginnings of tribal man. The painting showed Wawalag giving birth at the water hole with the dingo howling at the night. On the boulder down on the trolley hardly anything of it was seen but a few red spots marking the blood which had lured the serpent.

The remains of the sacred boulder saddened Gabo Djara, for it was there at the cave that the tribal elders gather to initiate the youth; they gather also when needing to remove a curse which might have been cast upon man or country. The ant had seen them often clapping *bilma* sticks against boomerangs to plead to him and other spirits' ancestors that no man should be left to suffer unduly, even one whose skin looked different.

Both of his feelers drooping with sadness, the ant looked down from his perch on the board, measuring the distance across the floor to the rock, but he quickly decided against trying to make the journey, for a trampling crowd of people had gathered around the trolley. Some of these had magnifying apparatus in their hands with which they examined, minutely, the surface of the rock as if unwilling to miss one single detail. Behind them, others shoved and elbowed their way forward to look; some pleaded in pathetic whispers to be allowed close enough for one quick glance. It was best to wait—Gabo Djara was loath to be trodden upon and to finish as a stain on a white man's heel.

Why should these people be so besotted about a rock? It had rough bare surfaces which could give no one, not even an insect, the hope of a meal, but no . . . on the edge of the rock was the green blot of a squashed leaf. It was not much but it might be enough to sustain an ant, for a day or two. Gabo Djara waited for the crowd to move away from the trolley and then began his descent. The clerk was already at his post, listing the names of securities: Black Uranium, Wawalag Mining, Namanama Prospecting. All appeared quickly under his hissing chalk, then more and more so that, as the ant crawled slowly downward, try as he might to find his way around the letters, the endless line of chalk crossed and recrossed his path. White dust from the words and figures formed a thick crust on his feelers . . . the left one quivered and itched . . . but not because of the chalk. Was it a sign? The ant stood still for a moment; perhaps the message came from *marngit*. Yes . . . Gabo Djara could not know how deep into the white man's world he had slipped, but however distant the tribal country might be, it seemed that the medicine man was in need of him. Maybe the elders were gathered for festivities, or perhaps *wardu*, the malevolent spirits, had stricken Namanama. Down on the floor a tall, dignified man made his way toward the rock. He had a white headdress which contrasted with his dark face. For a moment the ant thought of seeing his countryman and stretched both of the feelers to the limit. He assumed that the man had come to acquire the boulder and take it back to the sacred cave from where it had been plundered. Would the collar be *marngit* in disguise—the medicine man moves at will, talks lingo never heard of before, and puts on *balanda* clothes under which he must hide a spear-thrower. The thrower is small and cylindrically shaped and hides a spear inside, which no victim can see till it is pointed at him and then it is too late to tell anyone what the magic weapon looks like. A chubby *balanda* with a pair of mustaches, thick and white, bowed courteously as the man in the head-dress approached the rock: "It's a great pleasure to see Your Highness here—this is promising to be a great trading day." The visitor made a polite gesture but spoke no word. When out seeking a victim the medicine man remains mute, re-membered Gabo Djara. He moved further down the board, crossing Boomerang Exploration and Mogo Mining, and then, catching up with the clerk as he wrote Corroboree Uranium, the ant paused to groom his feelers. This display of bravado caught the attention of the clerk, however; his hand grew still, he stared for a moment and then, placing his fingernail under Gabo Djara's thorax, flicked the ant high in the air.

Gabo Djara landed on the top of the board, rolled over, and stood on his legs, shaking with fury. He looked downward to the floor to see if anyone had noticed the incident, but the staring people were occupied with the numbers, not with him. There were fewer people around the trolley now. The head-dress man moved away without anyone noticing his magic spear. The chubby host still moved about. "This could be the greatest boom to go down in history," he now spoke to a woman. It would be a while before Chubby feels pain—only people struck by lightning die instantly; hit by *marngit*'s spear, a victim could carry on for days before he falls down. The woman to whom the host spoke felt uneasy about the head-dress man; she slid her hand over the boulder as one would do to a piece of ceremonial finery: "You would not be selling this treasure to that Sheik Dollari." The host cautioned her that they were in public and pretended to be busy flicking off a speck of dust from the velvet, saying, "The Arabs could be our best customers; they could afford to buy the mountain." The woman wore a long fur coat at which the ant gazed with his bulging eyes. The garment smelled of Namanama but he failed to tell from whose back it might have been skinned. As she moved around the boulder the coat swung. "I don't like . . . those foreigners," she said. Chubby patted the rock, explaining that a good sale is worth its weight in gold, from whomever it might come. Besides, Sheik $-i could hardly be a foreigner, his ancestors have traded with Europe before Christ and they gave the civilized world the skill of numbers: "Without counting, my dear lady, we would not have gone any further than those Abos in the bush." The woman held that one must be fair when talking about people from the bush for they gave no rocks to foreigners. Sympathetic though she sounded, Gabo Djara felt certain that the coat had been fashioned from a tribal soul; it had a pungent smell which ran strongly against his feelers. Chubby explained that the Abos had dealt with the foreigners also, and looking at Recluse's picture on the wall, explained that he was helped by the natives in discovering the find. "That mountain—is worth its weight in gold." The woman hardly listened to him; she walked around the boulder, then leaning across it, asked, "Have they caught the assassin?" Chubby cautioned her not to talk loudly; he admitted there had been an incident in the Parliamentary chamber and, though the Speaker had been stung by *Oecophylla Smaragdina* no man had ever died from a green ant sting—the Nuclear Bill has been passed and is awaiting Royal Assent. "We shall be out in the bush soon to level the mountain," he said. The woman moved closer to the host: "There is more to it than an ant." She complained that her mink was infested by a strange bug which made balding patches in her fur and which, she asserted, had come from the bush. Chubby told her that the household moths had been about long before the uranium boom and should not be associated with the rocks. Angered, the woman showed a bald patch on her coat, asserting there was a phantom from the bush at large: "I shall be filing a claim for damages." Chubby, looking closely at her mink, held that his corporation could not accept responsibility for what the moth could do to someone's wardrobe, but suggested if the matter was handled discreetly, there could be some amicable settlement. The woman insisted on appropriate reparation and warned if the phantom were allowed to roam at large, no mink would be safe any longer. She was about to raise her voice and warn the crowd on the floor to be on the lookout for a bug from the bush when Chubby suggested that an appropriate garment would be on the way to replace the damaged one. "It has to be from dingo fur." The woman felt determined to settle for nothing less; she lifted her hand, making a gesture to attract the attention of Sheik $-i, claiming that the headdress could be infested by the phantom bug, as well as minks. "We shall get you a polar fox coat," Chubby tried to calm her. The woman preferred dingoes to foxes, claiming they had exclusive fiber and an aura of the desert which nothing else could match. Stroking his mustaches gently, Chubby confessed that no dingo had been sighted for years and the animal was likely to be extinct. The woman lifted her hand again and called out toward Sheik $-i: "Watch out for your headdress!" Chubby explained hastily that some years ago a dingo had appeared at the corporation's mining plant at the Wawalag Ranges; trapped, the animal chewed one of its legs off and fled to the desert. The dingo had been sighted again by P. Recluse who discovered a new uranium find in Wilberforce Gulf area. Hardly anyone else had seen the animal, but Chubby went to some lengths to explain that he personally was told by Recluse, who sold him the find, that the dingo was actually the healer of a tribe that once lived in Wawalag Ranges. Purportedly, the dingo carries the soul of his people under his tongue while seeking a new country where the tribe might thrive again. "There might be a whole pack of them by now, up in the bush," Chubby said optimistically. The woman failed to grasp the story, but the news that the dingoes might still be about calmed her for a time.

The ant looked at the picture of Recluse before strolling again. He felt much easier now, if not completely secure. Since the rock from his tribal country had met such a warm welcome there was no reason why he, a humble intruder, would arouse any hostility. Opposite, in the public gallery, the shape of a tall man wearing a silver safety helmet stood and raised a pair of binoculars. It seemed, at first, as though he, too, was watching the rock, but as the ant moved along the edge of the board, the binoculars shifted, too, tracking him. The thought that he was being followed hit Gabo Djara hard; if the whites were keeping him under surveillance, he might never be able to get to the rock, where those few fragments of squashed leaf represented the only available food, and his means of survival. The ant looked around in vain for something the same color as his skin, upon which to crawl and so camouflage himself against the prying gaze of the man with the binoculars. The only possibility presenting itself, however, was to climb downward on the shadow side of the bidding board, and at the bottom, to hide there behind a box of the clerks' chalks on a small ledge. The spot, about halfway to the rock, seemed likely to be within reach of the scent of the crushed leaf and was probably sheltered from the view of the man in the gallery.

The very moment that Gabo Djara began to climb down, trading took a rapid upsurge; as he crawled over the chalked figure $99, a sponge erased it and the clerk quickly scrawled three figures there instead. Though he tried again and again to cross part of the board, the figures were changing faster than the ant could traverse the bidding square. Then . . . the itch began again in his feeler. Gabo Djara cast his mind to Namanama, the tribal country . . . a bulldozer bit its way through the pandanus thickets at the foot of Mount Mogo, and, being dragged along behind it was Marngit, the medicine man. From his neck swung a *murga*, a dilly bag, full of *lida*, sacred objects, as he beat together two *bilma*, clapping sticks, and tried to throw his voice within hearing of the spirits. The machine jerked Marngit forward, drowning the sound of his chant with the rattling of the steel plates on its caterpillar treads, and behind them rose a trail of dust which blotted out all but the savage roar of the metal beast tearing the country apart.

His mind still on Namanama, his wounded country, Gabo Djara drifted across the blackboard, swept this way and that by the swift movement of the scribbling chalk. The trading figures spread, rapidly swallowing up the last blank spaces. Down on the floor the bank of computers hummed and, spurred on by the sound of the machines, the white tide of chalk swept higher. As the ant retreated, glancing about for a place to hide, the binoculars followed. Gabo Djara moved one of his feelers, and the silhouette in the helmet swayed a little. The ant paused and then made a dash for the edge of the board, but at that moment two sponges, aimed for the same number, closed in, leaving no alternative but to leap or wait to be squashed.

Gabo Djara's fall on to the clerks' platform landed him beside a sticker marked Trading Suspended and one of his legs became stuck fast on the gluey underside of the tape. The ant struggled to free himself but only became further enmeshed, so he rested quietly, contemplating what would be the wisest course—to chew off his own leg or to let the whites capture him. Down on the floor the woman was busy showing the damaged mink to Sheik $-i and loudly warned the crowd to be on the lookout for Phantom Bug from the bush.

Rocks and plants have lived forever; though the boulders might be older, the trees have grown wiser and have seen their way through drought or emerged from flood to bloom again. No trees die here until hollowed out by time. Even when struck by lightning the sooted trunk makes new shoots in no time. With a bit of luck I might be reborn as a tree and go on to thrive for centuries. That happens out here often—plants are relatives of yuln tribal man, I have been told.

From my shallow cave I can see a green plain descending from the foot of an escarpment. Scattered boulders lie about but there are bushes perching on them, for trees know how to get on with the rocks. As the plain unfolds, a green canopy darkens along a long stretch of billabong to grow into mangroves which, far out on the horizon, fade into—sea or sky, I cannot tell. Each leaf down there holds more secrets than we have ever discovered meddling with the atom. Trees grow often from the side of rocks and hug their roots around boulders to hold on; it matters little if the rock is uranium, and there is enough of that stuff around to mess a whole world—trees have long learned to handle that.

I, too, shall be branching out from the side of a rock, though a friend of mine thinks that no soul has ever died of radioactivity out here: "Plants have seen to it." Her name is Alba. Surprisingly, she is white and a missionary, but when in the bush long enough, plants have their way of winning you over. She was taught by Margnit, medicine man; he holds that people turn into trees, that is how tribal man has been able to learn various remedies which he would never know if he had remained solely human. Whatever shape you might be brought to live in, rocks harm no soul out here. Strangely, we have crushed rocks like this for a century and have tampered with the atom only to learn that it burns our skin and drains our blood.

Chapter 3

IT will never be known what brought Gabo Djara to the palace; perhaps it was the will of Jingana, the mighty tribal creator, or maybe it was the malice of the whites, but nonetheless there he sat in the shadowy nook formed by an acanthus leaf on the capitol of a Corinthian column in the Green Room. His feelers were testing the surrounding air for any imperial aura when, through the open doorway, echoed the voice of the Royal Usher announcing the investiture ceremonial for the newest of Her Majesty's knights, Sir Rock-Pile Ore.

Gabo Djara, feeling that he would rather find a way out of the palace than be concerned with royal pageantry, tried to climb down the column but not one of all his six legs could maintain a hold on the polished surface of green marble, and he slid to the pedestal and rolled to the floor. The fall would have been fatal if the ant's weight had been greater, but as he had been hungry ever since he came into the world, Gabo

Djara's weight was hardly more than that of the air space he occupied, and he hit the floor with the impact of a feather. The tiny movement was, however, detected, and Gabo Djara crawled scarcely a foot across the floral carpet when a monstrous self-propelled anteater in the shape of a vacuum cleaner rushed into the Green Room. From the drumlike belly of the machine protruded a flexible hose looking quite long enough to reach even the most remote corners of the ornate ceiling.

Gabo Djara waited, camouflaged by the green leaves amongst the floral patterns in the carpet. The monster stopped in the middle of the room, its hose upright and swaying like a snake's head seeking a victim. A fold of curtain material was accidentally sucked into the opening of the pipe, and as the silk choked the machine and it struggled for breath, coughed, and emitted puffs of smoke, Gabo Djara crawled away saved, for a while at least, by the mishap. Tempting smells of food drifted down the corridor and drove the ant's stomach into a frenzy.

It was hard to determine exactly from where the savory smells came, so, crawling slowly, Gabo Djara investigated several rooms—but with no luck. In one room, however, the ant found a stack of books and hoped to find a dead moth or possibly a fly among the papers, though the place was hardly an ideal hunting ground. One of the volumes smelled like . . . yes, it was . . . The Abolition of Slavery Act, 1833. Gabo Djara's feelers never failed to advise him correctly, even though the original title of this book had been obliterated and Atomic Energy Act written instead. The text was of no concern to the ant, though—he just hoped that a dead silverfish might still be found within the covers, and with it a safe sheltered place to camp.

The Act was on its way to gain Royal Assent and should it finally reach the royal desk, it could only be hoped that the Monarch would affix her signature without peeping inside to see what might be hidden between the pages. Labels carrying the warning "Confidential" were plastered across the edges of the volume and they looked very sticky. He might be able to squeeze in there without a feeler or a leg becoming caught, but Gabo Djara shrank from the possibility of being caught twice in the same trap, and walked purposefully away.

Back in the corridor, still tracking the savory smell, Gabo Djara peeped fruitlessly through several keyholes; then, unexpectedly, he was a witness to the investiture of the new knights. The Queen held a sword in both hands and let the tip of it touch her favored servant. "Our destiny is entrusted to you." She smiled as though meeting an old friend. Gabo Djara had thought it would be Chubby, but at the center of the scene being enacted before him was a huge rock resting on a royal blue velvet pedestal—the same boulder seen at the Stock Exchange earlier. "May no mountain hold you back," the metal rang as the sword tip touched the stone, and a fanfare of trumpets sounded—but there was not a crumb of food in sight. As Gabo Djara crawled on again, the monstrous anteater reappeared, sweeping along the corridor and probing every inch of the floor with its hose, and until it had passed, Gabo Djara froze, holding his feelers stiffly erect and his body motionless.

When he peeped through the keyhole again little was left to be seen of the ceremony. The Queen now leaned toward the newly knighted Sir Rock-Pile, whispering with motherly concern, "Don't let innuendo worry you." She told him that ever since she visited the Australian bush some years ago to open his first mine at Mount Wawalag, rumors had been floating around about a strange tribal phantom, which purportedly had intruded into the royal wardrobe. However, it has been a long family tradition not to comment on gossip and witchcraft. Then, smiling, she added, "We met no phantom when visiting you in that Australian bush." The visit was some years ago and the ant vaguely remembered, for he was resting then in the spirit world secluded from everyday life. The tribal elders must have felt uneasy seeing their country being inundated with *balanda*, for they tried to bring Gabo Djara from seclusion and kept clapping *bilma* for days to tell him that disaster was about to strike. Gabo Djara sent out *dodoro*, pigeon, to see if a storm or bush fire was threatening the country, but the bird came back telling that the whites had invaded the country and brought their Queen with them. He was told that the Queen worried the tribal elders more than any bush fire, storm, or flood, for it looked that *balanda* had come to breed. "They will eat every tree; the rocks will not be spared either . . ." worried the elders. Peeping through the keyhole the ant found the Queen now well groomed and fit, and thought that some-one looking like that would not have been brought up solely on trees and rocks. She spoke slowly: "His Highness Sheik $-i has been invited for dinner. When he sneezes we all catch cold, you know." She told Sir Rock-Pile that her guest was building scores of nuclear reactors to help him green the desert. Sir Rock-Pile rubbed his palms smilingly; when in the bush he showed the Queen Wawalag hills, claiming that a single boulder could melt winter snow, which is a hazard in her kingdom. When in the bush she wore a glittering dress which Gabo Djara was told was her coronation finery. She looked very young and it worried the tribal elders that, with a young and healthy Queen about, *balanda* will plague the country in no time. At Mount Wawalag Sir Rock-Pile had set his camp and cleared the surrounding bush with monstrous machines. The country, turned into a claypen, looked like a shorn beast. The trunk of a single tree was saved, stripped of bark and branches. It stood high in the plain of crushed rocks and dust. The day the Queen was brought to see the place, *balanda* raised the flag on top of the lonely pole and let it flap in the wind, signaling out to every white man and his machine to flock in and welcome the Queen. On arriving, she stepped on a platform behind the pole. In her hand she held a stone: "I was told to tell you that this precious ore is our destiny," she explained to the whites and the machine that, when crushed, the boulders are to melt snow and that in her kingdom no man or his machine shall ever suffer from frostbite. Now, years later, the Queen sounded even wiser and hoped that the rocks from Namanama would help Sheik $-i green the desert. "Hold on to him," she told Sir Rock-Pile.

His search for food brought Gabo Djara to the door of the State Dining Room, but it seemed that he could go no further without being invited. If there had ever been a keyhole in the door it had been plugged up; around the perimeter there was not even the tiniest gap, and though the door opened at intervals to admit guests, it immediately snapped shut again, operated by some magnetic device, and was airtight once more. Moving smartly, one might have slipped through with a party of guests, but for slow-crawling Gabo Djara, the feat would be nearly impossible and he feared a messy death on the edge of the slamming door. His chance arose, though, with the entry of two ushers wheeling Sir Rock-Pile Ore on his pedestal, and as it was pushed slowly through the doorway, the ant grabbed at the flowing blue velvet and clung there desperately. For a moment Gabo Djara hung precariously suspended, then gained a purchase and was aboard. The arrival of Sir Rock-Pile marked the high point of the occasion and the Queen and her guests welcomed him with applause. In his hiding place under a corner of the rock, Gabo Djara raised his head, his feelers swaying as he pondered whether to dread or to enjoy the situation in which he found himself. The guests all about were so obsequious . . . the gentlemen bowing and the ladies curtseying deeply. Sheik $-i came forward to congratulate Sir Rock-Pile on his knighthood. Sir Rock-Pile returned the compliment: "How dreadfully nice of Your Highness to green Texas." Sheik $-i explained that his nanny was from Texas and that from her he had inherited an accent and much of his business vocabulary. His desert actually lay half a world away and this he hoped to green with the help of a business associate who he met through his nanny. At this point Sir

Rock-Pile was introduced to a bespectacled man who preferred to be called Specs: "It's the trademark of my reactors—there are enough of them to ring the world." The man pressed his hand deferentially against the rock and pinned three of Gabo Djara's legs and part of his thorax between the stone and the sweating palm.

The ant slewed around, trying to position the sting at the tip of his abdomen, but thought better of it when he glimpsed the cruelty glittering in the man's eyes behind his thick spectacles. Lying pressed helplessly beneath Specs' palm, Gabo Djara tried to keep his feelers away from the brown stain on the greasy human hand and to avoid inhaling the acrid smell of tobacco lingering there. He resisted the impulse to struggle free, thinking it best to stay concealed in the hope that the hand would soon move.

"I gather you're fresh from the bush." Specs glanced at Sir Rock-Pile. "What was the name of that godforsaken place?"

"Wilberforce Gulf; it's remote indeed. It's only some years ago that the natives saw the first white man—actually it was the very man from whom I took the mine." Sir Rock-Pile spoke with a husky voice as did most prospectors who came to Namanama.

Specs polished his glasses to get a better view of Sir Rock-Pile. "How much of those precious rocks do you have there?"

Sir Rock-Pile was not able to tell; it could be perhaps the richest find known to man and there are some more mountains to come. "Our computers ran red-hot counting them." He smiled.

Gabo Djara had one of his limbs free and, clinging to the cloth on the table, tried to pull his body from the white palm when Specs leaned forward, flattening the ant's abdomen: "The Old Almighty was very generous there." Sir Rock-Pile explained that the natives have not adapted to Christianity: there is a missionary nun called Alba working in the area but she seems more interested in plants than humans. According to Sir Rock-Pile, the natives held that the country was made by their ancestral spirits and leased to them, figuratively speaking, of course. He mentioned Gabo Djara as one of the ancestors who had much to do with the shaping of the mountains and making the boulders. "Unfortunately the locals were unwilling to come forward and tell more about him. This had much to do with the tribe being decimated by disease and those who survived had fled deep into the bush, led by Marngit, their witch doctor." Sir Rock-Pile noted that even though information on Gabo Djara was incomplete, he hoped that the tribal creator, in spite of his color, should be given a proper place in the gallery of those who have shaped the earth. "He left us the mountains—enough to melt the snow of the whole world."

Gabo Djara had pulled out his other limb and struggled to break free when Specs leaned forward again. "You must have been most fortunate to buy the find from that witch doctor."

Sir Rock-Pile confessed that he settled the deal with P. Recluse, who discovered the find after he befriended Marngit and entered the local tribe while recuperating in the bush as a guest of missionaries—Sister Alba and Father Rotar. The news changed little and Specs still held that neither of those whites could have had any idea of the richness of the find: "You have had the right people to buy the mountain from." He smiled as though he knew the story. Sir Rock-Pile answered with a smile. Around him was an opulent sash lettered with his name and hung with a large glittering star, and behind the star was a hollow space into which Gabo Djara hoped to crawl. After a sip from his glass Sir Rock-Pile said calmly, "The man I got the find from shares the fame for splitting the atom."

Specs held that the prospectors would go to any lengths to extract a good price for their find. There are but few people who brought about an atomic breakthrough and their names

25

have been written in textbooks and manuals. "That man Recluse must have behaved rather oddly." Specs lifted his hand to reach for his glass.

Free now, the ant hurried across the sash and crawled under the star. In the whole palace he could not have had a better hiding place—so public, but so safe. Sir Rock-Pile went on explaining that Recluse did not claim any fame; he lived in the bush wearing only tattered shorts. Sir Rock-Pile learned about his identity much later when briefed by an officer from the State Security who had examined Recluse's file and identified him as the scientist of atomic fame. "The splitting of the atom happened before the war. The data are not easily verifiable." Sir Rock-Pile paused to sip from his glass, then went on to tell that Recluse bears scars on his body—marks from the war, most likely. As he put down his glass, the star moved slightly, tinkling as it touched the rock. Gabo Djara held his breath, waiting to be seen, but neither sound nor movement attracted anyone.

Specs must have moved closer to the rock, for the ant felt his breath under the shell as he spoke: "That odd prospector must have extracted a good price for the find?"

Sir Rock-Pile was about to stroke his white mustaches but his hand paused in the air; the ant felt *balanda*'s limb looming over the star. "He gave the find for nothing," he confessed.

Specs lost hold of his glass and it fell down. "Miracles do happen out in that bush."

The silence fell unexpectedly and it sounded, for a while, as if Specs might have dozed off while assessing the miracle when someone reminded him that yellow cake is being served. The guest hardly knew anything about the dish; a stiff butler appeared carrying a strange-looking lump on a silver tray. After sampling it, Specs looked at Sir Rock-Pile. "Fine grade; how many mountains can you offer?"

In the shelter of the shining shell, the ant's left feeler trembled, presaging another message from Marngit. Gabo Djara again directed his thoughts to the troubled country and his ear to the plea of the healer. Perhaps the country was struck by flood . . . the sound of the star striking the stone throbbed like a beating drum . . . perhaps fire had swept the bushland. The smell of smoke was overpowering, but when the ant peered out from behind the star he saw that the fume came from a cigar partly concealed in his curved palm. Gabo Djara retreated, though there was little space in which to do so. The twitching at the root of his left feeler became violent; Marngit's message . . . but at that very moment the pendant star lurched and a cloud of smoke filled Gabo Djara's refuge. The man's mouth, wet, gasping, must have been no further away than the edge of the medal.

Gabo Djara must have spent some time crouched inside the star, for when he dared to peep out again, he found that the rock had been placed at the dinner table, next to the Queen, and that the meal was almost finished. If he were to find any food the hungry ant must hurry. The Queen's left arm was resting on the rock so Gabo Djara made a circuit of the sleeve, using his feelers to test the atmosphere for the presence of food. A crumb of soufflé clung to the embroidered cuff—a crumb too tiny to be seen by a human eye, but enough to feed Gabo Djara for days. Jubilant, the ant dragged his spoils into the darkest corner of his hiding place.

Gabo Djara snatched only a mouthful before setting out to collect more food while the opportunity presented itself, and on his second try he passed the Queen's glass from which rose a strong, sweet, tempting smell that no crawling creature could resist. Gabo Djara climbed to the rim and dipped one of his feelers in the liquid below, but before he could appreciate the flavor of this nectar the glass was raised in response to a toast. As the Queen was about to sip from the glass she looked ceremonially serene, just as she had looked the day she opened the uranium mine at Mount Wawalag. The ant did not have the opportunity to see her face so close then, nor did the healer of Dingo tribe. The healer went to plead with her to leave the country, but, harassed by the whites, he lost his *djalg*, waist cover made from paperbark—the only piece of clothing he wore. The whites chained him naked to the flagpole and he was to be hanged the following day for insulting the Queen. No man breaks chain; however, Gabo Djara turned the healer into *waran*, dingo. The trapped soul was a good way through chewing his leg to break loose when a *balanda* crept in from the dark and set him free. "Head to the bush, I shall follow you," he told *waran*.

Perching on the rim of the glass, the ant looked into the Queen's eyes: You are swallowing my world; and yours as well. While she drank, it was an ideal chance for Gabo Djara to see from above the assembled company in its entirety, and also to witness the entry of the monstrous anteater through the farthest doorway. Servants rushed to intercept the machine but seemed powerless against its mechanical determination. Whenever it was approached, the contraption whispered some password and flashed numbers on an illuminated screen which so impressed any would-be interceptors that they fell back confused.

Gabo Djara crawled inside the tumbler, clinging to the rim with just one leg, but felt so vulnerable, protected only by crystal, that he finally plunged into the liquid below.

Through the polished glass there was a clear view of the anteater approaching to within a foot of the table before its hose snaked out, sucking up every particle of dust from Sir Rock-Pile, and whispering a recorded message to the boulder: "Sir Rock-Pile, your security has been infiltrated—repeat infiltrated; O.S., the phantom bug is about. Red Alert, danger—danger."

As the machine drew breath it sucked in the silken sash and then, with a gurgle, swallowed the silver star which tinkled as it went down the hose. The monster paused, wheezing, then belched loudly, twice. The room was hushed, perhaps in anticipation of a recorded plea for pardon, and in the silence the internal disturbances rumbled. In great haste the machine moved off in top gear and rolled quickly toward the exit, asking the way to the gentlemen's lavatory as it retreated.

The liquid in the tumbler had an overpowering smell and Gabo Djara felt he had bathed long enough in it, so when it seemed safe to do so he propped himself up against the glass and tried to climb. It was impossible to get a firm grip on the smooth, wet surface, however, and time and again the ant slipped back, until he at last realized that he must wait until the glass was full again and the rim would be within reach. Until then, there was nothing to do but wait, and to hope that he would not be swallowed in the meantime.

There is a colony of green ants moving about. They are coming down a tree, crawling over a rock to pass on to a branch and reach a new tree. They are presumably Oecophylla smaragdina species and little is known about them. According to Sister Alba, the ants are ancestors of yuln and have much to do with bringing about rocks and trees here in the bush. She thinks there are tribal remedies to make humans feel as vigorous as ants. Trees can heal even when science fails and you are cast out to die beneath a rock shelter like a mangy dog. In her young days Alba had worked at the Radium Institute where the nuclear curse was hatched; the curse has seen some of our best colleagues withering in the prime of their lives. That was far from here, though. "They'll provide you with galei, (young wife); she'd know all about healing." Alba told me yesterday. She must have told her friend Marngit all about me, for the medicine man has gathered tribal elders to clap boomerangs and blow didgeridoo down at the billabong.

> Trees green forever
> in country of Gabo Djara
> > green ant
> > gathers blood
> > from leaves

They chanted late into the night.

P.S. Alba had sent for my brother, he used to work as a missionary at Mount Wawalag but has since moved on further inland. He, too, believes the plants can cure where science has failed. I hope they are right— we split the atom from rocks like this to see our bodies eaten by the Rot. Why does Marngit call my brother wawa. It must mean a skin relative.

31

Chapter 4

BACK at Namanama, Gabo Djara climbed a tall gum tree, crawled along the top branch, and from the fringe of a leaf looked at his country. The trees are still about. Across the earth between trees marched a long row of surveyors' pegs marking the boundary of some white man's mining claim, and to Gabo Djara's affronted gaze, they looked like a line of *wuramu*, mortuary poles, placed in error on tribal land. The boulders were there, too, most of them scattered along a vast alluvial plain. Some of the rocks were scarred; parts of them had been blown out as though cleaved by an immense *galpar*, axe, leaving behind an open wound for the sun to blaze on. However much *wardu*, evil, has been taken away. We have to make *magarada*, and save the rest of the country. The whites breed fast and would plague a whole country if the peace ceremony is not held today, the ant thought . . . He crawled along the fringe of the leaf searching for food. The day set for *magarada* promised to be a long and laborious one and he needed a good morning meal before assuming his ceremonial duty.

The leaf looked dusty and tasted dry. The ant walked down the branch and, passing to another one, paused to look around again. Down on the ground under the tree whimpered Waran without properly waking from his morning snooze. Would the whites accept the treaty? It would cost them nothing and we both could live in peace. A good part of Namanama lay on a plain about a sky wide, and flanked by Mogo, the ranges looked like an immense dark cloud banked above his ancestral land. Waran whimpered again, the dingo had a habit of howling at night and whimpering during the day which Gabo Djara took as a warning about the whites. He hoped that by the end of the day, with *magarada* over, the dingo would calm down. From which direction would *balanda* arrive for the ceremony? he wondered. The Mogo Ranges rose sharp from a steep escarpment and climbed toward the sky with cliffs and boulders partly covered with trees and parted by steep ravines to trap intruders. It would take man or even a spirit many camps to cross the ranges if one ever made it. Even *balanda* with their machines were unable to beat their way through. Though they were in *waran* tribal country, which stretches further inland beyond the Ranges, they were bound to the camp they named Coronation at the foot of the Wawalag, a mountain towering over a vast inland plain. That mountain, though it looked big and tall, lasted only for a while, for the *balanda* and the metal beast they rode on ate rocks, and it was not long before the Wawalag shrank down into a pile of dust and the whites moved on further, sniffing about the bush for more boulders to satisfy their hunger.

The gum leaves have a greasy coating and taste bitter. Even with an empty belly, the ant found it hard to swallow what he chewed. In Namanama the trees have survived many storms, emerged from wild floods, and survived the longest drought the land has known—the food never tasted better. Waran whimpered again. Gabo Djara thought for a moment that the dingo might be pleading to him to remind the whites to pull out their *wuramu* pegs from the ground and, with the ceremony over, leave nothing behind. The pegs did not harm the land though he thought that Waran's wish should be fulfilled—the dingo came to Namanama from the Wawalag Ranges and had seen his own country turned into dust.

Later on, passing to a new branch of the tree to search for a better leaf, Gabo Djara tried to remember if his country had known such a great threat before. No danger came from inland as far as he could remember and the Mogo kept away man and spirits alike. However, at Dreaming-time, before the Ranges came to life, *mogo*, an immense crocodile, crawled out from the sea. As it made its way inland, the beast ate a string of low sandhills and wallowed about turning the ground into swamps—the kind of place they like. The monstrous *mogo* encroached upon the country eating land and boulders. There would have been no Green Ant people about had not *mogo* stumbled upon a hill called Ngaliur which was the home of Jingana, Rainbow Serpent. The crocodile was offered the boulders but they lasted him only for a short while and when the visitor asked for more, Jingana struck the ground with its tail, making the boulders roll down from the escarpment. "The more you eat—the sooner you will go," she told the intruder. No beast could swallow a whole country and get away with it—when Mogo tried to move on, the boulders rattled in his belly and brought dreadful pain. Feeling heavy from the big meal of boulders he had eaten, he could not crawl back to the water and, as the pain struck harder, his body grew stiff. His carcass still lies at Namanama, turned into ranges, and it towers above the country forever.

Down from the tree the ant crawled up a boulder and, by reaching the top of the rock, he reared up. The ceremony should soon begin, he told himself. Close to the fringe of a dry billabong, hardly a voice away from him, a group of tribesmen gathered under a banyan tree, their bodies painted with tribal designs. Each man held a spear freshly stained with red ocher and their leader—Marngit—wore the *murga*, a dilly bag, full of *lida*, sacred objects, swinging from his neck. It pleased Gabo Djara to know that every tribal elder had been invited; that message sticks had been sent to all the clans and across so many tribal dialects to ensure that every man would arrive in due time to witness the *magarada*. Whom *balanda* would send, Gabo Djara could not guess, but he expected them to come from the direction of the sea—Wilberforce Gulf was the name they had given it—and hoped that for once they might behave in accordance with the black man's customs. They might bring one of their masters with them—Jesus . . . or the Queen perhaps. The ant did not mind whose hand he must shake, just so long as he was not trampled underfoot in the process.

If he had a choice the ant would have preferred Recluse, whose picture he had seen hung in the Stock Exchange, to any other *balanda*, but he doubted that the whites would trust a man whom they worshiped to settle the peace, for he could just sit with Marngit in the shade of the banyan tree and chat in tribal lingo. Where would he be now? wondered Gabo Djara, feeling almost disappointed that the man was not likely to be about to see the ceremony.

Waran howled. He seldom does it in the daytime, Gabo Djara told himself as he ambled to the edge of the rock. The ant lifted up his head into the clean air and reveled in the deep blueness of the tropical Dry Season day. Nothing came out for a while but as the dingo howled again, from the direction of the sea, beyond the edge of pandanus forest, a metallic sound floated in the air. The ant looked toward Marngit for more information about protocol: could the machines have been invited to take part in *magarada*? Ever since they swept through Waran tribal country the mechanical monsters were regarded as beasts, and though it was suspected that the

35

whites might interbreed with them, it was always clear who was the master.

The sun climbed toward its noonday zenith; the boulder became hotter and Gabo Djara wished the *magarada* could have begun and ended while the shadows were still long. The surrounding area seemed an unlikely place to arouse a man's desire for possession. At the foot of the naked cliff lay the bed of a long billabong—dry now, in this driest of seasons—hardly a spear's flight wide but two voices long. A tongue of this waterless water hole licked at the mouth of a small cave tucked under the rocky walls, and from a distance resembled an immense serpent crawling from between the boulders to bask in the sun. In the Dreaming, before any man was abroad in this country, Jingana, the Rainbow Serpent, came from Waran tribal country carrying in her belly Wawalag, her child, and a dingo, whom she had swallowed there. As she coiled up on a slab at the cave's entrance to sunbathe, a *gabo*, green ant, bit her on the belly. The bite itched and she vomited her quarry. Thus the Wawalags were reborn and from them grew the Green Ant tribe. Some held that the serpent vomited because the quarry she ate was her own tribal relatives, but no soul in Namanama would believe that, for it was Gabo Djara who bit her belly.

Waran strolled down into the dry billabong bed. The dingo sniffed about and, finding no water, raised his snout in the air, sniffed, and whimpered. The billabong had never dried up before, remembered the ant, not even during Dreaming, the time when the crocodile monster came about. After the monster turned into ranges, the country grew abundant with water. During the Wet the water which washed down from the cliffs and boulders hardly flows away and stays in the plain, turning Namanama into a swamp. No ant could live in the water and that is why Gabo Djara had taken to the trees and had long learned to live on leaves—no flood ever troubled him. Should the tree die from drought, there would be no leaves to feed on or make the nest. For lack of water he blamed *balanda*, for, before they struck their *wuramu* pegs, the whites sank deep holes with their machines in the ground near the billabong and as the water from the sacred pool drained away, it left behind only dry crust. Still standing on that dry crust, Waran howled. Gabo Djara looked again toward Marngit: should Waran take part with other tribesmen or stay with him at the boulder to observe *magarada*? Waran was a tribal healer from the Dingo tribe who, by crossing the Mogo Ranges, had fled to Namanama. He carried the souls of his people under his tongue while searching for a new country. Gabo Djara gazed at the crust of the dry billabong; with no water about to quench the thirst, it would be hard to keep all those souls under a lolling tongue. The ant hoped, however, that *balanda* must have grown to realize now that the country reduced to dust could benefit no man. If the whites had been courteous to Jingana, the serpent could have brought about a new mountain range big enough for their people to live on. What a pity they did not see that Recluse led them in the settlement of the treaty; he would have been the right man to talk with. Recluse came to Namanama soon after Waran and he was thought to be the first *balanda* to cross the ranges. The newcomer had skinny limbs and a long bony neck, and when moving about he stepped slowly so that his weakened body did not snap. It was held that he could be a *mimi*, one of the spirits living in the rocky Mogo plateau. They hide among rock crevices and venture out only when there is not a breeze about, for the wind would snap their fragile bodies. None of the *mimi* wear the white man's shorts, though. Whoever he was, the newcomer did not scare Waran; the dingo was once seen licking his hand and that led humans, too, to trust him.

Blazed upon by the sun, the rock had become hot, the ant thought his body would be scorched. Gabo Djara climbed up the rock to shelter from the sun. The dingo gazed toward the pandanus forest and it was not long before a row of strange

---

silhouettes appeared, afloat in the heat haze and looking like a flock of monsters rising from the sea. Gabo Djara recalled the first *magarada*, the first peace-making ceremony, staged during the Dreaming, when a stranger called Luma came from the sea carrying *damo*, three-pronged spear, which he tried most persuasively to sell. The tool, it was said, could kill two *barung*, barramundi, with a single throw. Gabo Djara refused to buy, not because he seldom ate fish, but because he feared that should the spear be turned against mankind, there would be few survivors of such an efficient weapon. The stranger argued that his invention would harm neither man nor spirit, and finally he became so abusive that in order to settle the argument, a *magarada* was arranged. Gabo Djara, seated under a banyan tree, beat the *ubar*, a drum made from a hollow log, and Luma danced, pretending to hunt fish. The dancer brandished his *damo* to show off all its best features and shuffled and stamped to raise an impressive cloud of dust while the spear prongs flashed dangerously close about his head. At last one of the tines buried itself in Luma's throbbing throat, and though the stranger ran into the sea in an attempt to reach his own country, he stumbled only a short distance across the shallows before being transformed into a high cliff, in which guise he had stood near the shore ever since. Would this ceremony be any different?

The covey of metal beasts advanced across the plain, raising a cloud of dust above and puffing vile smoke from their rumbling bellies. No white man was to be seen; only the machines closing in—their huge steel caterpillar treads making the earth tremble and reflecting the sun, white-hot from their smooth, shining metal blades. Gabo Djara turned toward the banyan tree. The tribesmen had fanned out across the field, ready to meet the challenge and to stage a mock fight—the prelude to peace. To satisfy the white man's protocol, each hunter wore a strip of red plastic labeled "With the Compliments of J.C." wrapped about his waist, and ill-fashioned pants hanging so clumsily between the knees as to give the impression that fear of conflict had already taken its internal toll.

Sheltered by a small canopy on one of the machines rode Sir Rock-Pile—Gabo Djara recognized the sash and medal— and in front of him, in a threatening horizontal position, was poised a lance which swayed and gyrated as the caterpillar tracks struggled over the rough piles of heaped earth. Waran leapt forward, aiming at the throat of the intruders, but was met by the thrust of a lance. He clung to the rod by his teeth while his body swung in the air. The lance thrust upward, tossing the dingo into the dry billabong. The whites do not muck about, thought the ant, and he looked toward the banyan tree signaling his man to hold on against the intruders.

"Ngalor-gara, ngalor-gara," chanted Marngit, invoking the spirits, and the men threw their spears only to see them bounce back from the metal blades and caterpillar tracks.

Sir Rock-Pile cried, "Charge."

When the leading machine struck the boulder, the lance skidded across the surface of the rock, sending a fragment flying through the air. Gabo Djara clung to the chip with his jaws, while the rest of his body followed, inert, tumbling and spiraling as it plunged into a hole drilled near the billabong. The ant felt like a falling star passing from one world into another, yet he knew it was just the beginning of a long, long end.

Chapter 5

A T first it seemed that the place might be an anthill or a large camp. Gabo Djara sensed the presence of its inmates and could almost feel the warmth of his relatives. He struggled through the tightly packed pieces of paper and, butting his way through, laid both feelers back along his back to lunge forward and emerge from a file.

The filing cabinet drawer was crammed full; Gabo Djara crawled over the compressed edges of folders, dipping his head in here and there, behind the SS (State Security) insignia, to meet some of the inmates. Never before had he seen so many of his kind, and certainly not all cramped into one single chamber, and he felt somewhat reticent about prying into the details of their lives. Each dossier contained a profile imprinted on paper showing, by some magical insight, not only the outward shape of the suspect, but his inner workings as well, so it took no more than a glance to learn how long it was since each of them had eaten, and thus how far an empty crop might carry a feeble body. One of the files labeled "Highly Radioactive" intrigued Gabo Djara, and though he tried to crawl inside, the document seemed too well sealed. Then the ant discovered a small blot just below the file number on the cover, damp and smelling of stale coffee; a few nibbles with his jaws and the softened paper gave way. There was little enough inside the folder, except . . . a registration number and a blurred photograph. It showed Waran, the healer of the Dingo tribe, chained to the flagpole. From his neck hung a *murga*, dilly bag, in which he kept *dal*, a wound-healing magic. A note attached to the photograph said that the bag contains an unidentified but highly radioactive substance which, if used for evil purposes, could cause a plague of immense proportions. It warned that the witch doctor, who is very cunning and could strike at any time, is at large. Would they know that he is human no longer? Even so, one does not catch a dingo easily. Gabo Djara was overjoyed to see the healer from the bush, but an overcrowded filing cabinet was scarcely the place for a reunion. There was another piece of paper . . . with hasty writing scratched across it: "Dilly bag sent for fumigation."

Some days ago a message from Marngit reached Gabo Djara: "That *balanda* Recluse is on our side: he tried to be of help." Did the whites intercept the message? The ant had seen some of the traps and had heard of many others, but doubted that Specs and his man had mastered a device to track the spirit.

A humming came from outside. The ant discovered a peephole cleverly disguised as a crack in the paint at the top of the cabinet and, by peeping through, he saw two computers; the machines were working busily processing notes on the files. On the screen of one of them flashed the message: HE WAS CREDITED WITH DISCOVERING NUCLEAR FISSION IN THE 1930s. The other machine, hardly a handspan away, responded quickly with red lettering on its screen: CORRECTION: HE ASSISTED THE CURIES IN DISCOVERING FISSION.

41

Machine 1: WROTE POETRY IN SPARE TIME, GLORIFYING THE LOSING SIDE IN THE SPANISH WAR.

Machine 2: ANARCHIST.

Machine 1: DURING THE SECOND WORLD WAR HIS WHEREABOUTS WERE UNKNOWN. IN THAT PERIOD A POSTCARD FROM HIM WAS RECEIVED BY HIS BROTHER ROTAR, A MISSIONARY IN THE AUSTRALIAN BUSH. IT BORE THE POSTMARK JACKIMOVO, CZECHOSLOVAKIA. HE MUST HAVE BEEN INSPECTING A URANIUM PLANT THERE.

Machine 2: COLLABORATING WITH THE ENEMY.

Machine 1: AFTER THE WAR CONSCRIPTED AS DISPLACED PERSON AND BROUGHT FROM EUROPE TO AUSTRALIA TO WORK ON CORONATION MINE AT MOUNT WAWALAG DURING THE FIRST URANIUM BOOM.

Machine 2: DELETE MOUNT WAWALAG.

Machine 1: COMPLAINED ABOUT RADIOACTIVE HAZARD AT THE PLANT.

Machine 2: AGENT PROVOCATEUR.

Machine 1: MET ILLEGALLY WITH CONVICTED TRIBAL LEADER.

Machine 2: COLLABORATING WITH ENEMY AGAIN.

Machine 1: TERMINALLY ILL FROM RADIATION. FLEES TO BUSH.

Machine 2: CORRECTION: RETIRES TO BUSH. SEE ALSO FILES OF FATHER ROTAR AND SISTER ALBA.

Gabo Djara felt that the *balanda* must be afraid of Recluse and are meddling with his file. They would know by now that the man, even though being of the same skin as them, has his soul turned black. Crawling out from the cabinet and passing over Specs' insignia, the ant walked right into one of the computer installations. He must have made an unwise move, however, for the machine burst hysterically into a series of alarm calls and on its screen appeared a spate of code messages and signals urgently summoning every SS man in the country. Gabo Djara realized that he had touched upon a sensitive nerve in the white man's way of life and wondered what dreadful price would be exacted in payment for his error.

The ant had sat for a while on one of the machine's wires, afraid even to quiver a feeler for fear of making another false contact or blowing a fuse, when a panel on the computer face sprang open, partly exposing the interior workings. Through a narrow gap between two wire reels Gabo Djara saw, at a distance, a pair of binoculars directed toward him and, though no hand could be seen holding the glasses, the shadow of a safety helmet showed in sharp relief upon the wall. A message flashed on: WE HAVE AN URGENT ASSIGNMENT: GET ON WITH IT. The writing looked blurred, for it was brought to the ant after being reflected from a light object outside. It must be the machines hurrying each other. A drop of honey catapulted mysteriously from nowhere and landed on a silicon chip right next to the ant. It had such a tempting smell and spread its lure around the hungry ant. Although little light, apart from the flashing screen, penetrated the machine, and it was dim in the wiring box, Gabo Djara didn't know how well he could be seen. He was aware of a hole where a screw was missing, deep in one corner of the box, but hesitated to crawl toward it, fearing that some bugging device would detect the movement. It seemed safer to stay quite still and pretend to have disappeared or died, but there was small comfort in such a prospect.

The hurrying machine announced: THE CONTENTS OF THE WITCH DOCTOR'S BAG ARE MISSING. THEY INCLUDE A CONSIDERABLE QUANTITY OF THE LETHAL SUB-STANCE. Then came a persistent message: GET ON WITH IT; IT IS AN EMERGENCY!

Looking from inside, the ant suddenly saw, on the back of the screen, an X ray of himself clawing desperately at a chip; even his brain was showing as it slowly functioned. A bead of light; a missile of some kind flew across the screen toward his head and missed it only by a hairbreadth. What unspeakable silent weapon was this? Gabo Djara fought down panic, and remained perfectly still.

The machine persisted: TRACK DOWN RECLUSE. THIS IS AN EMERGENCY.

They don't say why they are gathering data on him and what harm a single man could have caused. They must have assumed that he is dead: why else would they keep that book written by him? Did Recluse write in that book about Marngit? He got along very well with the medicine man.

Machine 2 grew impatient: EMERGENCY!!!

For just a second the power supply faltered and in that moment pitch darkness fell. Gabo Djara started on his way to the screw-hole. A ray of violet light cut through the dimness and tracked the ant briefly, but its path was obstructed by a bundle of cables. Frustrated, the beam played back and forth agitatedly while a smell of burning insulation polluted the air.

Gabo Djara scuttled down the hole and emerged under the computer keyboard. All was calm and sheltered, but what would happen if the computer became active? If he was to be squashed, Gabo Djara would prefer it to happen in the open rather than in hiding in a dark corner. He came out from under the board, lifted his feelers, from one of which fluttered a white pennant of web, crawled on to the bench, and moved into the middle of a clear space. He allowed himself to be seen and, as though there was nothing amiss, the ant stretched out all his limbs to sunbathe beneath the fluorescent light.

RED ALERT: THIS COULD WIPE US ALL OUT. Machine 2 grew hysterical as its screen glowed red with the warning. Machine 1 remained calmer: IN HIS BOOK *HEALING NUCLEAR ROT* HE SPEAKS OFTEN OF HABITUAL FACTOR CLAIMING

THAT A LIVING ORGANISM COULD BE GRADUALLY ADAPTED TO EXIST IN RADIOACTIVE ENVIRONMENT. The other machine did not respond and still flashed RED ALERT. The ant wondered if it was he who had caused disarray among the white man's obedient servants, or if the breakdown had been caused by sheer strain from struggling over the Recluse file. For a while he stayed where he was, motionless, and nothing dramatic happened until, with a pattering like falling rain, drops spattered the surface of the bench. There was no need to test the liquid to know that it was unwholesome—one tiny drop which fell on the top of one of his legs burned like a glowing coal. Would Recluse help much? Though he is single-handed, wonders do happen, Gabo Djara reminded himself, perhaps not so much in the white man's world as in ours. He kept still for a while, feeling somewhat disappointed that Specs and his mates, for all the might they boast about, do not have the power to make a mountain rise; if they did, Namanama would be left in peace.

A strange silence settled; out of the corner of his eye, Gabo Djara glimpsed a telescopic lens trained on him—perhaps trying to determine whether or not he was finished—and he pondered if it was wiser to show signs of life or to stay dead. The white threads of his truce flag were still on his feeler, so Gabo Djara swung his head back and forth to brush the web off with the bristles of his leg, and when he straightened up again, he saw a gum blossom lying on the bench close by. It carried the strong sweet smell of nectar, tempting him to rush to it, but he controlled himself and pretended not to notice the flower, even when it moved so close that it was almost within reach of his feelers. Head down, Gabo Djara feigned sleep but remained alert enough to notice one of the computer keys being slowly and mysteriously depressed. Before the key was properly back into place, a great blast rose from within and echoed from one empty wall to another.

The screen on Machine 1 lit up again: ACCORDING TO

THE HABITAT FACTOR, GUM TREES GROW ON RADIO-
ACTIVE ROCKS AND BEAR HEALTHY FOLIAGE; THE BLOOD
OF GREEN ANTS WHO LIVE ON THE PLANTS IS A DERIV-
ATIVE OF THE FOLIAGE. THE ANTS LOOK HEALTHY AND
VIGOROUS. SO DO DINGOES WHO SHELTER AMONG THE
ROCKS AND GATHER THEIR FOOD ABOUT. On the other
screen only RED flashed as the machine lost its strength. A
noise like that of an insect caught in a web buzzed for a while,
then Machine 1 flashed: RED ALERT—DIG RECLUSE FROM
HIS GRAVE. The ant wondered how the whites did not know
that in the black man's country warriors do not die: when
you are hurt, you lick the wound and if the pain is more than
you can bear, the soul leaves the stricken body to search for
a new one. You can turn into a dingo or a tree and be part
of your tribal country, just as well a human being. RED was
about to flash but Machine 1 soon lost its strength, too. Smoke
gushed forth and a crackling of unseen flame was heard. Gabo
Djara wondered if the fire been lit deliberately or was an
accident—it mattered little; the ant knew that if he ran from
danger some trap even more terrifying lay set for
him . . . somewhere. Would Recluse be immortal? Gabo Djara
wished he was, for to him the white man's world seemed
hard enough even for a spirit to pass through unscathed.

Kind and numerous though they are, plants are not without enemies; they are afraid of cyclone storms and bush fires; they should be wary about humans as well. My tribal wife Jogu thinks that the trees have nothing to be afraid of—man makes his spears from bushes to hunt and fight but that is after the wood dries and has grown ngerdno, long dead. Besides, trees are kind to gabo, the ant—the tribal totem feeds on leaves and nests up in the branches. When she came to me Jogu wore around her waist a bush garment made of djalg, paperbark sheets held together with resin extracted from the spinifex. The garment looked short, covering hardly more than diridiri, her pubic hair; she does not wear it anymore, for the rock shelter is her home now. The day she came she brought new dry sand to spread over the ground. Here in the bush, humans, like animals, move from one camping spot to another before the bugs can set in; you don't move though if you are ill. Jogu brought an armful of paperbark, perhaps gathered from the same tree she made her dress from. When she was spreading it on the ground for me to stretch on, she reminded me of a nurse changing new linen in a hospital ward. She tries to tell me that no man dies from a curse if he is a friend of trees. When someone is sick gabo could crawl down from a tree at night and appear in a human's dream to tell what remedy is to be used and how. Since hearing it I have looked often to da, stringybark, growing next to the rock shelter and watched a column of green ants passing from a rock to a branch.

Plants and humans have been together since the dawn of time; science is uncertain when time actually began though it could be predicted when it would end. When up at the Coronation Mine, and before I contracted this Rot, I saw a cave revealed when they blew up a hill. On uranium rocks was a picture of a dingo, clear as though painted yesterday; below it were the remains of an old campfire. Scrutinized by carbon dating, the charcoal gave an age of one hundred thousand years—man and plants must have been about longer than the remains left behind; they might have been together since the drifting of the continents. No man could have moved a radioactive mountain with his spear and boomerang; he turned to the plains for a cure and looked for a way to live with the rocks. In that cave they found an ancient adze—rough cutting stone shaped from rare types of rocks never found on this continent. Men and plants have been together before the mountains rose up. I have thought much about this ever since Jogu came back from the bush some days ago with gargu, leaves of sandpaper fig. She heated them on a campfire while chanting:

> In bush of Namanama
> trees of gargu
> grow tough knees
> > stinging leaves
> > pungent smell
> > heal wound.

The leaves look dark green, and when Jogu wrapped them around my swollen joints, they prickled against my skin. When making their spears, men here use those leaves to sandpaper the shafts and smooth their tools.

The stringybark trees nearby have flowered this morning; this marks the middle of the Dry. Jogu thinks that most of the water holes will be dry soon except Jingana billabong. There are no bees about the stringy-bark yet, but I could hear a whole swarm of them humming around a single Woollybutt which has bloomed into an orange ball. They call the tree gunuru; Jogu had found a tiny red parrot feather and by sticking it to a bee she would be able to follow the insect back to the hive. Honey is used for food and remedies—she needs it for both.

P.S. When back from the bush Jogu told me of seeing balanda track. The people out here can tell the color of someone from his footprints, almost as accurately as looking into a face. The man had made short steps and was unable to walk straight; he, too, must be ill. Jogu assumes that the intruder must have killed a snake and carried it tacked under his waist belt—the hanging reptile had left a trail over sandy ground. She handed me a bag which she found by the track; it is filled with freshly chipped stones.

Chapter 6

GABO DJARA had never been in a white man's court before and it took him some time to learn its workings. Confined as he was beneath a bell of fine insect-proof mesh originally designed to serve as a food cover, the ant could see and hear but could not escape . . . except . . . the handle on top of the dome-shaped gadget had been partly damaged, leaving a crack in the brass where it sat on the bell. The gap the crack afforded was not large, but it was wide enough for Gabo Djara to squeeze through to freedom; he crawled cautiously toward the avenue of escape, stopping often to reassure himself that his movements attracted no attention from the court.

A guard stood next to the bell, holding a pick handle in one hand and a book in the other.

Dozing, the man wakened suddenly and, muttering, "In the name of the Queen," he swung the handle against the mesh bell. His right hand was covered with the tattooed message *Deus est Mecum* (God is with me). He looked as bold as a frog and, when again striking, his head smeared with ointment reminded the ant of a full moon looming over him. It must be Yudu—no man could be as bold as that fellow. When in the bush Yudu had hair and grew a long beard, but that was many monsoons ago. He appeared at Namanama on a sunny morning during the Dry and was believed to be the second *balanda* who walked across the desert and crossed the Mogo Ranges. From his shoulder dangled a strange box with which he dared not part even when stretching down on the ground for a rest. A cord hung from the box ending with a short rod which, when he walked about, swung above the ground like the head of a serpent poking rocks here and there. It was thought that Yudu was sent to look for Recluse and hoped to find him hiding behind boulders, for he hung around Jingana cave. Gabo Djara had seen him walking inside the sacred place; as *balanda* held his rod against a slab painted with Wawalag, the box hanging from his shoulder began to pip loudly. It was believed that the box housed a chicken encaged there to tell if Recluse was hiding among the rocks. On his shoulder Yudu carried a knapsack packed with gelignite; he blew up Wawalag slab but no man appeared from behind. "I'll get you, even if I have to level the whole bloody mountain," he muttered.

Gabo Djara was just about to crawl through the crack in the top of the bell when Yudu struck the pick handle against the wire mesh and, with quick glances into his book, began shouting passages from the Atomic Act. Suppressing his panic and the urge to run, Gabo Djara kept quite still and hoped for another chance. The movement of his feelers rising up in the air to gauge the danger was interpreted as an attempt to escape, however, and the handle struck again with such force that the ant had to grip the mesh with all his legs to avoid being thrown off.

When at Namanama, Yudu felt determined to blow the whole cave, and Marngit hurried to plead with Recluse to give himself up for the sake of *marain*, sacred place. The white man did not hesitate and walked into the cave without fear. "You are wasting your gelignite," he told the newcomer instead of greeting him. Yudu explained that his Geiger counter was running red-hot and expected the rocks to be uranium. Recluse held that the signal did not come from the boulders but from a tiny layer of red ocher the tribal scenes had been painted with: "They excite the instrument as soon as you touch them with the rod." Yudu thought that he would be still on the right track to discover the find. "Let's round up the local boongs—make them show the place the ocher comes from," he said. Recluse tried to smile, but being weak from protracted illness, he was out of breath. Leaning against a boulder, he explained that the red ocher is a precious trading commodity among the tribes and could often travel from one Australian coast to another, passing through many black hands. "Those paintings are generations old," he went on, explaining that when the cave was painted there were about five hundred tribes, most of which had become extinct, which made Yudu wonder how one could round up men who are around no longer. He stayed at Namanama, poking his rod against the rocks, when a snake struck back from under a boulder. "I should know the bush better, I grew up in it," he told Marngit later, as he called to the tribal medicine man for help.

The strains of "God Save the Queen" announced the opening of the trial, the court stood to attention, and that solemn moment of the white man's ritual gave Gabo Djara a rare opportunity; he dashed to the crack, squeezed through, and then, wasting no time, slid over the side of the bell, hit the pedestal, and rolled to the floor. Behind him came the reassuring sound of the handle lashing against the mesh, and a few more paragraphs of the Act—the court had been deluded into believing that the ant was still in the cage and it might be some time before the absence of one so tiny and with no voice at all was noticed.

In the judge's chair sat Sir Rock-Pile dressed in judicial regalia and appearing calm as though dazed by some magic spell. The judicial bench, though it seemed the most daring, was perhaps the safest place to hide, at least for as long as His Honor left his evil-smelling cigar unlit.

"*Oecophylla smaragdina*, you are accused of trafficking in the highly lethal substance found in the bag of one of your cult leaders." The judge wore an earphone and Gabo Djara's first thought was that he must be in contact with his master . . . God? . . . or someone else who was advising him on what verdict to bring in. The judge warned that unless Gabo Djara could prove his innocence, the court would . . . Wakened suddenly from a dizzy spell, Yudu shouted again, "In the name of the Queen," and lashed with the pick handle against the bell. It pleased the ant to be confined inside the enclosure, for Yudu seemed determined to finish him off. Would he know about me? wondered the ant. When in the bush Yudu had his mind set on finding the rocks he was after and it mattered little to whom the mountain belonged. It was thought the man had been struck by a curse and might not be around for too long. Marngit had helped him recover from the snake bite but hardly anything else was cured: since arriving at Namanama the man had lost all his hair, looked bloodless, and hardly moved about. "It's the Rot. Catches up with many of us." Recluse told Marngit that the man should be sent back to Coronation Mine so that *balanda* do not have to come for his remains. He held that Yudu, who had struck the find at Mount Wawalag years ago, had been sent by Sir Rock-Pile to Namanama to look for uranium again, and if he failed to return, a search party would be sent after him. No party arrived, for the monsoon set in, and as the country swelled under flood water, one had to be turned into a bird to get in or leave the place. Yudu camped beneath a rocky outcrop and Recluse told him of seeing a dingo sniffing nearby, the animal had fled the hilly part of the country. "It never attacks humans, not out here," Recluse assured him. That dingo was actually Waran, the ant reminded himself now, and he had known Yudu since the white man was a toddler. The boy grew up on a remote homestead not far from Mount Wawalag. Some tribal people used to go there during a drought and were given a billy can of flour to make damper in a campfire. The white man's food must have tasted strange, but no tribal soul lived to tell. However, the last time the food was given away no one had died; the people went back for more flour but found that the whites at the homestead had died. Even the rats who ate the crumbs from *balanda* table had grown stiff. However, *yudu*, child in a cot, survived, for it was too young to eat; Waran took him to a tribal woman to rear him. Though white, the boy did not mind nibbling a black nipple.

Reminding himself that he was on trial, the ant tried to move a bit closer, if not to crawl into the judge's wig, then at least to be close enough to hear some of the words whispering in his ear, when one of his feelers began to itch. There was no time to concentrate on the signal or even to decide who called—Marngit on the left feeler or Waran on the other—but whoever it was Gabo Djara felt sure it came from the tribal country and was a message of distress.

"You have no fixed address or adequate means of support. You have been found in one of the SS computers attempting to infiltrate programs with your black magic." Pointing his gavel to the bell, the judge stressed that ever since the Black Death had engulfed Europe, there has been no greater threat to mankind than the present tide of Black Magic outbreaks which were recorded some years ago at Coronation Mine. Shuffling papers in front of him, he read names of men who had contacted there a strange disease for which science had no cure. Among the victims appeared Recluse, and it intrigued the ant that he was listed as dead among others. The judge noted that though some scientists might differ in their personal view of what brought about the disease, however, it is now established beyond reasonable doubt from where the evil comes. The gavel pointed to the bell enclosure: "It hatched out . . ." The judge held his words as he hastily adjusted the earphone; a cracking whisper told him: "Black Uranium $95, Wawalag Mining $102, Namanama Prospecting $99." The judge said some flattering words and as the gavel pointed to the enclosure again, his face hardened: "The evil hatched from that dilly bag of yours." The bag actually belonged to the medicine man, but for once Gabo Djara found the white man to be right and, as the spiritual ancestor, he did not mind the sacred object being referred to as his. He crawled along the arm of the chair, searching for an inconspicuous bridge to cross over to the judge's back. One of his front limbs stretched out and clung to the judicial garment but it halted quickly, cautioned by the sudden words: "A generation of workers from Coronation Mine has been decimated by your witch-craft." A lonely voice from the courtroom shouted "Radio-activity" several times, but each time the judge waved a piece of pink paper repulsing the call, as though the word was a persistent insect inadmissable at the trial. When silence returned, the judge placed carefully the pink paper in a book in front of him. Laying his hand on it, he explained that a sinister force from the witch doctor's dilly bag had been noted long before the uranium boom. He opened the book where the pink paper was placed and read a passage about how the Aboriginal people knew for generations how to extract a certain substance from gum leaves which proved to be more effective than any drug of modern medicine. The ant recognized the book; it was the same one he had hidden in when hunted in Parliament House, though the title now lay concealed under the white fingers. "That substance when added to some other ingredients could be as powerful as strychnine." The judge cited a case on a remote homestead where the whites had been wiped out after a tribal witch doctor had placed the sinister ingredients in the flour. As he spoke, one of his arms moved restlessly, and when it came to rest, his elbow pressed against the ant's rear limbs. "We have here a lone survivor of that tragedy to testify to this court." Rousing from his dizzy spell again, Yudu hit the enclosure with the handle, but realizing what was expected of him, he bowed to the bench: "I ate no flour, this s . . . b . . . this . . ." Being told that the words were admissable in court, he followed: ". . . this son of a bastard here had poisoned the flour."

Yudu looked pale and stumbled over his words; Gabo Djara assumed that he might still be suffering from that long wet spell when trapped at Namanama. He was hardly able to move from his rock shelter there and had to be given *djungun*, young unmarried woman, to make his fire, gather food, and bring in dry sand which she dug from under the boulders. Fresh clean sand did not bring better rest, though—the white man used to mutter often during the night and swing his hand about as though still poking the rod of the Geiger counter into the rocks. Marngit was called several times by *djungun* to undo the spell of bad dreams, but not being much help, the medicine man consulted Recluse and was told: "It's the rock madness—we all suffer from it one way or another." Recluse thought that if Yudu did not return to the white man's world, with the monsoon over, a search party would be sent to look for him, for the *balanda* would assume that he must have stumbled on a find which he could not leave behind because of a fear that he would not be able to locate it again. To keep the whites away, Recluse sent a message to Sister Alba who had a place at Luma Cliff, some camps away along the bay, to come with her dinghy and take Yudu away.

The judge's gavel pointed to the mesh bell again but his eyes were on the pink paper. "Most of your cult-followers carry that lethal substance in dilly bags; they'll plague the whole world if . . ." An important news flash must have reached the judge's ear, for he cut off the sentence suddenly, his hand pressed against the earphone, while he peered at a list of mining shares scrawled hastily on the pink paper.

Gabo Djara crawled up the back of the judge's chair, until he was but an inch away from the earphone. "Black Uranium $180; Wawalag Mining $170; Namanama Prospecting $190" came the whisper. The voice was faint and distorted; the judge adjusted a dial on the bench and the voice came crisp and clear: "Mogo Enterprises $250, Repeat—$250 . . ."

The Judge leaned quickly toward a microphone on the bench and whispered, "Sell Mogo, all Mogo . . . sell now."

"Yes, sir, selling as . . ." The voice from the earphone was suddenly drowned in a flood of noise from the courtroom. The judge angrily slammed down his gavel, calling for order, and then watched while Yudu struck the pick handle on the floor and blew piercing blasts on a whistle.

"Your Honor, the captive has escaped."

The light went off suddenly, leaving the courtroom dark and eerie. The ant crawled across the bench with both his feelers stretched to the limit searching for cover while the dark lasted; about a handspan away Sir Rock-Pile mumbled the names of some of the securities and, angered by the inconvenience, slammed his gavel against the bench.

Discovering a neat round hole in the bench, Gabo Djara slipped in and found himself in the conduit that carried all the wiring systems for His Honor's sound equipment. It was dark and damp but safe in there and it seemed inevitable that Gabo Djara must cling to the slippery cable and follow where it led. He assumed that its destination would be a computer, but instead, after a long winding descent, the duct ended in a cellar.

Poor fellow Recluse, thought Gabo Djara; Namanama bush would be a fit place for him no longer. Once Marngit told Recluse the ancestral story of how Namanama looked at the Dreaming. Long before Mogo Ranges rose up, the country was but a flat plain which stretched many skies away, for there was not sea nearby then. Two ants inhabited the land solely:

gabo, green one, and his brother *galgal*, a white fellow who did not like climbing trees to look for leaves but crawled under the bark and chewed the wood of the trunk instead. He made his home there, had a young wife, who, being well fed, was made into queen and bore so many young that there were more *galgal* termites in the bush than grains of sand. They swarmed by day and bred by night; when the country ran out of trees they crawled into the ground to nest there. With so many about, they ate their tribal country in no time, leaving behind an immense hole which stretched sky-wide. Later, when the first monsoons came, the water poured in and turned the place into a vast sea. On hearing the ancestral story, Recluse kept quiet for a while and then, rubbing his forehead, said calmly, "The *balanda* have a queen, too; they could be here in no time." That sea, he was told later, made it possible for Mogo, monstrous crocodile, to come and eat part of Namanama. Recluse thought for a while and asked: "Is that where your ancestor sang that chant—'The quicker the evil eats, the sooner will he go'?"

The cellar resembled a long, deep cave, entirely devoid of sound and light. Gabo Djara crawled gingerly. Under him he felt the charcoal of long extinct fires; the smell of wine hung in the air, stale and sickly, and food crumbs littered the dusty ground, but they were so stony hard that, although his crop had long been empty, Gabo Djara had no wish to eat. As he crawled, the ant remembered that Marngit was told once by Sister Alba that according to the whites, the world had risen from darkness and it would plummet into it again if the humans did not remain grateful. The ant assumed that the missionary woman would still be about and wondered where she would go after the bush had been plundered.

In a shaft of light at the end of the cave lay a pile of skeletons, each skull decorated with a metal tab bearing a code number, and for a moment he expected to see the word "Namanama" but realized soon that the remains must belong to one of many extinct tribes. He felt that however ugly was the fate that had befallen them, he and every soul must embrace it, too.

I have to look for the Sister, the ant told himself. The flapping of a bird's wing echoed in the cellar; he felt uncertain whether the sound came from somewhere outside or from his mind. Whichever it was, Gabo Djara felt hopeful of meeting Sister again in the white man's world.

If rocks were pounded to dust, the plants would perish, too; with them would go remedies which have been about since the Drifting of the Continents. Left without a cure, the world would be engulfed by nuclear Rot. My friend Marngit hardly thinks of this—his job is to heal, not to prophesy. Some days ago a sick white man was found in the bush and brought to rest under a rock shelter hardly a stone's throw away from me. It was said that the man was hunting snakes and was bitten by one. In the hands of a good healer no soul ever suffers. With his spear Marngit cut the wound wide open and, holding a green ant nest over it, chanted:

> Gum trees are laden
> with nests of gabo
> > green blood
> > heals wound

He twisted the nest and let greenish liquid from squashed insects drip on to the wound and then the cure was rubbed into the blood. The box the newcomer had carried with him was a Geiger counter—you hunt rocks with it, not reptiles. The bite did not heal and grew into a wound. It dawned on Marngit that there was something strange about balanda whose blood did not mix with that of the tribal ancestor. He bound the wounded limb with lingar, vine, to prevent the snake curse spreading into the body and a message was sent to Sister Alba. When arriving she brought a handful of julunu, large leaves with ends round and lobed. The wound on the prospector's limb was opened with the spear again and heated leaves, which I was told were of purple beech convolvulus, were held against the wound. They eased the pain but did little to halt the bleeding. Alba resorted to munbi, fruit of styptic tree, partly crushed and sucked into a bailer shell, then the lotion placed inside the wound. It was commonly used to stop after-birth bleeding and was thought the remedy might work on an open wound, though Alba doubted. "Blood of balanda is different." She told Marngit that the whites held to a different god and the plants might not be as generous to them as to the blacks.

Though the two bloods seemed to have little in common the prospector began to recover. As soon as he was able to stand up again, the man limped to the wall of the shelter and began to chip the rocks. Marngit, who had to be called again, assumed that balanda had grown mad and if not helped could ruin a dry shelter which has comforted generations of families during monsoon rains. "No man in his right mind would do that." The prospector had to be taken down to the billabong where the tribal elders had prepared a fire already. Marngit had an armful of gunuru, greenery mixed with clumps of blady grass, thrown on the fire. The white man was dipped first into the billabong before being brought to the billowing fumes. Paperbark sheets were placed over his head to hold the smoke which cures the madness. The smoke helped the prospector regain some of his lost sanity, but he was barred from going back to the escarpment. He, too, was given galei to look after him and see that he harmed no rocks.

Marngit calls him Yudu: had the people here met him before? I shall ask Alba.

Chapter 7

THE ant found himself once again in that walled interior where the whites sit down to fashion their laws. He stood in the public gallery where he had first sprung into *balanda* world. The parliamentary chamber down below was filled with an air of business, less ceremonial and more leisurely than when last seen. The Speaker was puffing breathlessly after he read the morning prayers and looked toward the gallery to welcome Sheik $-i and the other guests who had traveled half a world to attend the occasion. "This was made possible by a special bill introduced by the Honorable Member for Virgin Bush." A short bald man rose up and bowed toward the gallery; the ant thought that he knew the man from somewhere but, now with no hair, *balanda* looked shrunken and had to step on to a chair to be properly noted. As the bald man rose, on the wall behind him a view of Mogo Ranges lit up; with a dark cloudbank behind, the mountain looked gloomy. Gabo Djara thought for a while he was seeing a painting of his country but he noticed *da*, gum tree, growing out from a crack in the rocks on the very edge of the escarpment, swaying with the wind. It is near Jangana Cave, the ant told himself. Everyone else must have had their eyes on the wall, for the Speaker explained that, as shown on the screen, Virgin Bush is a large constituency which had earned the Honorable Member, Sir Rock-Pile, a special place in the record books for representing millions of trees and an immense number of rocks which computers had not yet been able to assess. Hit by a sudden gale, the tree still swayed. There is a rock shelter down the escarpment where Recluse used to rest often. When Recluse drew a female face on the rock of his shelter with a piece of charcoal, Marngit thought that the woman portrayed must be the white man's ancestor, just as Wawalag is to blacks. The medicine man told his people not to trespass on the sacred ground of *balanda*. "No soul should be without a resting place." He held that even *mogo*, the beast which gulped part of Green Ant country during the Dreaming, had one.

The gale hit harder; some leaves flew from the tree and, tumbled about by the wind, disappeared across the plain below the escarpment. Gabo Djara was pleased to see his country, but he would have been even happier had Mogo been shown emerging from the morning mist while the sun shone on the summit. It took him a while to realize that the mountain was to be auctioned and that the man who was praised for representing trees and rocks would pass it on to the highest bidder. Sir Rock-Pile took the chair from the Speaker and, sitting down, swung the gavel to test the tool's efficiency. Sir Rock-Pile told the crowds that ever since the white man had arrived in the country he had been hounded by the mountain of gold which it was assumed lay somewhere in the desert or beyond. Generations of explorers and prospectors had tried for it and hacked their way through virgin bush, but their tracks often vanished in the desert. One man beat the desert, however, and beyond it he saw the mountain with a summit of gold glittering above the morning mist. Sir Rock-Pile halted in his story for a while, as though paying tribute to the prospector with a moment of silence, then, scratching the bare skin of his head, he explained that the prospector was actually Recluse. While crossing the desert he was harassed by a large dingo; the animal would creep into his camp as soon as he came down to rest, and steal his food and water. "It tore his clothes as well." According to Sir Rock-Pile, the dingo suffered from a little-known disease, almost as fatal as rabies, and as it had been in contact with tribal people it had passed the sickness on to humans. The disease wiped out the natives of the Mount Wawalag area. The whites like to make a story to suit themselves, thought the ant. Recluse and Waran were together in the bush, indeed. The dingo led the white man across the desert from one water hole to another—stretched camps apart and only known to a tribal soul. Recluse had swollen joints and traveled slowly; at night he quivered and thought he might freeze in the cold desert wind. Waran would dig a pit in the sand for balanda to lie in, then curl on top of him. After waking in the morning the white man felt stiff and the dingo would lick his joints to help him to move again. By the time they reached the Mogo Ranges Recluse felt too weak to move further and had to stay behind a boulder for days, unable to look around for food. No soul dies in the company of a good healer; Waran gathered some food for the sick balanda. No dingo could carry water, but there are always bulbs to be found growing in the sandy ground at the foot of the boulders; drink can be squeezed from them.

Sir Rock-Pile pointed toward the screen on the wall. "There it is, a mountain worth its weight in gold." He told the crowd that the ranges contain more uranium than the world could consume in a whole generation. Battered by the gale, the lonely tree swayed; a branch flew off and tumbled down the boulders. The Mogo cliffs are often battered by the wind and Recluse did not mind the gale against the rocks. The missionary's dinghy sailed up Jangana Billabong occasionally and whenever it came Sister Alba tried to make him leave the rock shelter and go with her where he could be looked after. Marngit told her that Recluse might never leave, for a man, fearing that he might die soon, does not like to be close to the shore for fear that his spirit could be hounded in the mangrove swamps by *mogo*, monstrous crocodiles. The medicine man held that when crossing the Mogo Ranges, the white man had had an encounter with *mimi*, spirits, who crept out from crevices at night and drank his blood. Some people do recover from such encounters but that takes time, remedies, and a lot of chanting; if Recluse has not offended the tribal spiritual ancestors, he should recover.

Gabo Djara heard Sir Rock-Pile inform the crowd that the mountain would be producing some of the finest "yellow cake," which the ant understood to be damper baked from ground stone. He had tasted damper once, and eaten several tasty crumbs given to him by the missionaries, but that damper was made from flour. Would the rocks taste the same? Sir Rock-Pile's hands played with the gavel as he explained that only bids in gold sovereigns produced by Specs' mint by appointment to the Queen would be acceptable. The Speaker leaned forward hastily and whispered something then as they both looked to Sheik $-i. Sir Rock-Pile added that convertible dollars would also be accepted providing the bid came from approved customers. An angry voice from the back bench interjected: "Would you sell it even to Genghis Khan?" Sir Rock-Pile looked around, as though trying to locate a prospective bidder on the floor of the House, and on hearing the interjection again, he explained that if Mr. Khan could come up with a tenable currency his bid would be welcome. The gale thrust harder against the mountain and as the lonely tree loomed above the abyss below, a limb split from the trunk and crashed over the rocks.

With the auction finally beginning, Sir Rock-Pile stood on

the chair and called out: "Do I hear one thousand gold sovereigns to start with—one . . . one . . . one . . . one . . . ?" Before the ant could comprehend the white man's system of trading, the figure rose to ten thousand. "Then . . . ten thousand sovereigns for a drum of yellow cake!" The Speaker of the House leaned forward again and Sir Rock-Pile admitted an error: the word "barrel" had to be used instead of "drum" as the House deals exclusively in imperial measurements. The bids hit one million and halted there while the auctioneer told the crowd that during a recent survey of the uranium deposit a painting of a lady was discovered on a rock wall of a shallow cave inhabited once by a man who discovered the find. A missionary nun verified that the painting portrays Madame Curie, ". . . a lady to whom the world is indebted for discovering the essence of uranium. We have named the mountain after her."

At Namanama, the rocks cracked, the boulder to which the lonely tree clung parted from the wall of the escarpment, leaving a fresh crevasse behind.

The white man chanted: "One—one—one—one million." As the words of the bid bounced off the walls and echoed through the House they reminded the ant of a ceremony at Jingana Cave near the escarpment when Marngit put on his finery and, while his men clapped with boomerangs and the didjeridu roared, he held up a seashell filled with crushed leaves:

> In country of *gabo djara*
> man hugs boulders
> —men harvest gum leaves
>> ancestral blood
>> makes soul
>> grow again

By the time the ant remembered the traditional chant the bids had doubled. Sir Rock-Pile announced that a large consignment of yellow cake had been reserved for the Holy C who had joined a European consortium to melt the snow and turn the continent into a warmer environment. "Ten—ten—ten—ten million." As the white mouth chanted, the split rock began to slide. The boulders rolled down the escarpment, but the uprooted tree caught in the rocks held fast; it still stood against the gale as darkness fell over the country. No soul dies without a fight at Namanama. When man had been turned into a tree could *balanda* tell if his skin was white or black? asked the ant.

It seemed that *balanda* knew so very little about Gabo Djara. His spiritual status and his sex were both ignored. In the beginning it appeared as if he was going to play a vulgar joke which only a few could have appreciated, that is, if they lived long enough to enjoy the laugh.

The ant, painted glossy black and led on a small chain by the Usher of the Black Rod, was brought into the State Hall of Parliament House. A tiny, specially tailored pair of pants was meant to cover his waist, but once placed on the abdomen the garment looked like a strip of purple bandage. "Don't let us down," pleaded the white man. "It is for the whole nation—yours, as well as ours."

Gabo Djara had no idea what the whites were after. Approaching the middle of the hall, the Usher released the chain and turned to one of the two men sitting on the floor. "Your Highness, Sheik $-i, the slave from the Curie Ranges." A sound of bugles, loud and piercing, was followed by a burst of drums and trumpets. The ant was lying flat on the floor, with both his feelers folded back. He was given a small tambourine, but he felt uncertain . . . was it an object of ritual pageantry, a toy or a dish? The brass disks around the tambourine's rim irritated Gabo Djara: he never trusted metal, though he was tempted enough to touch it. No one could have told precisely the color of Sheik $-i's skin. The man wore a white headdress, and as he sat with crossed legs, the width of his body appeared much greater than his height. Next to him sat . . . yes, Sir Rock-Pile, keeping his legs the same way as his companion. He glanced pleadingly toward the ant, silently asking, "Come on, show us that savage tempest."

Above the ant, loomed the Usher: "You have to perform a courting dance. Sheik $-i is your new master." The man's voice dropped to a whisper: "He and the Shah of Persia just about owned the world between them. We have lost the Shah, let's hold on to this one while he's still around."

Gabo Djara suddenly had a feeling that he was wanted at Namanama, his own world. Both feelers had grown numb from the fresh paint and there was no way to tell if Waran or Marngit were trying to reach him. However, once he focused his mind to the bush the ant saw Recluse near the billabong; a group of elders were smearing his skin with *malnar*, the red ocher, painting serpent Jingana across his chest. Yes . . . Gabo Djara reminded himself that the scene must have come from memory, for he remembered the day the white man was initiated; his *wawa*, brother, Rotar, was there, too, clapping a pair of *bilma* as the others chanted:

> At bush of Namanama
> country of *gabo djara*
> tall trees
> tickle sky

Sir Rock-Pile whispered to the ant, "If Sheik $-i is impressed he might take you on to his harem, as the bride or as an eunuch, whichever way it turns out to be." The ant was picked up and held by the feelers, with his back limbs slightly touching the floor. Only now he realized that every one of his legs had been tied to the end of a string, the other end of which was wound around Sir Rock-Pile's fingers. The white hand

68

moved—the ant was spun in the air with no object to cling to, he rotated helplessly.

"Do a belly dance, not a pirouette, you fool. Sheik $-i might turn you into one of his mighty falcons if you perform it well."

Still holding the tambourine the ant swung it around, accidentally brushing him with one of the brass plates. As it spun the disk jangled. The string tightened, directing the limbs and often forcing the tambourine against the abdomen. The instrument bounced on the body with a drumlike sound, while the plates whirled around endlessly.

Dancing on the floor, Gabo Djara swayed, then paused a foot away from Specs. The white man had no time to admire the dance. He held a copy of the Atomic Energy Act and, pressing the thick volume against his forehead, whispered out some figures. Yet no one, not even the obedient Usher, found this humming of commercial transactions of much interest. Specs looked at Sheik $-i and found his guest's face had bloomed into ecstasy, his eyes dreamily half closed. The white man tucked the Atomic Act under his thighs and stretched out both his troubled legs.

The white man at Namanama had already been decorated with an armband over each elbow and tufts of *bulg*, wild cotton, on his skin. The tribesmen led him to the billabong. Across the white expanse of water a dingo climbed up the boulder near Jingana Cave and howled. The animal stood looking across the country and waited for his call to echo from the escarpment, flapped one of his ears, then called again. From across the billabong the sound of *didjeridu* and clapping sticks quickened. The ant felt pleased, the white man had earned his place long before he came into the country. Had it not been for him, the healer of *waran* tribe would have been ground to dust; no soul, rock, or tree survived the white man's purge. The country would have descended back into a plain of dust as it had looked long before the dingo and other tribal ancestors were about to bring life to it.

"Sheik $-i will make you into a falcon. Keep dancing."

The ant felt breathless, the drawing pin holding the pants had pressed against his abdomen; whenever he moved, it drove deeper into the skin. The end was in sight, however; Gabo Djara had succeeded in chewing through two of the strings, the freed legs fluttered in the air, unable to reach anything to cling to. Four more cords needed to be cut—he hoped by then that Usher and the whites would be tired of the game and would not chase him.

From the bushes behind the billabong appeared Marngit. He had brought out *ubar*, cylindrical drum, made from a hollow log, and beat a palm frond against it as he chanted, directing his voice to the mountains:

> At Namanama
> Green ant country
> *gabo* nibbles leaves

For a moment Gabo Djara was uncertain whether the scene called up from his memory was an initiation or a healing ceremony; perhaps both? It hardly mattered. The ant cut the last of the cords. His freed body tumbled through the air, heading toward Sheik $-i's headdress. However, Gabo Djara fell short of the traditional garment and landed on the rim of the cup just as the guest moved to sip the last drop. The ant's legs tried to hold to the china's surface but, numb from the long strain of dancing, they lost hold and the body slid downward into a pool of dark murk.

As the sound of Marngit's drum echoed through the ant's feelers to refresh his memory of the past, he admitted that he did not mind Recluse being accepted by the tribe; Recluse's brother was admitted years ago and caused no harm to the country. It was expected that the white man would recover from the curse and in due course would take his place among others—having two more trees in the bush, or two more ants, for that matter, would do no harm to Namanama.

Gabo Djara struggled for a while, but as his body sank deeper he stopped, wondering whether it was wiser to come out, or hide and be swallowed. Above him a bronzed stony face loomed over the cup. The ant searched into the eyes to see the man's soul, but before he could notice anything, Sheik's mouth puffed a cloud of smoke into the cup. The fumes soon sent Gabo Djara into a dizzy spell.

PART TWO

Chapter 8

GABO DJARA awoke in a pool; the liquid around him had a foreign taste and was dark and greasy, reminiscent of the crushed fragments of some exotic plant. If he was to save his head the ant must swim, so although no end to the pool appeared in sight, he paddled forward, striking with all six legs.

"Keep going. The oil is charged with strength and power—it will turn you into a giant."

The voice of Sheik $-i floated across the murk and though Gabo Djara, his eyes irritated and inflamed by the liquid, could not see the man, he assumed that his new master must be on the edge of the pool.

The man coughed. "One of our great empresses, Cleopatra, used to bathe in milk, and oil should surely make you grow even more powerful than the lovely Cleo."

Gabo Djara made a few more strokes with his numb limbs and then began to gasp for his breath. His body, caught in a cramp, began to sink, leaving behind only the tips of feelers on the surface. The ant spun and struggled out of the murk. Above him loomed a long rod; Gabo Djara clung to it, waited a while to recover his strength, then crawled slowly from the pool.

"For a pool of oil like this I am offered all the rocks of your country—what magic boulders you have there: one of them could blow up the whole world."

The ant moved along the rod and walked up to the arm of Sheik $-i, who explained that it is a pity that the boulders like those at Curie Ranges do not grow; should they miraculously do so, he would water them with oil so that they might crop better. The man lifted his arm. "Your wings are growing fast and strong. We'll be hunting soon."

Am I prey or predator? Only now did Gabo Djara notice that he had grown to an immense size and had changed shape, not to that of an avian but rather to a strange crawling creature with the wings of a flying ant and the claws of a crocodile. He took fright at his own appearance, but soon realized that however monstrous he might look, little would change while he remained subordinated to his new master. Once freed, the old traditional shape would return, and with it would come back his spiritual status and virtues. Gabo Djara focused his mind suddenly to Namanama again; the dingo still stood on the boulder but whined instead of howled. The animal flapped both its ears and Gabo Djara thought the dingo was wet and trying to shake off the water. The billabong was dry, however. As he looked toward it, the ant noticed droplets of steady rain . . . no, it's dust falling.

"The world is our prey. We shall strike it in one blow." Gabo Djara was told by his master that one has to see what he is worth before he is passed on to Specs. What was expected of him the ant could not tell. The master's voice sounded firm, though it held a hidden rage, like that sensed only when a cyclone rolls across the land from a distant sea to punish the country for being good to every soul around.

At Namanama the dust has coated the billabong and covered cracks in the dried muddy floor. Would it ever rain again? Ever since the Mogo Ranges came to be there, Jingana never failed to bring the rain. As the Dry season draws toward end the days grow so hot that the ants can hardly walk across the hot boulders and have to crawl down to the cave. The serpent resting there has only her tail stretching out from under the boulder to sunbake. Bitten by the ant, she thrashes her tail against the rock and in doing so signals Jambawal, her son, who answers with thunder from far across the sea. It hardly takes long after that for a downpour to soak the country and as the stream runs into the billabong the trees wake from the long dozy spell of the Dry.

Sheik $-i watched Gabo Djara walking along his arm, coming to perch on his shoulders. "Those mighty rocks of your country . . . Don't tell me one of your witch doctors made them—Allah must have done all that." He told the ant that if Europe wanted to melt the snow it would have to pay dearly, for his thumb is on every drum of yellow cake made from the rocks. "Allah is with me."

The name Allah meant little to Gabo Djara, though he assumed it was perhaps his master's holy man or god and felt distressed that one of such high spiritual status had not instructed his followers not to snatch the land and the soul of the others. His anger at being enslaved, and that by being sent to Specs he would be passed on from one master to another, grew into a silent anguish, and the ant adhered to his tribal virtue of remaining calm. If ever he met Allah, Christ, or any of these gods, he would only voice his wish to be set free to return to Namanama. As for the rocks—the "uranium," the whites called them—the balanda could keep the lot, even throw them at each other when they felt like it. Near the dust-filled

75

billabong stood Marngit, his shrunken figure reminding Gabo Djara of a stump left behind from a storm-ripped tree. Wrinkled skin and gray tufts of beard marked his old age. Wind and rain had worn away *bulg*, tufts of wild cotton, from his armbands, the seamed skin had lost its ceremonial color, and a coat of dust had settled over it. Marngit's hand reached for something on the ground—something that looked like a spear thrower—but it was only after he had shaken a layer of dust from it that the ant recognized the cylindrical shape of the spear thrower which he had seen whenever there was a ceremony at Namanama.

Gabo Djara felt he had grown into a huge size, much greater than that of a man, and was still expanding. He stretched both his wings and flapped. Could he take off into the air? If so, would he be on his own, or fly as directed by the master?

"Let's see what you can do before I hand you over—go, strike the World!"

Here I go . . . Gabo Djara took off swiftly, swung into the air, making a half-circle, and, after gaining height, floated above the earth. His claws still clung to Sheik $-i's shoulder. The man struggled, shrieking for help for a while, but then grew calm and his yelling subsided into a whisper: a humble prayer to his god, asking to be neither carried further nor dropped to the ground.

The desert flowed in a misty ebb at the horizon. The land below grew little but the steel towers scattered over bare earth—the angry spears pointing toward the sky. Gabo Djara could not tell if they were planted by man, or by some malevolent spirit lusting to hound him. Whatever the way they sprang up, he felt sure these towers had much to do with Sheik $-i and his might.

Down below, panting across the desert, raced Specs while dragging behind him a carriage with Sir Rock-Pile sitting in it. The ant watched them; the men kept sinking into the heat haze and surfacing again while the desert unveiled. It is *waran*,

Dingo tribal country, or what is left of it. A cluster of iron sheds stood on the bare ground with several metal towers reaching far above and edged with rust. Behind them stretched an immense pit which, sky wide, resembled an empty sea coated with sand or dust, it was hard to tell which. A huge machine which had collided with a heavy boulder lay on its side in the middle of the pit. Is that how the rock eaters look? The ant gazed for a while at a shadowy spot left on the ground by an oil spill from the wreck. Around it stretched the desert— is it dust or sand covering the plain?

Distressed by the sight of Dingo tribal country, Gabo Djara forgot about his master, the grip of his claws weakened, and the load slipped away. For a time he watched Sheik $-i plunging down, and heard his call "Strike now!" but the mounting distance soon swallowed the words. The man tumbled through the air until he reached one of the towers, then slammed against the girders. The ground shook, and the metal frame slid into a sea of sand. Above it floated a lonely headdress, caught in the currents of a gale, tossed in the air—uncertain whether to fall or ride on the storm.

Gabo Djara tried to strike with his wing and . . . both gone! The powerful claws . . . nothing left of that monstrous shape. The ant floated through the air, carried by the current. He doubted he would ever reach his Namanama, knowing full well that being enslaved in the white man's world would soon lead to a trap, taken into the captivity of a new master—yet there was nothing he or the spirit world could do to keep away balanda. The only comfort was that no matter how far he was taken across the world, and whatever shapes were forced on to Marngit and the other tribesmen, they would always be with him—and as long as they were around, the white man's soul will have no rest.

Chapter 9

DARKNESS surrounded Gabo Djara, stale and so stifling it seemed that the world might never again know the light. A persistent ticking sounded, and though made feeble by the confined space, it seemed to the ant like a hammer pounding against his head: soon the whole world must blow up.

Fleeing from the dark, Gabo Djara squeezed through a tiny crack, passed along a cold metal chamber, and wriggled through a keyhole before resting awhile on top of the briefcase to catch his breath. Overhead loomed the great boardroom table like a threatening storm cloud. The sound pulsated relentlessly, and though it now seemed more distant, Gabo Djara still felt it would be safer to move on. The table, a daunting objective, but promising the best vantage point over not only the room, but probably the whole world, was not as satisfactory as the ant had imagined. As he struggled to gain a foothold on the polished tabletop the ant felt that the shiny board was slipping away, but at last one front leg reached a small brass plate and five others followed and then the ant's abdomen slid over. "The Chairman" was engraved in the metal.

Gabo Djara rested on a sheaf of white paper, stretching his body along the title "Namanama—Production and Marketing." Above swam a face—not old, but stiff and cold-eyed—and, though he could not remember seeing it before, the ant somehow sensed that this man, if he was not Sir Rock-Pile, was someone close and dear to that boulder.

Around the table sat a bunch of characters . . . for a moment the ant thought he was seeing Yudu. His head rubbed heavily with gulwiri, coconut oil, blazed like a full moon. Mixed with crushed minimbaja, green stems of porcupine grass or young shoots of spinifex, the ointment speeds hair growth before the onset of cold monsoon weather. The ant halted for a while with both feelers stretched out; the aromatic smell of gulwiri and crushed greenery lured him. Should I venture to that head? In the absence of gum leaves any plant from Namanama would provide a meal. The ant was about to move on, realizing that the man might not be Yudu, for every balanda around the table looked just as bald and had a heavily greased skin. Beyond the bald heads spread a panorama of Mogo escarpment and the hills beyond—covering an entire wall—absorbed Gabo Djara's full attention. He had seldom seen Namanama from the sea—from Wilberforce Gulf, as the whites preferred to call it—so, for a moment he was bewildered, but the country was certainly his. The picture showed part of the billabong and the cave beyond it but . . . the chairman's hand swept across the surface of the paper, shoving the ant aside to turn the page. It must be Sir Rock-Pile, who else would be so rude?

Gabo Djara felt furious; the paper had provided an ideal vantage point over his country. By the time he had crawled laboriously back, however, the picture seemed slightly awry. Along the escarpment line stretched Jingana, as though she had emerged from the cave; but instead of going to the billabong, she was heading toward the hills, and when he followed the profile of the serpent from the tail upward, past the middle of the reptile's torso, the ant's gaze came upon not the head but a cloud of dust. It looked as though the jaws were caught in a struggle with another reptile—a monstrous crocodile whose dark carcass lay above, banked against the leaden sky. Why had the *balanda* renamed the mountain? Curie stands for no crocodile in their lingo, according to Sister Alba. Something moved, the ant thought that the serpent was about to thrash with her tail. No, a tree swayed, it must be one near the shelter where Recluse used to rest, for the tree bore scars of torn limbs.

The tree still held to the boulder, determined not to fall. Someone whispered to the chairman: "We're infiltrated." Gabo Djara had little time to think of it; he held that there is a man in every tree that grows. Perhaps . . . the chairman's thumb swooped suddenly on the paper, and, caught under the white flesh, the soft curve of the ant's abdomen flattened and a drop of greenish substance flowed out through his back hole, making a blot which, though it was not large, neatly covered one whole letter. "Ooph . . ." The page turned quickly, leaving Gabo Djara enclosed.

"There's a corporate raider about" the whisper came.

Even though he was clinging upside down to the paper, it was still possible for the ant to see a slice of the picture; behind the billabong the large boulder guarding the cave's entrance had been blasted away. The light penetrating inside revealed a large slab covered with ceremonial figures telling of *yuln* being born to his Wawalag mother. Not many trees were about during the Dreaming but two palms grew near the water hole where she first gave birth. Both are painted on the slab of the sacred cave. The elders paint them always in *malnar*, red ocher, the afterbirth blood of the tribal mother. Would *balanda* harm the palms when they blast the rocks? They would be foolish to do so, as there would be no more *gulwiri* oil to rub on hairless skin; without it the whole white man's world could grow bald.

The rattling of metal caterpillar treads resounding in the ant's feelers could not have come from the picture on the wall but it seemed very close. Gabo Djara peeped out from under the paper to see a small monster rolling toward him. It was like an anteater in shape, but lacking legs, it moved on a pair of caterpillar tracks. The machine paused, while its still-beating heart made the same ticking as Gabo Djara had heard in the briefcase. Though much like the one he had encountered before . . . perhaps this was a young relative . . . this anteater had a long snout replacing the suction hose and a tiny steel bucket below a row of tough teeth with which to grab its quarry. The snout slammed down on the sheet of paper while a tongue flashed out, leafing through the pages. Gabo Djara flung himself over the edge of the table, fell, and landed back on top of the briefcase. Though the ticking sounded no more, the caterpillars still rattled across the table.

Lured by the scent of the coconut oil and the smell of crushed greenery, the little beast raced toward a *balanda*, stretching out his snout to mop up the ointment. Repulsed, the anteater halted for a moment, but, determined to persist, it rushed across the table to another man. The men must have forgotten about the ointment or pretended not to use the cure from the bush, for some of them complained to the chairman that the machine should be reprogrammed to distinguish a white face from a black. Gabo Djara expected that sooner or later the little beast would run out of steam and return to its nest. The ant gazed around in search of shelter, then scurried across the floor toward one of the feet under the table.

Climbing along a shoelace presents no problems for someone with six legs, and Gabo Djara quickly reached the top. Still heading upward, the ant glanced back to see the monster rattle across the floor, hesitate at the briefcase, then lift its snout to sniff the air and follow the scent once more.

For a moment the table trembled, so did the boardroom.

81

The ant thought that there on the wall the boulders had slid down from the escarpment and tumbled across the plain below. He wished he could glance at Namanama again, but thought that the whites might be trying to lure him from his hideout. I must crawl on further into the shadow, he told himself. Once he had scaled the shoe and negotiated the sock, Gabo Djara clung to the inside of the trouser leg, traveling rapidly upward and avoiding contact with the human skin. The chairman's leg had a strange powdery smell and, despite being covered with sparse hair, it proved no obstacle when the ant, crawling at last past the man's knee, was forced to travel on the skin. Sure that he had retreated deep enough inside his refuge, Gabo Djara stopped to catch his breath. A moment later the rattling sound floated up the trouser leg, followed first by the snout and then the body of the tin terror, cutting off all light from outside. The chairman's skin smelled of the bush also. Could that be perhaps . . . underneath the trousers it was hard to tell if the lingering smell came from *gulwiri* or some other plant, but Gabo Djara felt that *balanda* would be determined not to lose the hair on whatever part of their body it might be growing. They would care especially about *diridiri*, a patch of their hair below the belt. Gabo Djara scrambled to the top of the leg and crawled into the hairy forest, sour smelling and reminiscent of the judge's wig, and though he felt safe from the hunt, the ant wondered how long he could hold out before the vile atmosphere choked him. With his feelers folded back for fear of touching the tender human flesh, Gabo Djara crouched listening. The anteater, when only halfway up, was halted in the narrow passage around the chairman's knee. Having to burrow his way through, he pushed his spines against the soft white leg. The chairman moved restlessly, and Gabo Djara held his breath, expecting the man to jump up and roll up his trousers, but no . . . with admirable self-control and clenched teeth, he sat his ground.

Chapter 10

WITHIN the walls of the vault it seemed secure—they were solidly built and were surely thick and tough enough to keep out even the most persistent anteater. There was no need to fear, wind, storm, or rain either, for the white builders had taken great care not to leave one single crack which would let a breath of air in or out of the box.

Occasionally the heavy door opened admitting a beam of light from the office when bank clerks came in to remove or deposit papers, but as they were unconcerned with him, Gabo Djara ignored the intrusion. Apart from these occasional interruptions nothing else disturbed the ant. The temperature, regulated to a comfortable warmth, made Gabo Djara feel as though he was in his subtropical bush home. Although it was pitch-dark he moved easily with his feelers' guidance, climbing from one shelf to another, and squeezing in and out of the stacks of papers.

Prompted by this exercise, or the congenial temperature,

or perhaps reaching that time in life when one wants to settle down, Gabo Djara made a nest. A pack of papers bearing the "$" insignia was put to use and wound into a tubular shape, one leaf at a time, and sewed firmly with larval silk. Leaf after leaf was bound thus with the same substance, gradually acquiring the shape of a hollow ball. Gabo Djara had designed this nest with particular care, however, for apart from the main one it had a number of emergency exits; the ant was not to be deluded by the apparent absence of any danger.

Inside the vault day and night merged. There was little diversion in such a solitary life but Gabo Djara made the best of it, pretending that he was in his bush home, strolling about on a tree in search of leaves. The top shelf was stacked with $ bundles; the ant sat down on one and began to chew the notes slowly. The printed $ leaves had an unfamiliar smell and they tasted musty, but Gabo Djara attributed that to the lack of a fresh wind to keep them constantly rustling and prevent damp setting in. Unwilling to surrender the illusion of being on a tree, the ant, having dined richly, wondered whether to meander around in the outer branches, or climb down the trunk.

The news of his whereabouts must have been whispered abroad; or perhaps his crunching of the $ notes had been louder than Gabo Djara thought. The door of the vault opened wide and unexpectedly. A man—crisply dressed in a three-piece suit and a red tie with a white cross—picked up the fugitive with a pair of tweezers, placed him in a discarded tranquilizer bottle, and wheeled him away on a trolley. Gabo Djara stared in wonder at the strange storm raging outside, flinging flakes of snow at the windows of a great building and almost concealing its golden sign: Zurich Trust International.

At a murmured password the trolley rolled unchallenged through guarded doorways, past several barred gates into a basement where it was stopped at the last in a long line of vaults. If the intention was merely that of changing his location, then it was a change for the worse, and it upset Gabo Djara; for the atmosphere was an oppressive one of cold and gloom. The vault was crammed with gold bars, each stamped with the word *Namanama*, a number and a code occupying almost all of the available space. High above, though, on the topmost shelf, a small part had been spared to accommodate a miniature model of a bush settlement.

Gabo Djara was glad to see signs of his native country and the habitat for which he longed since the moment he had hatched. The greenery was represented by a number of plastic trees scattered about in a patch of sand—and though they were unnaturally still, nevertheless they were the appropriate color of leaves and bark. Among the plastic trees was the camp of a whole colony of green ants, with the same dimensions, smell, and behavior as his, and, overjoyed, Gabo Djara sought a way to join his relatives at last. The camp, however, was tightly confined under a glass dome in the shape of a church bell. In the background was silhouetted the outline of a slowly tilting safety helmet. Gabo Djara shuddered but the inmates seemed oblivious. His presence must have been sensed, if not seen, for the imprisoned ants rushed toward the visitor, thrusting at the glass and pressing their jaws against the smooth surface. A few circled the edge of the bell in search of a gap, but they could find no space through which even a feeler might be pushed.

Marngit sat under the glass dome, too. From his neck, where the *murga* should hang—the dilly bag holding magic objects to help heal wounds—dangled instead a metal plate stamped with a number. The medicine man blew into . . . not a *didjeridu* made from a hollow log, but . . . a piece of plastic sewer pipe. At the sound of the music the ants beneath the dome lifted a straw, and while one group of them held it up, others climbed along it till, reaching the top, they stretched their bodies and tried to form a bridge. Desperately the limbs clung, linked to form a span from the straw to the top of the glass; but the bridge sagged, gave way, and the ants slid again into the abyss.

The model, enclosed by fine insect mesh, was encapsulated within the metal towers of an ore-crushing plant. Gabo Djara, who had no knowledge of how he had arrived there, despaired of finding his way out to search for food. Though he could not yet tell if there was anything edible around, if he should find even a speck of fungus or a fragment of lichen, the ant planned to try to tunnel with it, under the bell.

A jingling in the locking system of the vault began outside, then the dial turned and a metallic clicking echoed within the confined space. The door sprang open to a new consignment of gold, each bar stamped with Namanama and the code number as before, and as Gabo Djara watched, the workers increased the level of the stacked slabs in the vault by perhaps a foot. Among those struggling with the load was a grotesquely fat man whose flame-red skin poured perspiration as he puffed and panted over his task. Sweat rolled down his temples, and as one large murky-colored drop fell on a gold bar, Gabo Djara tried to see where this precious liquid was stacked; but once it was piled on the shelf among so many he lost track of it. When, the job completed, the fat man admiringly tapped the stockpile with his long fingernails, each edged with a dark crusty crescent, a fragment of something slipped out, landing on the top bar. Gabo Djara waited only for the door to close before he scrambled down to grab the food.

Though the grimy crumb would not seem a feast to some, it was large enough to feed scores of his fellows and Gabo Djara began the massive task of dragging it up the metal girder of the crusher and swinging it over the fence onto the plastic tree. The journey took him hours . . . perhaps days . . . but finally it was accomplished and the ant leaned the crumb against the glass bell and prepared to start burrowing a tunnel underneath . . . but he was already too late. The ants in the colony could now scarcely be seen, so shrunken had they become. The flattened abdomens remained though the crops had disappeared entirely; the bright green color normally seen so clearly through transparent skin had faded; each thorax was quite deformed; and the spread-eagled legs and feelers resembled the threads of some strange web.

Gabo Djara slumped dejectedly by the glass bell while from beyond the great door of the vault, the stamping of booted guards echoed between the cold walls and piled yellow metal.

The Rot had struck Yudu hard. His joints had swollen and he had lost all his hair. His tribal wife Djarudu thought he might soon turn into a boulder, for his bald head looked like one. She was told by an elder woman that no bald man had ever been seen at Namanama before and she'd better do something before he became a rock. Though younger than Jogu, Djarudu wore maidja, breast girdle, made from bark of the fig tree though she hardly needed it. Her breasts, not yet fully grown, gave her the look of one who had not yet reached puberty. It remained uncertain whether the sick man would have any strength to sleep with his young bride. Yudu had perpetual diarrhea, and even if he tried to make love he would have to dash to the bush so frequently that he would have no chance to finish what he had begun. Djarudu tried to cure him with da, striped stringybark sapling, and while hammering bark between two stones, he muttered:

> In poor stricken belly
> wallows mad crocodile
> —da, tree of gabo
>   chase
>   beast
>   away

She left crushed bark soaking for a while in a large bailer shell before passing it to Yudu to drink. It brought no relief and they thought that the white man might have offended the tribal ancestor who in turn had withheld the curing power. The tribal people told Djarudu of seeing her husband on the trunk of a gum tree near the escarpment. A picture of him had been drawn on the bark and a small spear thrust to his head. Someone had cast a spell and that helped to explain the loss of his hair. He was to be ngerdno, dead, soon. Marngit thought it to be unfair; balanda was mad and so not responsible for the harm to the rocks. The medicine man went to the bush to rub the picture from the trunk and hoped to find the man who drew it and persuade him to withdraw the spell.

I struggled with my swollen joint down the escarpment one day to

89

see Yudu, and though it was held that the man was fast turning into rock, he remained much alive. "I shall strike it rich in no time." He spoke of discovering uranium earlier at Mount Wawalag and said that Sir Rock-Pile had sent him out to search for a new find. On crossing the desert Yudu had followed a trail of old campfires which led him across the ranges and into Namanama. Though he poked at every rock he passed on his way, his Geiger counter registered no reward, though he had found a stone axe at an old camp fire which excited his counter. The mountains do not walk away, he told himself, and went to search for the boulder from which the tools had been chipped.

No prospector could do much when pestered by diarrhea and with alien plants withholding the cure. Djarudu tried remedies of asparagus roots, tried also djalkurk, orchid, and remedy of jagnara, pandanus palm, but with those failing she thought that soaking dry dingo manure might bring relief to the stricken belly. A rumor had gone about that she might not be good with remedies because of being young. However, Djarudu still hoped to try jamba, tamarind, and thought of using medicine bean when Sister Alba, who knew just as much about remedies as any old tribal woman, suggested djumula, banksia corn, which was said to have magic which could drive away the diarrhea curse. She mentioned, however, that as the balanda wanted to turn into rock, plants could seldom help. Dry banksia corn was collected immediately in swampy bush adjoining the billabong and placed in a small pit dug in the ground. When lit, djumula gushed with thick smoke; Djarudu held her husband squatting over the hole so that smoke and heat surrounded his anus while Alba chanted:

> Out from your hollow nest
> malevolent wardu
> > smoke
> > drowns
> > pest

Caught in the fire, the banksia seed cracked and it was believed that the more sparks there are, the quicker the cure.

Chapter 11

T HE whites were playing a war game—strange and ghastly—
in which Gabo Djara had no wish to participate, but caught,
however unwillingly, in conflict with man and his greed, the
ant must find the strength to see it through.

Gabo Djara, hiding under a missile—a tiny model hardly
bigger than an index finger—peeped out now and then, both
to see what was happening to the world, and to ensure that
he was safely out of the white man's way. The battle-scarred
general studying the world, spread on a map-table nearby,
turned suddenly and the ant spied an ideal hiding place.

The soldier had one eye socket covered by a black patch.
Concealed in the hollow behind that dark shade, thought the
ant, he could have safety, comfort, and an excellent view.
Dangling under the general's chin, and plugged into a box on
the table, was a small gadget into which he barked code words
and, moments later, the tabletop before him trembled. The
commander yelled more orders, and each time he did so a

part of the earth changed shape and color. As Gabo Djara watched, a group of missiles sprang from one end of the table like a flock of grasshoppers and where they landed on the other side of the map became flooded with a rising orange tide. "Off we go." The general's voice was dry. Have I met this man before? That seemed to matter little, *balanda* were like a clutch of turtle eggs, and from a whole world of them, only a few stand out.

An aide to the general leaned over the table following the spread of the orange tide with the device which, though smaller, looked much like the Geiger counter which Gabo Djara had seen carried by Yudu at Namanama. When in the bush the white man stumbled through the foothills of Mogo's slopes, poking his mechanical rod among the rocks and making everyone believe he was after snakes. It was good that he was bitten by one—eventually. You can fool a tribal elder but it takes more to trick a serpent. It came as no surprise to Gabo Djara to see Yudu now dressed in army fatigues and trembling at his master's command. Not far from them, two pictures on the wall of the bunker shook under a sudden explosion and one of them tilted. Yudu held up the rod to straighten the frame. "I know this man from the bush," he said. Doubtful, the general explained that the man in the picture had dedicated his life to nuclear science, not exploration. "Had it not been for this guy and our good old Specs we would still be fighting with stones; I gather the natives still do that in the bush Down Under." Yudu claimed that Australian tribesmen seldom fight. "Even if you blast the cave they live in, they would rather move off than charge at you with spears." Worshiping the plants as they do, the natives would hesitate to waste the spears. Besides, the natives do not see the mountain as worth fighting for. The only stone they use is a flint to help them shape the boomerang.

The general sent several more missiles from one end of the world to the other, then turned to the picture of Specs hanging on the wall opposite Recluse. "Thanks to those governors here man fights star wars now." He wondered how some people could still believe that when you blast rocks in the Australian bush, tribal phantoms hatch from the dust. He recalled someone who said he had seen the shadow of a huge dingo traversing the ravaged country. "Bulldust." Yudu scanned the world again, then confessed that he, too, had seen a phantom dingo while at Coronation Mine. The shadow, almost as big as one from a cloud, moved slowly over the dust-clad landscape. "Ginger in color—it could only have been from the bloody dingo." The general found the story strange, for shadows have no color; he grew upset, but less so over how a shadow should look than over people believing they had seen something which did not exist. Yudu explained there are hardly any tribal people left in the bush and dingo, whether alive or just a shadow, would soon go, too.

After firing a few more missiles the general primed his pipe. "Your buddies must have been very fast in firing Down Under." Yudu, turned toward the bunker's wall to take hold of Recluse's picture shaken by a new blast, failed to hear his master. He swept fragments of dust from the picture and wanted to know: "What do you use to split an atom?" The general puffed his pipe. He felt uncertain but held that God had entrusted some men with greater wisdom than others. Still in his hideout, the ant assumed that the *balanda* talked of the white man's God only, perhaps the same God as Sister Alba had talked about when she first arrived at Namanama. In her bag she had carried a bottle of iodine, some stuff to help with leprosy, and a pack of smallpox medicine. A metal cross hung from her bag. "It is the totem of my boss and every *balanda*." She told Marngit that no soul in the bush would suffer pain.

The general persisted: "Your buddies must have been very fast in firing, I'd say." Yudu explained that bullets were often in short supply Down Under. It was much cheaper to chuck a jar of strychnine into a water hole or put it in bags of flour.

"We often infected blankets with smallpox before giving them to the natives." The general spoke a coded message into the command box and, after a bunch of missiles had flown off, he said, "I much prefer technological to biological campaigns." He believed that star wars could not be won with a jar of strychnine.

The rod tilted over the table, stopping hardly a hairbreadth from the missile. Though one of Gabo Djara's feelers were protruding, to move it might attract the man and his machine. It seemed best to pretend not to be there and to hope that someone so small as he, and with no voice at all, might be considered beneath the contempt of the whites. The shadow of the rod moved away and for a moment there was such profound silence that it appeared that neither the whites, nor their machines, could draw breath. Gabo Djara peered out; Yudu and his boss were whispering together and, with grim faces, watched a huge screen upon which a host of missiles darted to and fro. Gabo Djara watched, too, as missiles sprang up, traveling across the dark sky trailing tails of flame, and ending in a ball of light on the rim of the horizon. "The world will be ours," declared the general. A whole flock of missiles flew out but one exploded on takeoff.

The white man's God dwells in the sky, Sister told our people. She tried to convince Marngit, too; no good healer would let himself argue with a woman, but he let her set her camp by Luma Cliff near the shore. Sister had a tea caddy and would boil the billy whenever someone called to see her. She gave children a lump of sugar if they wrote God on the sand for her. She hoped to have him persuade the Green Ant people that God is in the sky. Marngit could not believe it, for the sky is the place of Jambawal, our Thunder Man. Son of Jingana, the serpent, he dwells on the high peaks of Mogo but goes often to sea to fish with his *larpan*, magic spear. You can see them about at sunset during the Wet; that is when Jambawal calls to see his mother down at the cave, dragging clouds behind him from the far sea as he comes. Marngit tried to warn Sister Alba that the monsoons were near and, as Jambawal would be coming soon, it might be wise for her God to keep out of his way, for our ancestors could tear the sky into pieces with their *larpan*. Sister Alba would not have it any way other than that the sky was hers. As the two were arguing, a lightning bolt hit *djalg*, paperbark tree, near them. "It's from my God, definitely." Surprised, Marngit looked at her: "Has He any tree of his own to play with?"

More missiles crossed the sky; something was amiss, however, for two more exploded on takeoff and subsided in a tide of flame which lit the entire screen and shook the bunker. It must be Jambawal knocking down the white man's toys; the monsoon is getting close, you do not mess the sky around when the Thunder Man is here.

The general's shadow fell across the map and Gabo Djara, dashing for cover, found a hole hardly wider than a straw, but deep enough to accomodate his length. With feelers and limbs clutched tightly to his body, the ant squeezed in and was met by such strong odor of Namanama, reminiscent of the billabong and escarpment, that he felt he was hiding in a gap between those very rocks, while his tribesmen were hunting in the bush. Jambawal was being slow. Why was he so long arriving? He had never been late before and had always brought this son Ngaliur, the Lightning Man. The two of them sweeping the country and tossing their *larpan* would make *balanda* run in terror—and their machines would be tossed into the sea like broken toys, for when he is angered, Jambawal has power that can uproot a tree or split its trunk from the topmost branch to the stump with a single blow from his spear. The whites know him well; he can split rocks faster than they do, flatten the hills, and flood a whole world if he has to—have the *balanda* forgotten this?

The two mighty sky ancestors live high up at Mogo so as to see Namanama, and bring the rain when the trees begin to wither after a long dry spell. They would chase away an intruder who might rise from the sea to eat the land like in the old times. The two have their cave below the mountain peak in which they sleep throughout much of the Dry; Marngit is about the only tribal man who may climb the Mogo crags and approach them to ask for the cloud to be brought to the land. Being old and human, Marngit would not always struggle over the hot boulders but would sit down near the billabong with his ubar, while one of the tribal elders played the didjeridu and another clapped the bilma sticks making music loud enough to reach the summit and wake up the ancestors. After the whites swept through the Dingo People country, Marngit climbed up to the cave with Waran, the healer of that poor tribe. Angered for having to be awakened, Jambawal went out to sea and mustered some of the biggest clouds the sky had ever seen. When he rumbled to the land, he uprooted trees that lay in his path and shook the mountain so that boulders slid from the escarpment. "Cyclone—a dreadful storm!" cried Sister Alba after her hut blew away under the onslaught of wind. Jambawal did not aim at her, though. The clouds passed Namanama quickly, blew over Mogo, and stormed the Dingo People country beyond the ranges. As angry as a mighty spirit can be, Jambawal tossed away the white man's home, twisted the metal towers, and wiped out every single dwelling they had put up. The machines with which they crushed the rocks were tipped over, and as the hills of bare earth slid down beneath the heavy rain and mud, the country turned into a murky swamp and buried them. Such was the anger of Jambawal that balanda never came back to Dingo country. Besides, there were hardly any rocks left, for they had eaten most of them.

"Hey! You're not getting a free ride, friend! Out of there." The general turned the missile upside down, trying to shake the ant out. Then, when one of Gabo Djara's clinging legs appeared, gripping the outside edge of the hole, the man took them between finger and thumb and pulled. The limbs stretched to their limit and finally the body came with them. "Hah! Caught you! You bugging device! You miserable little crawler!" The white man's hand closed; and pressed inside, with only his head free of the tightening fist, Gabo Djara felt that his end must be very close. The man's forehead and his bald scalp stretching beyond looked much like a bare boulder, and the scar slicing across that expanse could only have been made ... yes, surely the general had already met with Jambawal, whose flashing *larpan*, though it had cut a mighty groove across the white man's face, had not bitten deep enough to finish him.

The mighty ancestor from the bush flashed again on the screen, and other missiles blew up.

"We can make you talk, you know. Who sent you here to spy? Tell me! Tell me! Nothing must stop me. I will flatten the world!" The general stamped in frustration, tightening his fist, and shouting even louder: "No one can stop me destroying the world." The dirty fingernails crushing him smelled to the ant like Namanama earth but soaked with blood, such as might be found under *barg*, slain kangaroo. The fist tightened again, then sprang open as the ant's sharp and angry sting found its target.

Gabo Djara descended on the blue paper sea, sped across the word *Atlantic*, and met head-on a white hand drawing a new defense line across the map. An advancing column of rattling caterpillars forked as it approached, intending to impale this enemy in an area of ridged terrain; overhead hovered a white hand trying to trap him in an empty glass, but Gabo Djara reached a green patch of the map and disappeared into a forest the same color as himself. The electrical wiring box was close by, and having listened until the rattling column passed by, the ant made a dash for this shelter.

It was dark inside the wiring box and as he lay there panting, Gabo Djara wondered what really was happening to him, and to the rest of the world. By climbing on something—the ant could not tell what, but it was slightly warm—he could see through a tiny crack in the box, the screen and its field of dark sky. Several missiles started up but they soon met maramara, the lightning, splitting the sky in half and made by Ngaliur, who goes first, to make a pathway through the clouds for Jingana, the serpent. The ngambi, stone blades, tied to his knees and elbows clash together as Ngaliur moves and leave a trail of flame for Jambawal. Would the mighty ancestors chase the whites from Namanama?

"Come on out, little creeper. I'll flatten you and the world."

The lightning flashed again; it was Mother Jingana following Jambawal and one could see her djeno, forked tongue, flicking between two split masses of leaden cloud as she headed toward Namanama to settle in the billabong. The serpent always comes at the start of the monsoons, restoring life, so it may flourish the whole season to follow. Gabo Djara waited to hear the chant of the tribal elders, who never failed to bring out the ubar, didjeridu, and bilma to sing welcome to the Mother and thanks to Jambawal and Ngaliur for bringing her home.

The general turned to the wall, facing the pictures of two men: "Why can't I do it? Why not let me flatten the world?" He moved away nervously and his fist slammed against the wiring-box.

Lightning flashed again but faded quickly as a great rainbow arched across the sky, and where the strips of bright color touched the ground, tribesmen appeared. They were shrunken and deformed and could hardly crawl, but those who could still move had piled up the stiff bodies of those already dead and climbed up on the heap. A white hand holding a grain of wheat tied to a string dangled the food suspended in the cage, until every ant was clinging to it, then withdrew the bait with its light burden of bodies clustered like a swarm of bees.

The general faced the pictures again: "Let me flatten the

bloody world. You must have some secret weapons in that lab of yours. With two of you behind, I shall win star wars in no time."

Dust from crushed rock lingered in the air, mixed with a bitter smell of charred flesh. Gabo Djara debated whether he should dash again across the burning world to see . . . but there was no place left in which to shelter; he must stay and await his fate just as man and insect alike must always do. In his mind he tried once more to call on the mighty ancestors, despite knowing all too well that against some of the white man's machines, the spirits could be powerless.

Chapter 12

WHAT place was this, where the whites had him trapped? Gabo Djara was repelled both by the smell of the stale air and the feeling that he was shut in a box; it was too dark to see the walls, but the strange odor of sweating concrete and damp earth suggested they were not far apart, and though there must have been a door through which he had been thrown, the ant could remember nothing of it.

"*Oecophylla smaragdina*, confess all." The inhuman voice, dry and stilted, came from a suddenly glaring bowl of light which looked as though the *balanda* had brought the sun to blaze there, suspended only a fingerspan above the ant.

Gabo Djara turned his head away, but found that his body was immobile on a table, his spread-eagled limbs fastened and held down stretched out with high tension wire. I must be trapped in a cellar, he thought, for the air smells like a mangrove forest. When at Namanama, Gabo Djara had once seen Sister Alba showing Marngit a picture of her brother Jesus, who she claimed had died stretched on a cross. Did they hold out his limbs with high tension wire also? wondered the ant. The light tilted, shining in his face again. "We tracked the dingo, that phantom of yours. Speak up." What secrets were left to give away? The whites are tearing the guts out of the country and dragging it away, leaving only the ant with an empty crop—the whites would not be keen on hearing about that.

On one of the walls, the shadow of a safety helmet appeared, huge and dome-shaped like a sandhill. It swayed for a moment. The table beneath the ant jerked and the cords tightened again. "What's the way to trap that beast. Tell us?" Gabo Djara noticed only then that the words appeared on the screen as they were spoken. On his left he was flanked by another screen cross-questioning him. "We'll be doomed if that beast is not trapped." The machine on his left had tightened the ropes and he felt that his body was about to part in two. The screen blinked, and instead of words, there appeared the large boardroom table the ant had encountered earlier. Around it sat a bunch of directors rubbing their bald heads with *gulwiri*, ointment, each one of them naked and hairless like a frog. Something tickled his left feeler and Gabo Djara thought it might be the scent of the coconut oil lingering about. No, it must be from Waran. Dingo fur catches dust easily; it smells in the bush more than anything else. The dingo stood under the table with his jaws half open and eyed the row of bare white knees hardly a whisker away. No *balanda* is much good at noticing the scent of the bush. You have to know how something smells before being able to tell it is about. The jaws closed around one of the knees but the leg failed to twitch. When he is about, the tribal healer carries a tiny spear made from a single stem of grass, very pointed but packed with pith inside. When struck with this spear, the victim would not notice it; as the spear breaks through the skin the pith squeezes out *malnar*, red color of blood. Though

101

the victims still have their blood, it grows colorless like water. The dingo on the screen grew suddenly larger with a row of white knees within reach of him, each with joints appearing swollen: "Does the beast respond to any call—a whistle perhaps?" Gabo Djara learned from the screen that a whole generation of workers from Coronation Mine had been wiped out by this swollen knees complaint. They also suffered from Diridiri, loss of hair.

The whites would not believe in a cure even if they were told about it. After arriving at Namanama, Sister Alba asked Marngit to tell her tribal words for smallpox and leprosy so she could apply a remedy from her bag. Marngit called them *wardu*, but the tribal word meant "evil" or "curse." The white woman wanted names of a particular sickness and kept nagging our healer from one monsoon season to another. This came to an end when her friend Rotar explained to her: "They don't have a name for something which is not theirs." According to him, both sicknesses had been brought by the whites. Though Rotar had skin the same color as hers, it was held that his soul had long been black. It was he who, years ago, led Waran to see the Queen at Coronation Mine. The whites did not like to hang a man of their own color; however, Rotar was handcuffed and escorted out into the desert.

The ropes on the right limbs tightened as another screen lit up: "The phantom has offended our best customers." The words faded fast to give room for Waran again. The dingo ran across the desert with something in his mouth, leaving only a faint trail behind. Gabo Djara reminded himself that when you are a spirit, you can move about without trace and that no soul can catch up with you. A naked fat man, stumbling forward, tried to follow the dingo. His skin looked slightly darker than that of *balanda*, and as he halted to catch his breath, a line of sweat streamed down his chest and ran over his belly button to drip finally from his long drooping penis into the sand. The man had not a single hair left on his *diridiri*; the ant was puzzled that the puffing man was circumcised. Would that be anyone I should know, a half-caste or a tribesman deprived of his color? Only after the dingo appeared on the screen again did the ant realize that in his mouth he carried away the headdress of Sheik $-i. Waran halted and, using both of his front paws, quickly dug a hole in the sand, placed the headdress in, and, after pushing some sand over it, lifted his leg to mark the spot. "What that piss smells like; you have lived in the bush long enough to know." As the steel rope tightened, the shadow of the safety helmet swayed again. The burning butt of a cigarette emerged from the shadows and thrust its red claw against the ant's abdomen; Gabo Djara clenched his jaws to grind out the pain. Where did Jesus go when the *balanda* had finished with him? That Sister must have talked about it. She had stayed in the country for years, seen the arrival of many monsoons, and learned the tribal lingo. She had come often to the *barura* and the other non-sacred ceremonies, and had even chanted with the black women. It was just as well that the white woman had worn long clothing that covered most of her skin, though, and *boberne*, the mosquitoes, had a hard time finding a bare spot to sting. The insects, craving for white skin, would swarm around her and Gabo Djara thought that perhaps she tasted sweet, like the lump sugar she carried wrapped in a cloth. The ant had twice ventured out under Sister Alba's skirt. The first time he had crawled on her knee and around the place where her garter had left its groove in the soft skin, he noticed scent of crushed leaves of an aromatic bush which the tribal women rubbed their skin with to keep away the mosquitoes. The other time, he ventured much further, reached the top of the skirt, and wandered into *diridiri*. After using the last piece of soap, she had to resort to *worki*, lotions made from leaves of flat wattle, with which the tribal women wash themselves. Give them time, thought the ant then, the plants are on the way to winning her over.

The glowing butt was still against the ant's abdomen when one of the computers asked: "Most of the mongrels respond to a call or whistle—what do you use to sound the dingo out?" The machine complained that the Queen had been molested recently by the dingo. Gabo Djara thought that at last the opportunity had come to meet an old acquaintance and whatever reputation he might have earned during earlier encounters, she might now be moved by his people's misfortune and reprieve him from the torture table. The Queen appeared on the screen in her coronation dress just as he had seen her at the opening of the mining plant some years ago. That was in *waran* tribal country: now the dingo stood next to her on the screen and looked as though he was about to wag his tail. She gave him a good pat and told him to fetch something that she threw—a stone or a piece of wood, the ant could not tell. The dingo leapt on her instead; his claws clung to her shoulder while his jaws tore the coronation dress in a single stroke. Shocked, the Queen stood naked. Her body appeared to be covered with patches of peeling dry skin. A wig she wore had been pulled off with the dress and there was no hair to be seen on her; even where her pubic hair should have been was bald as a rock. She broke down suddenly: "A wig! A wig! My kingdom for a wig." The monstrous vacuum cleaner which the ant had encountered at the palace rushed to her aid, flashing a Red Alert. The machine propped up the sucking hose, and as it loomed over her, it spewed out a fire-extinguishing foam to cover her bare body.

Before the Queen faded from the screen the ant remembered Sister Alba again, for she, too, was white. Once, while looking after her visitor Rotar, the woman had brought out a damper which she had made from *dalangurk*, crushed seed of kurrajong. Before they ate she murmured words of thanks to her god for making the food available. Her guest noted politely: "You should compliment Gabo Djara, actually. The food is from his tree." It surprised the ant that most of the whites had so little understanding, not only of the black man's ancestors and the world they had created, but of humanity and its ways. They could have learned much from that fellow Rotar and Sister Alba about tribes and life in the bush, and how to live in any world; and she spoke so softly that her words could not harm the spirits, black or white. The woman had come to Namanama looking in the bush for her brother, whom the elders assumed had died when mobbed by his own people, and whose spirit had come searching for a better country in which to spring into new life. He was a good medicine man, this Jesus that the Sister had talked so much about; she told how he could breathe life into the dead, but the Sister was something of a healer herself. She had helped Marngit with a broken leg once, and whenever the tribal women were in pain, and they sent for her, she had come carrying a basket filled with her *lida*. The magic objects did not look like Marngit's but they worked very well, even healing snake bites sometimes. Slowly she grew to see the plants for what they are and what they stand for.

The computers wanted to know whether the dingo would be likely to drink stale water and what his favorite prey was. They assumed that he even hunts grasshoppers though the grasshoppers might not be most appropriate for a bite. "You better speak fast, your skin is very thin," the glow whirled against his abdomen.

Sister had thought that insects have no soul, but that was only when she first arrived in the bush. The elders had helped her to raise a cross, her totem, on the Luma Cliff, facing the sea. It was quite a log—that one they had used—and every man was gathered in from the bush to lend a hand with it, first stripping the bark, then staining the wood with *malnar*, a bright red ocher, to make the log *marain*, sacred and strong. Marngit (*wawa*, brother, the Sister called him) brought our *ubar* and beat upon it with a palm frond to tell the spirits not to harm the woman who kept away from the billabong, not wanting to upset Jingana, and who had never killed a single reptile, not even *boiweg*, the gecko. She ate no meat, only sometimes a little fish, but she never stepped into the billabong to look for these. Gabo Djara had seen her in the bush searching for *gugu*, yams, with Marngit's two wives, and the Sister had wielded the *djad*, her digging stick, just as well and as fast as did the others. She seldom baked her tucker but would rather boil the yams in her billy can with a sprinkling of salt. The tribesmen had built the Sister a hut, at Luma Cliff, large enough to accommodate Jesus, too, should he come, though a man wounded on a cross and speared by his own people could not be expected to return and live amongst them again. Where would she be now? The bush is no longer a fit place even for *boberne*, mosquito, to be about. The ropes tightened, forcing his abdomen against the glowing butt. "Did you ever see Sister Alba feeding a dingo?"

Gabo Djara expected the white woman to appear but instead of her they brought the general on to the screen. Still soldiering in his bunker, the man was trying to move one of his missiles from one part of the world to another, when he discovered the dingo curled under it. The general swung his swagger stick to hit the animal: "Out of here, you imposter." Cornered, the dingo quivered, then, when hit again, leapt forward. It went for the general's throat but instead grabbed his face, tearing out the remaining eye. The general leaned against the bunker wall trying to stem the flow of blood with his hands. "How can a blind man win star wars?" he cried. Above him a picture of Recluse shimmered for a while.

"That nun believes that dingoes are attracted to the scent of a certain bush—it must smell like a mating lure." The machine wanted to know the name of the plant, and urged Gabo Djara: "You'd better hurry. The boss might burn you in one of his reactors." The ant smelled his skin burning as the computer explained that the dingo had been seen at the Holy C; intending to poison the pontiff, presumably. A grotesque man with a bulging belly appeared on the screen. He had just been served a drink and complained that the water in the glass looked unusual. A nun inspected the glass, found the drink to be somewhat cloudy, and explained that the water had come from the melting of snow by nuclear fuel. She seemed unclear about how the melting process worked but thought that the color had something to do with fallout of dust from the Australian desert. "It is quite safe. The whole of Europe drinks it." As the pontiff looked into the glass again a shadow hovered about and a moment later the dingo emerged from the water. The animal hung by his front paws on the rim of the glass; his head was wet and he flapped an ear while gazing into the white face a whisker away. "A miracle!" The glass slipped from the pontiff's hand on to the floor.

The ropes holding the ant's limbs tightened again: "You know the whereabouts of that nun from the bush?" Gabo Djara was not sure whether the woman seen with the pontiff was Sister Alba; she was lightly dressed and seemed younger than before. However, the pontiff appeared strong and healthy, and it seemed most unlikely that he would employ an old woman.

"You'd better talk, and be quick about it! The boss will burn you if you spoil his breakfast." A jabbing pencil darted out of the darkness, poking and prodding at Gabo Djara's abdomen. "Where's your male organ? You should have something left, no matter what shape you've shrunk to."

On the wall the silhouette of the dingo appeared. It faded as quickly as it had come but the ant stretched one of his feelers toward that dark corner and hoped that he might see his way out after all. The computers told him that at the Holy C a peculiar bush was discovered growing in a pot in the nun's room. One computer showed the shrub while the other read a catalogue of suspected plants from Namanama, each described by a white man's name. "Identified!" insisted both of the machines. Why have they never learned the proper names of the plants, names they have been known by ever since they came to be in the bush? One of the computers blinked, and then a moment later, the light blazing above Gabo Djara went out.

A pointy object poked into the ant's back: "I'm not going to castrate you—I'll just tickle the spot and then you'll tell us everything . . . even how you bit your old mother's nipple."

What madness was this? Gabo Djara sighed, lacking the strength or means to enlighten the whites that though he was male he was only ritually so, enabling him to carry out his ceremonial duty when gathered with the tribal elders; his status had nothing to do with that of the winged reproductive male, which mated with the queen, and, then as his destiny decreed, died. Gabo Djara had lived millennia—ever since the Dreaming—since the beginning of the black man's world—and it puzzled him why the whites, knowing this, could not deduce his sexual status.

The pencil point forced itself into his back hole and Gabo Djara tensed himself to bear the electrifying pain. "Speak. Tell us about the phantom Dingo." Could *balanda* talk to the spirits? The Sister often had a lot to say to Jesus, but she read most of the words from a book. Marngit's wives went to the Luma Cliff; they helped Sister to chant and call on the woman's brother to come to life by his strong magic, which seemed to be something like *dal*—the power to heal and breathe life into a man, a tree, or whatever one should choose; but Gabo Djara wondered why Jesus should have been crucified at all, this man who harmed nothing, and was even said to have restored life.

The computer screen flickered for a while and *bilma*, the clapping sticks, tapped out Marngit's call for rain in the dimness. Gabo Djara closed his eyes, visualizing his spiritual fellow, and wondering why he was using not the *ubar*, but the sticks. The medicine man appeared on the screen, he sat in a pool of dust near the seashore, surrounded by heaps of freshly dug rock—the remains of Luma Cliff. The great log which was once a cross stood no longer proudly erect. Only scattered splinters of crushed wood remained and Marngit held two of them, one of which showed traces of *malnar*. Though his call traveled across the sea, the eyes of the medicine man gazed toward the sky for, while he asked in vain for rain, he nursed a hope that Jesus might turn up and use his powerful magic to heal the country.

"Tell us word for word now—what do those tapping codes mean?" The screens went dark suddenly.

Silence fell at last and Gabo Djara was comforted in the knowledge that whatever power the *balanda* bred into their gadgets they have failed. In the darkness that followed, Gabo Djara felt the breath of the dingo against his feelers. A good tribal healer would always be about when needed, he thought, as the dingo's sharp teeth snapped the rope to free him.

Chapter 13

THE day of the sorcerer—the soul hunter—had arrived and though Gabo Djara had never in the white man's world known one, he sensed that before he had learned about the magic or was even aware of any harm, there would be little enough left of his fast shrinking body.

The ant lay on an operating table, covered with a cloth in which he had shrewdly chewed a hole only big enough for one eye to peep but still large enough to frame his fate. In one corner of the room a doctor and nurse sniggered at childish jokes about his six legs. The woman held a pair of scissors and Gabo Djara guessed that as soon as he was put under anesthetic, one of his feelers would be snipped off, for she had stroked the antennae greedily, sliding her fingers back and forth whispering, "Priceless antiques—fifty thousand years old."

The doctor thought that the ant would be much older than that and might even date back to an earlier period of evolution,

Ocophylla smaragdina in particular. He believed that the species must be ancestral ones. "To develop an immunity system against radiation, one would have to be as old as rocks or plants." The doctor's head jerked perpetually as he spoke; even his limbs moved unexpectedly now and then, and Gabo Djara feared he might be accidentally struck by a pair of pincers from the white man's hand. The nurse helping with the operation held that the ant is the ancestor of humans, assuming of course that one considers the black people to be such. She thought that the ant could be the cause of Diridiri's symptoms, for *diridiri* means hair. "Pubic hair as well," she said. The nurse claimed that the disease was spreading fast and could have devastating effects on the birth rate. The doctor warned her that his task was to cure, not to panic. He admitted to being unfamiliar with this patient of whom nobody seemed to know much. "No one except Sir Rock-Pile and his tycoon friend, that is." The nurse glanced at the patient's file and muttered some words as she read them for herself, then looked at the doctor: "He is classified as a black—he must be related to the tribal Abos." The doctor, eager to get on with the job, rattled his surgical instruments, but the nurse reminded him that before you cut open someone's belly you have to be certain if the patient is human or animal. "The bureaucrats have to tell us this, so let's wait." The doctor lay down his tools. "To hell with the politicians."

Gabo Djara had no time to consider the implications of this conversation, for both his feelers began to itch simultaneously, signaling that Waran and Marngit were on the move. The ant, lifting his head, could see no windows, and the only door looked so tightly sealed that even if his friends had changed into flies or birds, they stood small hope of gaining entry. The itching suddenly ceased and both feelers fell forward, drooping over the ant's face like two withered stems. The whites' trap seemed impregnable and it must only be a matter of time before their machines squeezed out his soul. Then, if Waran or Marngit did arrive, they would find little of him, except shrunken skin or perhaps fragments of dust to blow in the wind and mingle with the dust that Namanama had become.

Into the operating theater marched Yudu, swinging the pick handle and bearing news: "All clear, Doctor B. You've got your go-ahead." He explained that the ant had been classified as an honorary white. "It's all legal and aboveboard now." The doctor's head jerked. He kept quiet but the nurse worried aloud that Diridiri would soon engulf the whole world and lead to human extinction. She believed that hairless people have no desire for intercourse: "Man makes no love to a frog."

The doctor jerked his head again and lifted one end of the cloth covering the patient. "Well, let's hope all goes well—I have never operated on one of this kind before.

Yudu knocked the pick handle against the floor. "You'd better be sure—the chairman wants a classy job."

Gabo Djara feared that the white sorcerer's surgery might be painful and rough. In the bush at Namanama the man who practices magic is called *nagigid*. It is actually Marngit who does it, but before he could assume the job of sorcerer, he has to go to the spirit world, secretly at night, and be given *dal*, power to perform. Once told by the ancestors what to do, the sorcerer stays away from humans and sneaks into camp only to collect the soul of someone who has harmed *djang*, sanctity of life, or one who has hurt the country, and always he leaves the camp without being seen. Some people have tougher skin which cannot be pierced by the tiny spears made from porcupine grass. Our *nagigid* has to use *bogo*, shovel-nosed spear, instead. He stabs his victim in a limb, sucks blood through the wound, and spits this into the ashes on the campfire. He then heats the blade of his *bogo* in the fire and, pressing it against the skin, instantly heals the wound, leaving no scar to tell of his work. Before he slips away *nagigid* breathes life into the bloodless body, but only enough to sustain the victim for several days. No man can survive for long without his soul, and within a short time withers like a branch severed from its parent tree trunk.

The doctor glanced at Yudu and then at the door: "You can wait outside. I shouldn't be long."

The pick handle knocked against the floor: "I'd rather stay here—I don't fancy getting into trouble for a missing kidney or a slimy liver." Yudu asked the doctor if he had washed his hands.

The doctor's head jerked. "It's a heart I'm taking out."

Yudu produced a bucket and dumped it under the table. "Any good parts—just drop them in there. The boss wants all you can get—the blood, too."

"What for?"

"For transfusion and research—the chairman's life is in peril, yours and mine might be the next." The nurse took it that Yudu had already contracted Diridiri symptoms and wanted to know how one can cope with hair loss. The man told her that losing all hair is like living without teeth. He explained how he had survived some of the worst monsoons by rubbing his skin with coconut oil, which kept him warm. That was while he was being held captive by the natives at Wilberforce Gulf.

How long will it take them to do the sorcery? wondered the ant. Our *nagigid* seldom leaves any evidence of his job. Should a drop of blood fall, a serpent or a lizard summoned from underground will lap it up and crawl back into its burrow, but what would the doctor do if blood should be spilled on this floor? Gabo Djara wondered if the nurse might stand in as a goanna and mop up the stain or would they summon the anteater? That little rattling brute with steel caterpillar feet and snout made from flexible hose would suck up worse than blood and never even hiccup.

"I hope you fastened the little bastard really well—we don't want him at large again." Yudu rolled up his sleeves and checked the knots on every limb.

The white hands were broad and stubby, reminding Gabo Djara of *mogo*, crocodile claws, and the arms were smothered in tattoos. Each tiny dot told of *nagigid* trying to suck out the man's soul, but it seemed that our man, despite so many attempts and such rows of punctures on the white skin, had failed. The *balanda* must have learned someway to outwit the sorcerer. Though Yudu had looked as pale as a shadow when he left Namanama, he had returned to the bush some monsoons later looking fit and had regained weight. His hair did not grow again, though; perhaps *balanda* prefers to remain as bald as the boulders. With him Yudu brought a bunch of friends to stick pegs in the ground and set their claim on the mountain. He had a corrugated iron shed built near the billabong, and when he crept in there for the night, he barred doors and windows. Gabo Djara doubted that *nagigid* would be deterred by a few bars. The sorcerer could creep through a nail hole and though the *bogo*, shovel-nosed spear, might not be able to follow, he also carries one made from the porcupine grass which could serve him equally well. At night the shed was as dark as a burrow; no light from a campfire shone to reveal the potential victim, and Yudu always kept two tribal girls in his bed, one on each side, and, imprisoned by his arms, they protected him as he slept.

The doctor tweaked at the cloth, exposing most of the ant's body. "He's terribly green. His blood might be that color, too."

"It's from living in the bush all those years. Anyway, red or green, it all goes into the bucket, Doc," insisted Yudu.

"Shouldn't you have taken him somewhere else? I mean . . . really I'm a heart surgeon, you know."

"Come on now, Doc, you're getting well paid for this. You ought to be proud of the job—this fellow is older than all of your other patients put together and in much better shape, I reckon."

The feelers itched again but Gabo Djara could not tell which, if either, twitched more strongly. Perhaps Waran and Marngit were traveling together. The nurse held a damp cloth and pressed it against the ant's jaws and Gabo Djara shied away from its evil, powerful smell reminiscent of petrol . . . or gunpowder. No—it smelled like booze. Yudu kept a stack of flagons inside his shed, drank the contents of each at one go, and made the girls do the same. Some of the fiery stuff splashed on to the floor, making the shed smell like the inside of a bottle, and that was Yudu's way to keep Nagigid at bay. The tribal spirits will not tolerate booze and even the smell of it keeps them at a distance.

"That anesthetic doesn't seem to be working. What if I dong the bugger over the head?" Yudu swung his pick handle.

Out there in the bush after failing with his *dal*, Marngit resumed human shape, hoping again to get rid of the bottles and the smell of alcohol before he could try his sorcerer's magic again. He made his way to the white man's hut to retrieve his daughter. The girl, grown enough to be *bala*, the initiated, lay on the dusty floor, her body covered with pustules and her tongue too swollen to do more than mumble— a curse the tribal elder had never seen before. Yudu did not like Marngit coming in, he hit him with the pick handle and chased him out from the hut. It looked as though the girl suffering from the white man's curse might never recover. Sister called the curse "plague" and feared a flare-up which could wipe out black and whites alike. She had a bottle of iodine which she used to rub on the youngsters in the camp, but that bottle had long been empty. Wishing to help the sick girl, Sister knelt by her all night and with her eyes closed prayed to her God and to the tribal spirit bosses to cancel the terrible spell.

Marngit's wife held that the sick girl would recover if proper remedies were applied. She brought *jamba*, tamarind fruit, which was soaked in water and drunk. They also tried *lingar*, snake vine, which, softened by hammering, was wound around

115

the girl's head. The tribal women were going to try some other remedies but Sister convinced them that the "plague" had been brought about by *balanda* and the whites might be the only ones to remedy it. She walked to the Luma Cliff, and sat there for days. Though Marngit's wife took her *gugu*, yam cooked in hot ashes, and coconuts of water, and even *jurdu*, honey wrapped in wild banana leaves, she would take nothing. Face upturned to the sky, the white woman whispered day and night, but whether she was calling on her brother Jesus to send more bottles of brown stuff, or begging him to visit Namanama, Gabo Djara could not guess. Perhaps other whites were asking help with more important worries and the more Sister nagged and begged, the longer it seemed she must wait.

The doctor was worried that Gabo Djara's blood was green. "It might be the work of the tribal sorcerer." He repeated that he had never had a patient whose blood looked green before. Yudu explained that his boss had swallowed a mountain so it was unlikely a single ant could bring harm. He himself, when held by the natives, had used the ants for a remedy which had cured him. This prompted the nurse to ask if man could be cured from Diridiri effectively, she understood that people who lose hair have no further interest in sex. Yudu told her that has not been the case with him, and that sterile people are sexually very active. "It's like eating watermelon without pips."

Up at Namanama, Marngit went to Yudu's camp pleading that he and the other men might go away, and take the terrible spots with them, but the whites do not like to be told what to do, especially by black men or spirits. Even when Jambawal, the Thunder Man, had been about, all the white man's fear—every trace of it—was forgotten as soon as the storm had passed, and the work of ripping up the country began again, as though the trees, rocks, and earth had no soul at all. Yudu had called Marngit to come closer, chinking two bottles together as if that might lure him inside the hut, but the medicine man was not to be led so easily into a trap; he could see into the mind of a man from whatever color or world he came. Spirits might outwit humans, but no one knows the mind of the machine, and a flock of those crawling beasts had set off in pursuit of Marngit, across the plain, through the pandanus forest, and still further, to the shore. Left with no land over which to flee, the man had skirted the water and headed toward Luma Cliff, calling out for Sister, but the machines flanked him, and from the one upon which he rode Yudu threw a lasso. The noose slid over Marngit's shoulders, tightened, and, as the machine-beast rolled forward, dragged the medicine man behind in the dust.

The surgeon's face was gloomy and his voice breathy and nasal. "No heart here . . ."

Yudu kept knocking the pick handle against the floor. "You'd better keep searching, Doctor. There has to be one."

"I've laid him open—have a look for yourself."

Yudu poked his finger into the ant's abdomen: "What about here then? This part's swollen up like a balloon."

"Just guts and muck—I'm not going to mess up my equipment with that rubbish."

The two men argued loudly, but Gabo Djara cut himself off from their angry words and concentrated on his own world. His feelers itched again, even more strongly than before, but who was on the way to see him? Was it Waran or Marngit? Perhaps it was both and, though their help could not matter now, the ant would be comforted to have his spiritual relatives' company while his abdomen was being ripped open by whites. His countrymen must first sneak inside the theater, and this seemed impossible when the walls looked too solid for even spirits to penetrate, and the door, so tightly sealed, was without even a keyhole. Ah! The ventilation duct in the ceiling! As Gabo Djara watched, a *bogo*, a shovel-bladed spear, edged its way slowly through the metal grid for a few feet and then stopped, suspended in mid-air. Nagigid must be tired after such a long journey and would rest until, under cover of darkness, he could strike.

Gabo Djara heard a noise and thought it was just a white man's belly rumbling, but a moment later he heard a clattering which sounded like bilma, clapping sticks. Dingo could make noise like that with his teeth, he told himself.

"You've stolen that heart, haven't you? Come on, Doctor, tell the truth."

"How did I get involved in this? You're all raving mad," said the doctor.

Two shining eyes appeared from the darkness of the ventilation duct. They halted, looking down on to the operating table. Waran and Marngit—they both must be about. With two of them coming to help, there might be a way out.

Yudu still complained about the missing heart: "Something like fifty thousand years old and still beating—I'll bloody blow your head off for this."

The room plunged into dark suddenly. "What the hell is happening!" shouted Yudu.

"There is a big storm outside; the lightning must have struck the line," explained the nurse.

"What about the emergency power?"

"That has failed, too," said the doctor.

"This is all your trick, Doc. I'll get you for this."

As the two men tussled they crashed into furniture and equipment in the dark. Gabo Djara felt the warm touch of the shovel-bladed spear passing swiftly over the open wound on his thorax and the skin healing fast behind it to the sound of Nagigid's chant. The sorcerer moved with delicacy in the dark, unlike the stumbling humans, and with a single accurate stroke, severed the rope that imprisoned Gabo Djara. The ant, glorying in his freedom, clung to Nagigid's blade and held fast as he was carried up to the ceiling to be led along the ventilation duct.

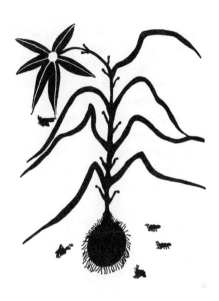

The plants are forever kind to humans, Jogu tells me. If they fail to heal a man they see that he springs somewhere in the bush and, by joining their lot, he might help his human relatives later on. From our rock shelter she can tell where each of the trees stood and how green it looked. When getting up in the morning she will rest her eyes on da and mutter chants to charm the tree as though greeting an old relative. The tree often answered her back with swaying branches and let her know if the flowering is soon to begin and how plentiful it would be with nectar. The plants flower throughout the year to tell man that the monsoon might be over or the Dry should be around soon. By the bush calendar no flood goes away or drought comes without the trees being first to know about it. From our rock shelter Jogu was able to tell if a water hole half a country away is dry by looking at a gum tree nearby. When expecting a child some monsoons ago, she dreamed of a kangaroo eating gugu, a large yam, and thought Gugu would be a proper name for the newcomer. The child turned out to be a boy, but since yams do not have anything to tell whether they are male or female, she opted for barg, black kangaroo; it lives among the rocks above the escarpment and comes down to hunt near the billabong when the country goes dry.

One morning Jogu noticed that balbak had turned a pale green—the termite tree was actually flowering to tell that the monsoon should be about soon. She rushed down immediately to help Djarudu make a shelter, but as we were suffering from the Rot, neither Yudu nor I could strip the trunk of gum tree and prepare the bark sheets for the roofing. We watched the women as they stuck two fork poles in the ground and set saplings on top of them for the main ridge. Several lighter saplings were laid against it, forming a tent-shaped frame. The dwelling looked familiar to Yudu and he admitted to living in a similar one almost all his life—that dwelling was of canvas, though. The women covered the hut with djalg, paperbark sheets, and laced them together with jagnara, pandanus fronds. Man has split the atom but the shape of the home one lives in has changed little. A small platform had been erected inside the dwelling with shorter pieces of sapling covered with dry grass and paperbark for humans to rest on. Yudu found the dwelling as comfortable as one he slept in when at Coronation Mine. Though the new shelter held against the monsoon showers, the ground did not. As the wild plum trees in the bush finished their crop and gugu shot out from the saturated ground, the billabong swelled. The water rose to the platform of the hut. Marngit told Djarudu to move her husband back to the escarpment but to keep an eye on him to see that no harm is done to the rocks. Though he restrained himself from chipping the boulders, Yudu poked the rod of his counter in the rocks whenever he found enough strength to move about. Most of the boulders hid their secrets, but not one that was covered with old tribal paintings. As the white hand held the scanner over an immense crocodile portrayed on the wall, it trembled; it trembled even more when it moved on to an ancient tribal scene of a woman, her newly born child and a dingo being swallowed by a serpent. "The counter clacks red-hot." Yudu hoped to round up the tribesmen as soon as he recovered and hoped that they would lead him to the find. I told him that the painting must date back to the Ice Age, and though the tribesman who painted the scene might be reborn as a tree, he would not be able to lead us. Yudu explained to me that before he took off for the prospecting expedition Sir Rock-Pile had told him that if there were no tribal people to be rounded up, Yudu would have to look for ocher himself. I tried to convince him that, according to science, the sea rose at the end of the Ice Age and that is the period where the myth of tribal creation led us, too. People and the plants have been about since the drifting of the continents, but to a tribesman it matters little if his ancestor was a tree, insect, or human—we all owe our origin to someone. Yudu admitted that the prehistory is beyond his understanding; however, since he was told by Sir Rock-Pile that the hills do not walk, he expected that the rocks he was after would be hiding in the bush.

Chapter 14

WHAT the rocks turn into when they are crushed and what pounded dust tastes like, Gabo Djara was to find out on three occasions. Although he learned about the white man's greed and hunger for the boulders and the trouble he goes to seeking them, it still was unclear to the ant how one can live on the dust alone.

According to Sister Alba, rocks have a magic of their own which is even greater than *dal*. The magic lies dormant in the boulders and has been there ever since the mountains appeared. "It's the world of science," Sister told Marngit that in her younger days she was taught by a woman called Curie, the first human to know about the magic of the rocks. That magic could reshape the earth, make new mountains, lakes, and even bring about new stars, just as the tribal ancestors did during the Dreaming. "Your world and our science are not far apart." She showed Marngit a picture of the Curie woman which she kept tucked inside the Bible in her hut; it had crumbling edges and looked blurred. Sister explained that her friend Curie was searching for the secret of how to lure *dal* out fom the boulders. "With that power at hand the world could become a better place to live in—at least Madame Curie thinks so." Sister Alba tried to be impartial.

Gabo Djara came to remember Madame Curie clearly as he would remember every *balanda* who has meddled with Namanama rocks. He first met her while she sat by her workbench. The woman was pounding a handful of rocks in a metal bowl with a small club-shaped implement. Woken by the pounding, the ant stretched out both his feelers, but in the dust-laden air he could not tell whether there were any cracks through which to crawl to safety. Next to him a stone struck by a metal tool was crumbling into grains of sand. Choked by the dust around him, the ant felt his rear limbs grow numb "Get out of my mortar!" Curie tried to remove him from the vessel. She jabbed again with the club: "Stay away from the pestle." She had a faint voice and looked weak as people do after a long drought or illness. Curie dipped a loose leaf from her notebook into the mortar and let the ant cling to it. Though white, she reminded Gabo Djara of a tribal woman crushing cycad nuts to make them into *ngadu*, damper baked in hot ashes. The page rested on the bench and the ant crawled over hastily written numbers, symbols, and words before sitting down to clear the dust from his feelers. "There must be quite a colony of yours down there in that bush. That's surprising— my dear friend Rutherford mentioned nothing about you." She told the ant that the rocks were a gift from her colleague Rutherford who, although white-skinned, came from the same part of the world as Gabo Djara. She felt indebted to her friend, for the rocks were better than any she had crushed before. Madame Curie peered at the loose leaf. "That land of yours must be very rich in boulders." She had actually been told by her friend Rutherford that there were mountains of good rocks in the Australian bush which, if crushed to dust, could melt

123

the snow over the whole world. "In time to come, no man shall suffer from frostbite," she told Gabo Djara, trying to compliment his country. The ant would have been much happier if he were told about gum leaves which remain green through the monsoon and can survive drought; when flowering, the trees drip with nectar. Why would the *balanda* prefer rocks to them? His hostess must have sensed that he was thinking about his empty belly and handed him a crumb. The food had a tempting savory smell, but the ant had never tasted croissant before and he feared that the food could be a bait to lure him into something that he would regret. Madame Curie thought that he must have been hurt while he was between the crushed rocks in her mortar and handed out another crumb which she had dipped into her tea. "It will go down much easier." The wet food made a blot on the paper and she suddenly grew angry seeing her writing blurred. Gabo Djara did not want to cause his hostess any discomfort and tried to leave. He crawled to the edge of the bench and looked through the window at the world outside. Instead of trees, tall gray buildings stood about, crowded together like a dead mangrove forest. "We, too, have our anthills," Madame told him. She let him crawl over her hand to get a better view through the window. The ant noticed later that the white hand that held him was covered with discolored spots, marks which he had never seen before on human skin, but had seen on leaves after they had lain for too long in the sun and were soon to drop off the stem. She told the ant that the humans, cramped in their anthill, might begin eating one another soon; then she corrected herself, explaining that they had been doing it for generations. It was a cold winter's day when the ant visited her, and as she spoke, Madame shivered and kept apologizing for not being able to light the fire: "After we melt the snow, the world might be a cozier place to live in." She went back to crushing the rocks and her teeth chattered from the cold as she struck them again and again with the metal implement. Later on Gabo Djara was placed in a little tubular passage through which he had to crawl while his hostess adjusted the dial on the machine. "Extraordinary—you're more radioactive than anything I have encountered before." She rolled the ant over, holding a magnifying glass above him, but could discover no spots on his skin. That, too, was "extraordinary."

Gabo Djara stayed on the bench for some days, watching fragments of pungent fumes rising from test tubes; steam rising from a boiling flask traveled through a system of glass piping and dripped into a glass container—the drops reminded him of morning dew trickling down the leaves. The water looked the same and tasted the same as that from Namanama: it seemed for a moment that his world and *balanda*'s world are not far apart. The ant preferred the bush, however, where he could climb a gum tree and feast on green leaves and nectar; these foods tasted better than croissant. Madame showed him some strange substance held on a tiny plate and kept in a glass enclosure. The substance had a light of its own and shimmered in the dark even when hardly anything else could be seen. "It comes from the rocks," Madame told him. So, she got her hands on *dal*, the magic, thought the ant.

Years went by before Gabo Djara saw his hostess again. She now walked gingerly as though stepping along a rotting log over a deep ravine. Madame led the ant out from the workroom to show him a rose she had planted in a garden next to her window. The plant had green leaves and white flowers: the ant watched the aged woman watering it and noticed that the spots had spread and there was no longer a single hair growing on her skin. Madame explained that in spite of her growing bald and old, science had made progress: "We might be getting ready for the snow, forever." The ant was told to crawl up the spiky bush and help himself to leaves and flowers. Though he preferred gum tree foliage to rose leaves, the ant anticipated a good meal just the same. The white flowers looked large, but had a strong scent which irritated the ant's eyes: one of his feelers grew numb and drooped. The leaves had an acid taste and, after chewing one, Gabo Djara developed a sneezing fit and thought his crop might never be good for a meal again. When some days later his hostess came out to the garden to see the ant again, it looked as though she, too, was kept on the wrong food. In spite of her sickly appearance, she tried to water the rose again, but noticed that the white flowers had withered and were quickly drying in the sun: "How extraordinary." She explained that she had to write to her friend Rutherford, for now it seemed that the melting snow might not bring any comfort after all.

Gabo Djara did meet his hostess again, but this time he saw only her picture hanging on the wall of her workroom. Many of her old tools still remained on the bench; the notebook was there, too. A younger woman, looking very much like Madame, stared at the pages of the notebook, muttering, "Let's try—it should split." The new woman was about Sister Alba's age and, though it seemed unlikely that the two of them could be siblings, Gabo Djara felt that both women must have been raised to believe that one can live on the dust of crushed rocks. When she first arrived at Namanama, Sister went around renaming the plants and cursed them for being wild. She had many nice words to say about the rocks: though the rocks provided no leaves or nectar, she hoped that the boulders might repay her with kindness, and whenever she passed by a rock not seen before, she knocked a chip off and placed it in her bag. It was only some monsoons later, when she learned that the rocks do not heal man, that the plants won her over.

Gabo Djara was still reminiscing about the Sister when the new hostess, flipping through the pages of the notebook, came to a loose leaf with a blot where the ant had once nibbled. "The world should be freed from snow: the boulders will see to it."

A young man who was helping the new hostess thought

the same. He felt sure that the rocks, being so old, had a wisdom that no human could match. The man had combed oily hair and a freshly shaved face; had it not been for his voice, it would not have dawned on the ant that he was seeing Recluse in his younger days. "Let's help the boulders free the world," he told the hostess. The woman looked at the notebook and chanted some words and numbers: Recluse joined in the chanting while his hand adjusted a machine on the bench. The machine failed to join the chant but buzzed instead like a trapped insect. The ant remembered the sound from his earlier visit and drew back his feelers to shield them from the irritating noise. He was about to crawl away and look for shelter when a flash of light flooded the room. The flare faded away just as suddenly as it had come, but a smell of molten rock lingered in the air. The ant rubbed his front legs across his bulging eyes and held them closed for a while. When he was able to look again, the balanda were hugging each other and chanting jubilantly: "We've cracked the atom." The hostess then looked at the picture on the wall: "I wish you were here, Mother, to share the joy."

Looking through the window, Gabo Djara noticed that the leaves on the rose bush had suddenly lost their green color and were covered with dark spots, and some were falling off. The ant remembered the Sister telling Marngit once that if the whites freed dal from the rocks and used the power unwisely, there would be no green plants seen ever again. As the ant stretched out his feelers again, the smell of the molten rocks still lingered about; he reminded himself to crawl carefully and stretched one limb at a time—a single mistake could lead him into the white man's oven.

Chapter 15

THERE in the auditorium nearly nothing was known of him, so Gabo Djara hoped that nothing would be expected, either. From behind the emblem hanging above the wooden statue of Peace, where he clung to the U of UN, the ant eavesdropped on the gathering of the General Assembly. Into this ceremonial, witnessed by such cold human faces that they might be wooden figures carved by their spiritual ancestors, Gabo Djara had walked uninvited and, with luck, unnoticed.

The wall below looked like a slab of Jingana's cave, covered by a large mural set with mosaic, and as Gabo Djara crawled slowly across it, he recognized *magarada*—the peace-making ceremony. He stared into the faces of his ritual ancestors, puzzled how they, too, happened to be there, in the white man's world. No one but the spirits knew when and how the ancient figures were painted in the cave, but from the time the pictures appeared on the wall, telling the story of the first peace-making ceremony, no clan or tribe had ever needed to fight. Common sense had always prevailed to settle any dispute which arose.

Below, in the Assembly auditorium, and beside a small Australian flag draped on the table, sat Sir Rock-Pile. Behind it . . . or him—Gabo Djara always found himself in this dilemma over how one should refer to a boulder—appeared an object the size of a human head which at first seemed to be a half-moon sitting behind the rock. The object then rose slightly, turned and became—Specs . . . without a single hair left on his head apart from his eyebrows, and these had grown, or been bleached, white. The mural exuded a companionable warmth for which Gabo Djara was grateful but he was bewildered by its presence in the Assembly hall. Perhaps the painting had been brought in with Sir Rock-Pile, in order to explain his origins to the gathering but, on reflection, Gabo Djara doubted that Specs and the other *balanda* would bother. It seemed more likely that they would prefer to have the whole mountain and Namanama to themselves without sharing any of its secrets.

The ant's right feeler itched and trembled like a stem caught in the wind. Waran must be close; seldom before during any of his wanderings in the white man's world had the message reached Gabo Djara so strongly. The sensation seemed to come from below so he glanced down; surely Sir Rock-Pile could not be the cause. Beside the pedestal stood a log stained with *malnar* red ocher, and coiled about by a painting of Jingana—the *ubar!* The log was *ranga*—most sacred of all objects and only brought out during certain ceremonies as a tribute to newly initiated men, to seal tribal friendship or to welcome the arrival of the rain. The same log—the uterus of the mother from which all black men come—would be there again at his departure for the spirit world to accompany him with the sound of its beating but at other times lay silent, guarded by spirits at the *djang*, the sacred place which only the elders knew.

Gabo Djara crawled around the curves or ochered wood to the end of the coiled rings; the log had been sawed, taking the serpent's head off at the neck. How, even if Marngit came to lash it with palm fronds, could the *ubar* restore life to the country without Jingan's head? Gabo Djara, desolated, squeezed himself into a crack in the log, for there was no object closer to his heart, or more precious, and he felt he must cling to it at least until the white man forced them apart.

The feeler itched again. Gabo Djara watched Specs' hand sneak under the table to toss down some scraps and slip back quickly to rest against the *ubar*. Sir Rock-Pile, sitting on his pedestal in an aura of self-satisfaction, and spotlessly sashed and tailored for the occasion, was attended by a black man wearing a white bow tie. Leaning forward, deferentially, this man patted the boulder, whispering words of respect which Gabo Djara interpreted as no more than a polite gesture, expected of one who seemed to be the host. The ant stretched both feelers out to learn more of someone whose skin seemed so much like that of a distant relative, but at the same moment Specs' hand plunged inside the *ubar*. Discreetly, the white man drew out a small stone and, rubbing it with his fingers, awaited an appropriate moment to slip the ore sample into the black man's eager hand.

"Please, dear President, accept this as a token of tribal respect."

A shadow cast on the floor appeared first, and a moment later, the ant saw *dodoro*, pigeon, under the table shyly picking crumbs before fluttering quickly away with her prize. I must know that soul; only a girl with pigeon totem could turn into a bird of that kind. Gabo Djara pictured the bird making her way out of the United Nations building. She would be searching for somewhere to perch, but would only hover above the bronze statue of a man forging a plough from a sword, hesitating to rest on the cold metal of the raised hammer, for tribal man knows neither steel nor plough. *Dodoro* still fluttered in the air. She had twice tried to land on the statue but had sprung back, shocked by the coldness of the metal. Which girl had the pigeon for her totem, the one who married Recluse or the other who tried to heal Yudu from the Rot?— the ant tried to remember. Both of them belong to Dingo tribe but had fled to Namanama after the whites leveled Mount Wawalag into dust. Whether the girls were human, or were spirits seeking a new country to be reborn, hardly mattered, for you remain a tribal soul even though you have been turned into a bird. Gabo Djara watched the pigeon hovering above the statue—no tribal soul likes to perch on metal. At Namanama, the land had stayed a part of Jingana ever since it was created for man by the spiritual ancestors. The black man does not make furrows in the earth, ripping open his own mother's belly.

Somewhere, half a world away, the pigeon landed on a wire cage inside which rattled a bulldozer no bigger than a fist. The machine dug a ditch and then swept the area around, piling up shrunken bodies. Gabo Djara saw some of his countrymen wandering about in the tiny compound, but with barely the strength to drag themselves along. In a corner of the cage hung a nest with a little chick inside. Featherless and weak, the chick lifted its head but failed to open its beak wide enough for the food. The crumbs from the beak of *dodoro* rolled through the wire mesh, missed the nest, and fell down on the naked tribesmen who stretched upward to catch the food. The pigeon cooed softly before taking off to return for more. It must be Recluse's wife, thought the ant, she was the one who had youngsters.

When the bird flew back, a grain of wheat lay seductively on the floor under the desk and, as Gabo Djara watched, Dodoro first pecked and then lunged backward, fighting against a tautened fishing line which pulled its victims toward a briefcase marked "J.C." Out of the case poked the probing snout of the anteater, looking longer than ever before, as it swayed and swept, almost to the floor.

It was not until much later, after he had wandered about the Assembly auditorium and reached the top of the President's desk, that Gabo Djara saw Dodoro again. Suspended on the wall behind the black man with the bow tie, the bird drooped, its wings pinned behind it with a large bulldog clip, its body hanging exhausted and motionless. The pigeon held something in its beak, but as his view was blocked by the man's shoulder, the ant could not tell what this might be unless he found a better vantage point. Gabo Djara climbed on to a microphone, but the object in Dodoro's beak was still out of sight and, as he cast about, searching for a higher observation post, the ant's glance returned to Specs sitting in the front row of the auditorium and busily dipping his hand in and out of the ubar whenever a delegate rose to pay his respects to the rock. With eyes only for his ranga, his sacred object, the ant did not notice that the presidential bow tie had moved forward, bringing the presidential mouth within a palm's breadth. "On behalf of the General Assembly, I bid welcome to Sir Rock-Pile and stress how touched we all are by his compassion for Progress. He has been on the moon quite recently, as we all know, and made an astronomical mineral find—ha! ha!—quite a revitalizing experience for the whole field of human endeavor. We . . ."

Specs crooked a finger and whispered into the presidential ear and, though unable to catch the words, Gabo Djara guessed from his expression that Specs was disapproving. "A slight correction there," apologized the President. "It was actually in Australian bush at Wilberforce Gulf, not on the moon—a printer's error—do forgive me."

The orator coughed nervously and Gabo Djara, blown through the mesh of the microphone head, found himself swung across a metal partition with his abdomen on one side and his thorax on the other. By the time he had righted himself and lifted his head again, the ant found he was face to face with an attendant bringing the presidential throat a glass of water. The man—the Usher of the Black Rod—blinked his eyes so beadily and so close that Gabo Djara, fearing he would be spotted, withdrew inside the microphone.

"That native girl from Wilberforce Gulf is awaiting you at your apartment. We trapped her at last." Lowering his voice, the Usher of the Black Rod reiterated that the tribes of Wilberforce Gulf had been about for three thousand generations and have perfected their erotic rituals—something that no man had experienced before. "It's a pity there are only a few of their females of entertainable age left about." The Usher mentioned that some unsubstantiated rumors had been floating about of a so-called Dirigiri complaint; it relates to lack of hair, but that it should be of no concern. "As you'll see, she is furry all right, sir; they say that even the man who split the atom fell for her and changed his faith." Some more words were whispered close by the presidential ear and, judging by his happy smile, they were those he wished to hear. The ant turned to inspect the interior of the microphone and immediately felt apprehensive of the metal mesh looming overhead, like the walls of a trap. In a panic, the ant crawled clumsily about searching for a hole or a crack that would let him out, but only succeeded in getting one of his feelers jammed in the mesh and his whole body entangled in a tiny roll of wire.

The President's voice flowed on: "While spreading progress Sir Rock-Pile traveled under the alias 'Dr. Livingstone'—as we all presumed. Ho! Ho!"

No laughter, but shouting rose from the auditorium, then whistles and howls like the noises of a hunt.

The orator snatched up the microphone in the hope of

raising his voice above the hubbub. "We are all truly grateful to God, and to Mr. Stanley who saved Sir Rock-Pile from the savage natives."

When the noise from the crowd rose again, the presidential temper was finally lost, however, and the black hand raised the microphone and smashed it against the desk. As Gabo Djara felt streams of electrical current running through his body he knew that he must now decide whether to spring out among his enemies or stay to be charred.

An amplified whining noise echoed through the auditorium like the sound of a lonely dingo caught in a trap. Gabo Djara thought that it must be Dodoro crying, the pigeon was no longer hanging on the wall, though her shadow remained there with wings held by a bulldog clip.

Chapter 16

ARE the legislators, the pundits who make the law in the white man's world, immortal? Gabo Djara met one of them; the man spoke softly and only kind words: "In the eyes of justice all men are equal, at last."

The ant had no desire to dispute the law the whites have set for themselves and others, and looked blankly at the man sitting by a heavy oak table. I came here as a friend, he reminded himself, and lowered both his feelers.

His host was in the process of writing something but laid down his quill, the freed hand rose up and, tapping a globe on the desk, spun the earth: "We struggled to free your kind." The man looked an exact copy of the picture bound in the volume coated in dust in the parliamentary library. His old-fashioned garb (perhaps made soon after the ant encountered the first white man) looked well brushed now; the creases and occasional greasy blots seen earlier on the paper print had left no trace—William Wilberforce, alive and well. His index finger followed the line of the equator while the world kept turning in front of his spotty nose: "Every black soul has been freed."

Hasn't he heard of five hundred and fifty of our tribes? Gabo Djara was going to say, but then reminded himself that he had to show some gratitude, not to give rise to anger. The ant began to move his feelers signaling out: "I came to thank you, sir, for making available the *Abolition of Slavery Act*, 1833, such a fine volume. It saved my life."

Mr. Wilberforce held his hand against the jabot covering his chest. "Most obliged, dear brother."

The ant wondered whether he ought to explain how, long ago, during the passage of the Atomic Act in the Australian Parliament, he had had to shelter in a burrow which silverfish had mastered through the pages of the *Abolition of Slavery Act*, when a picture behind the host caught his attention. It covered a good part of the wall, yet it portrayed only one man—a mosslike clump of curly hair perched over a dark face. The forehead of the man had a fresh wound with a trail of blood running over one of the temples, diluting in the drops of his sweat before sinking in the bushy hair below. Whenever he faced a soul stricken by pain Gabo Djara's limbs quivered. Now his feelers trembled, for the man in the picture reminded him of a dingo caught in an immense iron trap. Gabo Djara stared at the picture. Had he seen him before? The saved man looked familiar, almost a relative, though it was hard to say whether he was the President in his young days that he met earlier at the auditorium, or a mutual cousin of him and the ant.

"That man is chained to a galley—a nigger, not one of yours, though."

The ant compared his skin to that of the distant cousin seen on the wall and, though there was a fraction of difference, he felt as though the soul could have been the same. Gabo Djara had learned long ago that it was not so much the color but the world and the country a man lives in that shapes his life; the more precious little things one has in life that can be robbed, the deeper the pain a man will suffer.

The white hand rested on the globe. "The other blacks were less fortunate than your people. Many of them were enslaved." The globe spun for a while on its own while Mr. Wilberforce's hand reached for a book.

Gabo Djara watched the globe. Will men ever find the way back to our tribal country? At Namanama, the boulders forming Mogo Ranges are immense ant eggs. When a man dies, his soul splits in two. One turns into a boulder and waits to be reborn, just as plants do from a seed; the other part returns to the Land of the Dead to join the tribal ancestors, and thus the human seed will never be lost.

The host waved an old copy of the *Abolition of Slavery Act*. "This book, this alone, wrecked every galley."

With all the boulders ground, the tribal souls will be reduced to specks of dust before the white man scatters them all over the world. Though made to look so little, the souls will have to struggle back to Namanama, for you can be reborn only in your own country. Gabo Djara looked at the globe, trying to determine the length of the equator so as to know how many camps the straining souls will have to journey before they are back home again.

The white hand swept the dust from the cover of the book. As the shine returned to the old volume a new title emerged, *Atomic Energy Act*—written in the same lettering as Gabo Djara saw it at the palace long ago while the bill awaited the Royal Assent. However, in the hands of the man who had championed the cause of the blacks the book appeared much larger, as if every single word had considerable weight, and looked more a block of precious metal—so close to the white man's heart—than a volume of paper. "The title has been revised, the essence remains the same, though." Mr. Wilberforce's voice sounded apologetic. The painting of the man in the gallery behind him swayed slightly as though some unseen power in his words was trying to tilt it. "Would you like a cup of tea?"

Kind words were seldom encountered in a relationship with the whites—offerings were uncommon, too. Gabo Djara wondered for a while what to say to the host. A cup was inappropriate for an ant to drink from, though he did not mind having a lump of sugar; he had tried that food once long ago and the sweet taste tempted him ever since so that he often thought apart from their strange habit of eating the rocks and obsession with strange metal tools, the crumb of sugar was about the only thing he could share with the whites.

Gabo Djara's shape amused the host's housemaid, she gazed at him for a while, then, leaning toward her master, whispered something, giggling unceasingly. "It's his totemic appearance—no harm in that." The host rustled uncomfortably in his chair but the servant persisted: "Sir, can we be sure it is safe?" Part of Mr. Wilberforce's chin twitched and, struggling to prevent it spreading over his whole face, he said loudly: "I would like you to meet Mr. Dj— D— G— Geargy—the spiritual leader of the black Australians. He's very pleased with your sugar." The maid curtseyed and left the room while the ant waved one of his feelers as a friendly gesture. He knew now, just as he knew centuries ago, that it will be long—very long—before the whites could come to terms with his appearance. When they finally did, there might not be many of his tribesmen about. The ant looked at the picture on the wall behind the host, thinking again that his distant cousin chained to the galley might be more fortunate if the sympathy of the whites was any comfort.

Mr. Wilberforce laid his index finger on the globe again. "It's very rich country of yours here. Nowhere else has He been so generous."

Gabo Djara disputed the view that Namanama was created by anyone else but Jingana and other tribal ancestors. Instead of raising objections, however, he took a bit of the sugar.

"I was very honored when they named that gulf there after me. It lies northeast of your sacred place at the Curie Ranges. If it was listed on the map it would not be further than a fraction of an inch." The white man stared at the globe.

Does Mr. Wilberforce know the country of every black man so well? Gabo Djara looked at the picture on the wall again.

"They're going to build a whole chain of lighthouses along the gulf's coast. The waters there have grown so busy with shipping lately. The beacons will be seen from beyond the horizon." The man wanted to point his finger to a certain spot but was unable to find the place. He spun the globe again, complaining that the people must have fiddled with the maps. His index finger landed on Specs Cape and the name angered him. "A forefather of this man was Washington's lieutenant. No decent English gentleman would have the name of that rebel on the king's map."

It is Luma Cliff he is talking about, thought the ant. Why did they rename it? That man Specs never set foot on the bush there; besides, he eats rocks and it might not be long before he ground Mogo mountain into sand—the cliff would be ground, too. The sea would remain, however, and might stretch inland to engulf the land, just as it did in those mythical days. Gabo Djara reminded himself that the man whose name the sea bears was the one now offering him tea and sugar. Perhaps the man is not so sinister as the other whites and might like to help. Now that his name is pinned on the map next to Namanama, the ant thought of him not as balanda but as a tribal neighbor who could help when the country is struck by drought or flood. He had heard of the man long ago; the name was referred to in the parliamentary debate while he hid in the *Abolition of Slavery Act*. Later, the name was rumored about at the Stock Exchange and . . . Wilberforce Gulf had been mentioned several times at the royal dinner. In the bush, Recluse used to talk about Wilberforce often. "He should have been here long ago," he told Sister, and wondered what might have kept Wilberforce, for it was believed that the man had called just about everywhere else excpet Namanama. Sister, too, thought if Wilberforce had been about he would have helped the tribal people to hold against the whites. With him about, Sir Rock-Pile might never had set foot on Mount Wawalag. The mountain would have still been there instead of a sea of dust, so would Dingo people. "Even the souls of the dead have fled the place," she often cursed, and told how she heard the howling of dingoes at night—the soul of people driven from their country and lost in the bush. Sister prayed that Wilberforce might come and save Namanama and asked her friend to do the same. Recluse told her that the white God had long abandoned him, but some days later when Sister pleaded again, he considered: "I suppose there's nothing to lose by being courteous to Him."

His host sipped his tea while his eyes rested on the globe: "Thank heaven those ships do not traffic in slaves anymore. It's a mere industrial commodity." The man brushed off his jabot. "The experts believe a shipload of that precious rock dust from your country could generate more energy than all of black mankind chained to the galleys would do in a whole year. No wonder they call that god-given substance 'yellow cake'."

The picture on the wall quivered and the face of the unknown black man faded away. The sea behind him was still there; so was the vast empty space. Something floated in the air, Gabo Djara reared up. A swarm of gnats hovered above the water drifting slowly to the distant land. He quickly glanced back at the host; does this man know that every rock or tree at Namanama has a soul?

Mr. Wilberforce leaned forward. "We will see that your people receive a fair deal. That mineral find in your country is astronomical, I gather. Do not let it fall into the enemy's hands." The man then mentioned something about George Washington again.

The swarm had spun over the sea like an immense serpent heading toward the edge of the horizon. They are coming back, all of them—Gabo Djara assumed that the gnats were flying ants, the souls of his people returning from the white man's world. Their shape was reduced, for it contained only a part of their spirit that had traveled to the Land of the Dead to join the tribal ancestors.

The host sipped his tea. "We can commission the Canterbury bells to ring for a week—beg the Lord to accept every black soul into His Kingdom."

We have a world of our own. Mr. Wilberforce's shoulders shielded the view and Gabo Djara swung his head to see the picture on the wall. Far ahead of the gnat's swarm, the land had appeared, though too far off to tell if it had sprung from the sea or the mist beyond. Luma Cliff!—the ant recognized his Namanama.

We can build a chapel at that cape which they called after that blooming chap Specs; every black soul will flock there. The mountain they are quarrying the rock from is not far from there. The man sipped his tea again and asked how far a boomerang could be thrown to knock down an enemy effectively. Talking about warfare, the man asked how many boomerangs Gabo Djara could muster and if his warriors would fight against George Washington and the French: "It would be for God and king."

On Luma Cliff Marngit sat, looking toward the sea and clapping two wooden sticks together to accompany his voice while he chanted. Next to him sat Waran, the dingo tried to chant, too, but made only some throbbing noise and, not happy with the sound, turned to howling . . .

The host held a box of biscuits toward Gabo Djara: "Have some, please . . . Don't let that sadden you—there's room in

141

our world to accommodate every black soul." The man spoke again about warfare as though it belonged to the past; nevertheless it pestered his mind and he asked, "How effective is black magic?" He had heard from some earlier explorers that an Aborigine points the bone toward his enemy and that enemy dies instantly, even though he be a half country away. "That would bring an end to Washington and the French." The man promised that after a successful campaign, the warriors would go back to the bush and legislation would be amended to give the right to the natives to live and worship on their land. "You and I could draft the Act of Human coexistence. You have to help . . . all black mankind would be grateful to you."

Gabo Djara felt uncertain if his host was talking about the white man's heaven or the kingdom down on the earth. However, neither of them were worth thinking about, and Gabo Djara concentrated again on the picture on the wall. The swarm of gnats had already reached the land, passed Luma Cliff, and flown over dust-veiled Mount Mogo, heading to the alluvial plain beyond covered with rain forest.

On the cliff Marngit, helped by Waran, still chanted, summoning the souls of the dead back to the land. Next to them Dodoro perched on a rock. She, too, tried to sing the people back by long, soft coos. Behind the pigeon, the naked chick squatting in the nest opened its beak now and then to join the others, but the voice of the infant was too weak to be heard. Should there be two chicks in the nest? Dodoro had a boy first, he must be in the bush playing with toy spears or Marngit might have taken care of him—he needs a boy to teach him the secrets of healing. The ant looked at Dodoro with gratitude. It is good someone was there to call the tribal people back. No tribal soul dies beyond Namanama, he told himself.

Gabo Djara knew the swampy part of Namanama well. It stretched eastward on Mount Mogo and was covered with a canopy of tall paperbark trees providing safe places for his people when they departed. The spirits of the dead retire there, hiding in the shadows around the billabongs, and wait to be ferried to the Land of the Dead. However, the ant could not see much of the place now—the billabong, long dry, had a crusty surface of hardened mud. Instead of the trees only dry skeletons showed here and there. Above them hovered the swarm of gnats searching for a place to retreat. They came down to squat on a dry branch. Nearby a willy-willy raised a column of dust from the dry ground. The swooping wind came against the trees, first a branch snapped off, followed by the whole trunk. The handful of gnats was seen for a while, whirlpooling in the dusty abyss. Gabo Djara stared at the willy-willy swooping around but he did not see his tribesmen again.

The white man leaned forward again. "Have you ever thought of entering politics? We can assure you a safe seat in Parliament. Once in, you can help your constituents. We can draft the laws together—for the blacks and the whites."

This man assumes I will defect, or have done that already. The ant felt surprised that his host did not know that in the tribal world, though the man could change into a tree or a rock, the spiritual leader holds no more privileges than the others.

My brother Rotar who is held inland wrote a short letter which was passed on to me by Sister Alba. "Have faith in trees; they'll lead you out of despair." He might be right: the night after Yudu had detected the radiation trace at the cave a green ant came to see me in my dream. He descended from a nest of da branches, crawled across the rock, and reared up. He clattered for a while with his jaws and it sounded as though two boomerangs were clapping against each other. A chant was heard:

At Namanama
country of Gabo Djara
monster gulps boulders
    quicker he eats
    sooner he dies

    I must have slept hard that morning and failed to hear Jogu leaving the shelter. When I woke the sun was already high up, for Marngit's

144

shadow fell over me. He came in to tell me of a message from my brother who he referred to as wawa, skin-brother. Knowing that both of them are expecting to be reincarnated as trees, it was no surprise to hear that they had become kinsmen. Marngit told me that I, too, am to be taken into the Green Ant clan, and now that the plants are curing me I should make the bush my home. He expected the flood waters to ease as soon as the spear grass stopped flowering and he held that by surviving through the Wet one recovers during the Dry. Since I have been here for years he told me that, like the plants, people thrive after the monsoon and that dal, curing magic, is especially strong then. "You'll be healed in no time," the medicine man said. He smiled and it looked as though he knew that I have been visited in a dream by Gabo Djara.

My wife held that if a man dreams about the tribal ancestor, he is not to talk to others and has to remain silent just as a tree would do. Marngit told me that a ceremony would be held soon after the flowering of the bloodwood to initiate me. I will be taken into the Green Ant tribe just as my brother and Alba were years ago, and no soul or a tree had regretted letting them have Gabo Djara for their ancestor. He asked about Barg, who after we become skin-brothers, is to be his waku, nephew. The boy was out in the bush with his mother. He was already grown enough to toss about the stem of the dry grass pretending it was a spear. Marngit thought that one could become a healer if he learns early to like plants. The medicine man expected that he himself would age and die, just as any other tribal man, and when that happens dal, the healing power which he believed belongs to the spirit world, would have to be passed on to a younger man.

Jogu expected to have another child at about the flowering of ga-dayka, bloodwood tree. She thought that if a child did not have gabo, green ant, as an ancestor, when grown he might turn into rock instead of a tree. Rocks do not grow and if you are not to flower or green ever again, there is no need to have a country of your own; perhaps that is the way the rocks crumble and turn into a pile of sand eventually. Unlike plants, rocks have no soul. I heard Jogu once muttering in her dream, "No man lives without soul," and thought that she, too, might have been visited by Gabo Djara. She held that for someone unrelated of plants it would be hard to tell where in the ground the roots to be dug for food are, and which berries on the bush are safe to eat. Man could easily be lost in the bush, in mangroves especially, if the trees do not tell him the way out. "No soul could make fire with unfamiliar trees." Jogu collected her dudji, a pair of fire-making sticks from worki, which Alba identified as a species of wattle: it had smooth bark but twisted twigs. Jogu thought that the twigs look that way because the tree grows on the rocky hillsides below the escarpment where no other fire-making bushes were about. She believed that being a faithful relative worki had followed her to the higher part of the country and had dry branches so that she could pick them and make fire even on a rainy morning. Had not the tree followed her about, Jogu would have had to walk down into the flooded part of the country and look for dudji. I was told by Alba that the women make the fire in teams of two. Jogu managed on her own, though. She would hold one stick firmly against the ground with her foot and sprinkle a pinch of sand on a cut notch before forcing into it the end of another stick which she holds between her palms. As the stick in her hand twirls, she leans on it and breathlessly mutters a chant, the words of which could be understood only by her faithful cousin worki. She did not have to chant for long, for the smoke often rises quickly, showing that dust from the whirling friction had caught the glow. I hardly thought much of her faith in the fire-making tree until the middle of the last Dry when worki showed itself scattered through the bush as it bloomed in a bowl of golden yellow. Jogu told me that the tree displayed the flower so that she could memorize the spot it grows on and go there when in need of dudji.

Plants are more numerous than humans. Although they were her relatives, Jogu felt that there were some trees in the bush with which she felt less familiar than others. Some days after Gabo Djara visited me I saw her and Djarudu led by Alba as they stripped the bark of minda, mistletoe tree. I recognized it, for I was told before that the tree is used for the peg of spear throwers and it was seldom cut for anything else. The people were often told that if you put minda on fire the smell and smoke would spread fast through the bush and no green ants would ever hatch again, nor would there by any newborn children. The women were in need of inner bark only; scraped from the trunk into a bailer shell, the bark was left to soak for a while. Alba had some seeds picked from the same tree and shook them into the shell. Long before I fled to the bush I was told that she once published a paper in a medical journal about the leaves of a certain bush utilized effectively by tribal women to prevent pregnancy. She held that the practice of contraception dates back before Christianity and has often been mentioned in the myths of tribal creation. Poor old Alba, she told the truth and lost her veil for revealing the secrets of lharang bush; the tribal women have known the plant since the Ice Age.

The remedy from minda was meant for Djarudu. After she drank the liquid with her eyes shut, the shell was then buried in the ground and some words were uttered to thank the tree for being helpful. Later that night I thought that Djarudu must be aware that her husband had no faith in the plants and that he may never come to think that the bush might cure him of the Rot. Like the plant of the bush Sister Alba wrote about, and which lasts only for a season, minda was said to keep a woman childless forever. Jogu told me that using the remedy was better than having children with balanda who lost all his hair and is on the way to turning into a boulder. "Rocks are ngerdno," she said, and from dead things, raise no family.

Chapter 17

AS Gabo Djara went down the long narrow passage, such silence throbbed that he knew no man, beast, or reptile accompanied him; yet for a time the ant was unaware that he was in danger of drifting beyond any possible return. At last, however, he realized that unless he soon found an exit, he would be nothing more than a fragment in a pile of fresh dung.

The passage had a slimy surface over which limbs and feelers slid easily, so, though the journey was like descending into an abyss, it proceeded smoothly. Gabo Djara wondered at first if he were not traveling through an underground anthill along a tunnel which connected nesting chambers excavated by his countrymen, for a strong smell of Namanama—the home country—lingered around. Not a single chamber showed itself, however, and, in truth, the place felt too damp to be a home for ants. The journey continued and, from the depths of the seemingly endless pit, came a rumbling as if some beast wallowed there in the darkness. "No need to worry, Chairman—it's just an upset tummy; nothing serious, I can assure you."

"There's something creeping about in there, Doctor."

"Could you have swallowed something?"

"Well—we all have to do that in the business world, you know."

"Been fiddling with any silver coins lately?"

"Of course not! I don't handle such low-grade tokens."

Gabo Djara slid further and came to a narrow passage lined with a thick layer of . . . ugh . . . the ant felt as though he was making his way through an oil slick which forced his feelers backward and pasted them to his body. A vile smell penetrating like a ghastly tide nearly drowned him, but to Gabo Djara it seemed as hopeless to try going back as it was to be sucked further. A tablet came bubbling to rest on the ant's abdomen, melting quickly, pouring over his thorax and head—and as Gabo Djara felt the sting of effervescence irritating his skin, the layer of slimey mush around him opened up.

The ancestors' trip through the serpent's belly must have been better than this, Gabo Djara thought, as he remembered how his old cousin Wawalag was swallowed by the python. Though that had happened in the time before the mountains and the trees came about, the belly of the beast would have been just the same. Desperate and helpless the woman must have been, just as he felt now; Wawalag managed to come out, however, and after being vomited, she, her child, and the dingo were licked dry to begin a new life. Would he, too, be given this grooming courtesy by his captor? No, *balanda* do not lick, they tread on you.

The chairman coughed. "I have heard that the natives of Wilberforce Gulf practice some kind of metamorphosis—they can plant a new soul in a man half a world away, even when he is dead."

The doctor thought that might be possible; some years ago

he had heard rumors that a tribesman at Coronation Mine had turned into a dingo the night before he was to be hanged. This was later confirmed by a certain man called Recluse whose papers had been found in a cave at Curie Ranges and who was purported to have had an insight into the power of tribal healing and witchcraft. The doctor held, however, that since the tribal man believes that he is descended from an animal or a plant he expects to reclaim the old ancestral shape when he dies.

"It's a very sound belief," said the chairman.

"You're surely not planning to change your faith?" The doctor asked the chairman to open his mouth so that a certain gadget could be passed down his throat.

"Well, I wouldn't mind being incarnated as Curie and have mountains packed with all those precious rocks named after me." The chairman ran out of breath after this long sentence. He belched, shaking Gabo Djara out of his reverie and tumbling him about just as a long, flexible rubber tube came inching down the man's throat, moving gently lower and lower. The gadget, which looked like a tiny snake creeping inside a burrow in search of prey, had a narrow metal head and a sinister eye which kept blinking while the head moved. "Watch the screen, Chairman, this picture shows exactly what is happening inside your tummy."

"That's a jungle, isn't it, Doctor? Everything normal, is it?"

"Well, you have swallowed rather too much . . . a little fasting would do you the world of good."

"It's all that yellow cake, I suppose, and I was assured it was quite harmless."

"Popular scientific belief had that opinion, sir."

"And now the stuff not only tastes terrible, but give me guts ache."

"You were so fond of yellow cake, too—and made tons of it to give away to poor and rich alike."

"That man Recluse shouldn't have been trusted. No man

gives away a mountain of precious ore without good reason." Gabo Djara wondered if he was in the belly of Sir Rock-Pile or Specs, but that would hardly matter. *Balanda* bellies must all be the same—all packed with the dust from the rocks. As the metal head of the tube bumped Gabo Djara, he toyed with the idea of clinging to it as it was dragged out, but rejected the theory. Contact with the white man's gadgetry repelled him and the *balanda* would certainly grab him as soon as the tips of his feelers appeared out of the man's mouth.

The chairman wanted to know whether, when man becomes incarnated as a tree, he must live in the tribal bush or in the country of his choice: "That man Recluse should know."

"I'm afraid, sir, that man is a quack." The doctor felt uneasy and turned his attention to the gadget, trying to manipulate it through the chairman's stomach. The metallic head butted its way downward pressing against Gabo Djara's abdomen with such force that the ant's sting sprang out involuntarily.

"Hell, that hurts!"

"Be still, brave Chairman. Remember when you swallowed whole mountains without a murmur."

"It's not terminal is it, Doc?"

"Don't alarm yourself, please. I'll get the devil, or whatever it is which dares to harm you."

The chairman complained that his stomach looked like the interior of a mining shaft. "And a rotten old shaft at that." The doctor tried to calm him by suggesting that the picture on the screen might be out of focus and that, at any rate, intestines are not the prettiest sight even to professionals. He was muttering encouraging words but the chairman stopped him: "What is that little insect doing down in my belly?" The doctor insisted that it was only a shadow on the screen and no cause for panic, but the chairman was adamant: "A bloody ant inside me—couldn't you see it?" The doctor pleaded for calm. Ants live in mounds that they build for themselves, some inhabit hollow logs and there is even a species that purportedly live on the leaves of gum trees in the Australian bush, but none have been found in human intestines: "We must have faith in science."

The chairman objected: "To hell with science—I have to get rid of that Rot from inside me."

The ant's right feeler itched a little, bringing a message from the far world, and though the call was rather faint, it was persistent. Gabo Djara was filled with despair—not only because he had wandered into this putrid jungle of a human belly, but also because Namanama seemed always just out of reach. Was his country drowning, too, in some murky sea?

The doctor explained that his instruments ran red-hot, and if the measurements were correct, then there must be considerable levels of contamination inside the body. "That'll be cured, I assure you." The chairman wanted to know if the doctor had read Healing Nuclear Rot. He had been told that the book elaborated on unorthodox methods used for generations by the natives of Wilberforce Gulf. "I have heard no man ever died there from contamination rot."

Painstakingly, Gabo Djara gained a foothold on the passage, heading upward, driven less by the hope of finding an exit than by an urge to stay well away from the man's stomach. After a long climb, the ant reached a small cavity and, after poking both his feelers inside to probe the shape and safety of the shelter, he crawled inside.

The doctor insisted that the book was a hoax written by a quack. It was actually found in a cave where he supposedly lived and had no scientific merit. The doctor stressed it would be absurd to expect something progressive from a people who had not even discovered the simple bow and arrow, let alone a means of combating nuclear disease. The chairman refused to budge; he held that the man who gave the mountain of ore for nothing had a sound scientific background and had been credited with taking part in the splitting of the atom.

The doctor's voice rose: "Man cracks acorns when he accidentally steps on them."

Gabo Djara's right feeler became itchy—would that be Waran on the way? No, Marngit would be more likely to come. The good *nagigid* could creep in without shadow or sound, carrying both of his spears, though the ant realized that spears alone might not be able to fetch him out. If *balanda* dies, I could be trapped inside him. Gabo Djara could feel a draft blowing along the main channel suggesting that an exit was not far ahead, and this premise was confirmed by the buzzing of a fly near the chairman's mouth, savoring his bad breath.

"Exterminate that pest."

"Yes sir, chairman, sir. May I use insecticide, sir?" The butler's voice was whining and servile, yet Gabo Djara recognized it as that of the Usher of the Black Rod. Realizing that he must have dozed off and that the doctor had gone, the ant concentrated deeply in order to picture the chairman's battle outside. It was the Usher, indeed, but dressed now in a dark suit and bow tie. The Usher raised a can and releasing a jet of mist, tracked the insect until its buzzing stopped. Gabo Djara was sure that the fly was wise enough to keep away until the contaminated air dispersed; Dodoro the pigeon would be no less clever though changed into an insect, and would undoubtedly lie in wait until a chance arose to dash into the chairman's mouth. With a fly in his mouth, a man must cough—be he black or white—and eject anything stuck in his throat.

"Dinner, sir. A choice of yellow cakes from the virgin bush at Wilberforce Gulf—especially for you, sir."

"It smells good!" As the chairman spoke, the fly swooped toward the moving mouth and Gabo Djara lifted his head, in readiness to catapult from the throat with the force of the expected cough. The lips snapped shut abruptly, however, and the insect was dashed against them. The chairman was offered the morning paper but asked instead that *Healing Nu-*

clear *Rot* be brought to him. Told that the book was out of print, he insisted that a copy be obtained through interlibrary loan. "Someone must have a copy." He grew angry. The Usher remembered the book from the Parliament House library. He had seen politicians reading it, but that was before the uranium boom and passing of the Atomic Act; the book had long been withdrawn from libraries and to read it would be in contempt of the law. "That man Recluse is a quack, sir . . . may I say your breakfast is getting cold." The chairman ate while the Usher informed him that Recluse was being pursued by the State Security as an alleged imposter. Angrily, the chairman sputtered, food still in his mouth: "Bugger State Security, I want to live."

When the food from the chairman's meal began to pour down, Gabo Djara jammed his thorax inside the cavity, leaving only his abdomen sticking out into the half-chewed mass sliding by, squelching and gurgling. If the fly was buzzing, the sound was drowned by that dreadful interior noise. A stone chip joined the procession, forcing everything else ahead of it, and swept the passage like a bulldozer blade. The ant tried to hold on, but presently he, too, tumbled.

The Usher knew that a certain missionary nurse, Sister Alba, who had known Recluse from the bush, had previously refused to cooperate with the State Security. He suggested, however, that there might be a way to obtain some information from her. The chairman said loudly, "Find me that woman. I want to see her."

"I shall contact the Holy C immediately, sir. The people there have been cooperative in the past." The Usher was about to leave when the chairman stopped him. "Get me the pontiff on the telephone but bring me my drink first."

Gabo Djara imagined, vividly, his fate if he accompanied the digesting food, and the thought of the disgusting mess in which he would be excreted made him retch. Spurred by this threat, the ant headed upward again. Now he had to struggle against rushing torrents—burning and smelling like a brewery—which cascaded down the passage. Gabo Djara stiffened his limbs, rigid and disobedient, as though they had ceased to be a part of his body.

The Usher informed the chairman that the line to the Holy C was busy and that he must try again. The butler brought another drink and whispered something into his master's ear, and both men sniggered. Perhaps they were plotting against the fly, and Gabo Djara hoped that nagigid's wisdom was equal to the cunning of the white minds. The ant reared up, trying to hear more of what was happening outside, but no sound reached him. Down the passage rolled a cloud of fumes, bringing the acrid taste and smell of burned tobacco, and though Gabo Djara searched for shelter, he soon learned that the whole area was as full of smoke as a fumigated chimney. Lying flat and tucking the tips of his feelers beneath his body to shield them, the ant hoped that whatever brand of nicotine the chairman was enjoying, he would tire of its pleasure before a point of asphyxiation was reached.

"Has that line been cleared yet?" The Chairman sounded tired of feasting. The Usher apologized for the hold-up and suggested another drink.

The sound of snoring began to rumble, so loudly that nagigid must have heard it, too; Gabo Djara sensed the fly floating about, alert and waiting to slip into the sagging mouth. The man's teeth clicked together suddenly and his lips shut tight to the hollow echo of an insect trapped in the vise of a human jaw. The ant stabbed, the mouth opened quickly as if to release the pain, and the fly rushed out, its buzzing growing fainter and fainter, then fading altogether.

Later, much later, when the telephone line did clear, the Usher woke his master to say that the pontiff was having a bath and might be available some hours later.

It was now doubtful that the Holy C would be as cooperative, as first thought. Once they learned that the Sister held the secret to tribal remedies for Nuclear Rot, certain demands might be made as preconditions for cooperation. "They need plenty of uranium to melt all the snows of Europe," advised the Usher. Stricken with sudden pain, the chairman held one of his hands against his belly, pushing the ant upward. "Damn that bloody pontiff," he gasped.

Gabo Djara could not tell how long he had been inside—time meant nothing to one so cut off from life outside and forgotten by humans. The food came regularly, in quantities large enough to feed a whole tribe of ants—not just one—but much of it smelled putrid and had an acid flavor. It seemed that the chairman had quite forgotten his suspicion of an invader in his interior, for he seemed cheerful and laughed often. That changed, though. Just as Namanama country turned from drought to monsoon flood, so may the human condition alter at one stroke, but what was happening in the white man's belly was too ugly even for the mighty Jingana to have foreseen. The chairman grew more and more taciturn, speaking only when addressed and then only in a whisper or a sigh. The gross body withered, the fat melted away, and the whole frame trembled uncontrollably. Day after day he pleaded with the Usher: "I want to be incarnated, even as a tribal fool, if nothing better—get me a witch doctor." Gabo Djara knew that death was near, and when the white man's blood cooled and the flesh began to rot, an ant could easily burrow his way out . . . Would the *balanda* body turn into a boulder? The ant reminded himself that monsters had eaten the tribal land before but none had filled his belly with loot and got away with it. The ant focused his mind on his tribal country to gaze at Mogo—the mountain—veiled in a dusty haze at the line of the escarpment where the long body of the mother, Jingana, still lay. It looked as though a huge cleaver had chopped here and there, hacking the body of the serpent into pieces. Parts of the mountain seemed so shrunk that gaps had appeared, revealing the leaden sky. Marngit was nowhere to be seen, but Gabo Djara knew that wherever the medicine man might be he would sense his country's wound, and mourn. It should not be for long: Gabo Djara told himself that when the white man died his carcass would turn into a boulder and from it would grow a new mountain.

Chapter 18

THE visit was not arranged so there had been no time to seek an official audience, but the news that Gabo Djara was on his way must have preceded him. The host waited, ceremonially dressed, and had already rehearsed kind words not only to welcome but to soothe the visitor who had traveled halfway across the world dragging his wounded soul. "I have prayed for your people, and asked my followers to do the same. We have even programmed the computers to say nice words." The man who spoke was human, not a spirit, yet he possessed the rare privilege of the power to tell his own God how to behave.

Climbing slowly upward, Gabo Djara reached the top of the baculus—the apostolic rod—to where, only a palm away, gazed a face, tranquil and filled with quiet purpose, as if the whole world had fallen asleep and he had been charged with keeping the fire alive to warm each drowsing soul. "There have been improvements in human rights, I'm pleased to hear. Emancipation is our earthly objective."

Had Sister not told him that so few of the tribe were left? That the handful of blacks still dragging their souls about the compound had long since shrunk beyond human limits and that even they, had they not learned to live on sand and wind, would have been long gone. Gabo Djara remembered how Sister once chided a tribal woman for using *lharang*, the quinine bush. "Thou shalt not kill. That is what our brother Jesus tells us." She believed that bark, leaves, and the fruit of *lharang* which our women used to prevent them from becoming pregnant killed unborn children and that is a sin.

The pontiff raised the stick level with his forehead and Gabo Djara, feeling the man's scrutiny, worried that he was being reproved for a breach of protocol. The ant wondered if he should climb down from his present perch and look for somewhere more conventional, but decided to stay rather than cause more inconvenience by disappearing from sight and then requiring his host to stoop in order to hear his words. The man's belly, smooth and round like a boulder in the river, would make bending an uncomfortable and undignified move.

The host wanted to know: "Did you shrink of your own free will—or by coercion?" Sister should have told him that, thought the ant; she had put on paper all that she had learned from the tribal elders. When she complained to Marngit about the tribal woman using *lharang*, the healer explained that the bush existed long before the mountains. In the Dreaming, when the monstrous Mogo rose from the sea and began to eat the land, Jambawal created a huge storm to sweep the country clear of intruders. What a storm it was—stripping the country of trees, bushes, and even of soil, leaving nothing but bare rock. Gabo Djara clearly remembered that storm. He was human then and had made his campfire, chanted, and hunted just as any other tribesman, but after the storm his life changed, as did his shape. Scarcely any food grows on bare rock. It takes time for seeds hiding in the cracks of boulders to sprout and much more time for a tree to grow and bear fruit. Gabo Djara shrank into an ant then, and though there was scarcely any food, cracks in the rock still hid morsels of life, and the newly grown plants, though young and feeble, contributed a leaf or two. Anchored on bare rock, the trees grew slowly, and the ant feared that if the hungry mouths of his countrymen should nibble each emerging shoot, then Namanama would remain bare forever. Luckily, however, a tree emerged which thrived among the boulders and soon bore round yellow berries among its small shiny leaves. Gabo Djara could no longer remember why the bush was called *lharang*, but it saved the country from growing bald, for it helped man and ant to breed only when there was food enough on which to live. Now perching on the apostolic rod, the ant thought his host must be aware of the traditional life in the bush, for the man sounded sympathetic: "You understand that I have to treat this visit as unofficial till . . . ahem . . . our doctrine undergoes some amendment. Soon, I hope . . . you take my meaning?" It dawned on Gabo Djara that the pontiff might be feeling uneasy not only about *lharang* but also by the ant's shape. According to Sister Alba, when she came to the bush and before she grew to understand plants and animals, only humans have a soul. The ant did not mind being told again that he did not have a soul; should he have become a kangaroo or whale, the treatment would have been just the same. The host felt uneasy about something else, too, though. "Your remarkable age confounds your followers. Sister Alba suggested that you have been in existence for forty millenia but we deleted one zero—just to be on the safe side of the premise."

Gabo Djara recognized, with amusement, that the amended figure bore some significance.

"And, of course, He created the world about that time, so . . ."

Gabo Djara looked his host full in the face: "You mean . . . white man's world." His gaze implied, "Only your world."

A stony-faced man entered, accompanied by two guardsmen dressed in glaring yellow, orange, and blue uniforms. Gabo Djara, suddenly wary that his thoughts were offensive to the Holy C, wondered what price he would need to pay. Years ago Sister had told Marngit how the people of her faith must see the bush in the way their masters dictated, not as they really see it. "You can end in hell for a single sin," she complained once, yet she felt for the plants and it was not long before she, too, thought *lharang* had saved the world from growing bald. "I must collect some seeds of that shrub; the whole world would benefit." She sent a message to her friend Father Rotar, who lived then at Mount Wawalag with Dingo people further inland, to come and take the seeds: "The tree shall bring peace to the whole world; let's spread it about." Now feeling that his host might be as harsh with him as he had been with Sister, Gabo Djara was about to slide from the baculus rod, and escape. The ant realized that whatever horror this incident might bring, it could hardly be more painful than those previously encountered, so he stayed.

The host inclined his head, listened intently while the newcomer whispered into his ear, and then replied slowly, "You're quite right. We should take no chances."

The stony-faced man took the ant by the tip of one feeler, lifted him from his perch, and ran a detector rod along the suspect's body. The machine gave out pipping signals which, though they should have sounded similar to those made by other Geiger counters, seemed louder and more menacing there in the confined space of the Audience Room. Gabo Djara, back again on the baculus rod, lifted both feelers to acknowledge the apology he expected for the disturbance, but the man was not finished. The detector rod pressed against one of the ant's feelers, pipping even more loudly, but when it swung again, Gabo Djara quickly lowered the other feeler and the rod flashed past some distance away.

"Come now. You must turn the other cheek," admonished the host. The pontiff sounded almost human to Gabo Djara, though Sister thought differently. In the bush she told how her Boss never smiled and she feared that she might never be able to convince him about *lharang*. "I could lose my veil because of that shrub." Marngit, who understood that Sister might be condemned never again to wear *balanda* clothes, offered comfort by telling of tribal women who had lived for generations wearing no more than a piece of paperbark to cover their genitals, and that she would be welcome to make such "clothes" from the tree of her choice. The host repeated his advice that the other cheek should be turned and the ant obediently lifted his feelers—though not quite high enough to be hit—and the pipping began again, shrilling its loudest as the detector rod swooped past the ant and touched the host's belly; perhaps there really was a boulder inside. Gabo Djara lifted his feelers high, giving the security officer every chance to scan again, but confident now that this was only a pretext to run a check on the pontiff himself.

Later on that same day, Gabo Djara was carried along when his host performed a canonization ceremony, for though he cared little how the whites regulated their saints, he had to cling to the rod or else wander about on the stone-paved ground and risk being trampled. The host, in ceremonial garb of dazzling white, with red shoes, was too dazzling to look upon, but Gabo Djara's eyes strayed often to the hat. Its shape seemed to him much like Mount Mogo, though its surface was much smoother and the shining cross perched on top . . . well . . . Really, the two were different in many ways, but the ant had drifted into a dreamlike state of mind where any similarity to his native bush brought sad memories of

Namanama. He remembered Sister again and the day her friend Rotar came in from Dingo country to see the tree of peace. "The plants have won you over at last," the man told her. Though white of skin, the man must have had a black soul, for he wore the hair belt of a tribal elder and marks on his chest to tell of the tribe to which he belonged. The man explained that though lharang did not grow at Mount Wawalag there was another tree of peace quite as effective to ensure that only as many people were born as the tribal land could feed. He believed that the trees were relatives of humans, however different they might look, and cared about the country in the same way. "No tribes have ever fought one another—the tree of peace has seen to that." The man told the Sister that she should write about lharang and spread the virtue of peace throughout the world.

The host, leading the procession, was seated on a canopied palanquin, with Gabo Djara—also carried along by the perspiring bearer through the welcoming crowd—clinging even more tightly to the baculus. If he should tumble to the ground, the ant knew he would perish under the heels of so many boots. The procession reached an open court and wheeled around a heap of boulders piled up to look like . . . Luma Cliff!

Gabo Djara brightened on seeing a relic from his Namanama; every flake of it, even to the mussel shells on the lower rocks at the tide mark, had found their way to the new site. "Peter's penance," whispered the host. Gabo Djara did not comprehend the meaning of these words and stretched his feelers to hear more. "Peter, the Rock. The gift from Sir Rock-Pile."

The ant was baffled by the allusion to Peter, for on top of the cliff sat not a man but a large woman petrified in bronze—Sister! The wind from the open sea had torn away some of her clothes, leaving only enough to preserve her modesty. When the clothes Sister brought with her wore out, she stayed in the bush and Marngit's wife helped her make a skirt from paperbark. The tribal garment was too short to cover her white thighs and the Sister had to rub her skin with the crushed leaves of an aromatic plant to keep *boberne*, mosquitoes, off. She still wore the cross, though, for its metal was much stronger than cloth and might last a lifetime. Gabo Djara remembered Sister telling her friend Rotar, who came occasionally to Namanama to see her, that now that she had lost her veil she had sworn allegiance to plants. "That tree *lharang* should grow in every family, white or black. Plants, being older than humans, are much wiser and could pass on the secrets of how the world might live in peace." Looking at Sister now, as she perched on the cliff, Gabo Djara saw that she was holding on to a bush which, though meant to be *lharang*, grew stunted and twisted and its branches, bare of bark, bore neither flower nor leaf. It seemed not to like growing in the white man's world, thought the ant.

The baculus rose toward the bronze Sister and, swaying in the air, made the sign of the cross as many voices droned in unison. "That thou art Peter and upon this rock I will build my Church; and the gates of hell shall not prevail against it."

That being the way the whites made their satins, Gabo Djara had no objection to being involved, but should Namanama ever become his again, and the opportunity of a similar gathering arise, he would see to it that the elders sent out message sticks to invite the pontiff so that he may witness something more impressive. Marngit would play the *didjeridu*, and beat the *ubar* to tell every *djang*—every spirit—in the country to be kind to the stranger, and the tribesmen would bring *barung*, barramundi, to cook in the hot ashes for a feast. The ant puzzled a moment over how the food could be boiled to suit the visitor, for the tribes possessed no cooking vessel, metal or clay. The pontiff must be asked to bring a pot with him, that was all, but it had better be a huge one, for, at ceremonial festivities, the fish were always bigger than usual.

164

The rod rose again: "*Urbi et orbi.*" (For the city and the world.)

The words reverberated against the cliff and returned. "Habemus the Rock (We have the Rock)," chanted the crowd.

It was only when the procession moved around to the other side of the cliff that Marngit came into view. The medicine man clung to the boulder, trying to crawl forward, upward, his bronze lips drawn back, gasping for breath in a manner which reminded Gabo Djara of a hunted possum trapped in a hollow log. Above him stood the *lharang* tree and from the boulder at its roots gushed water. The torrent swept against Marngit's face, cascaded over the rocks below, and gathered in a large pool upon which clots of foam whirled. There were no *jogu*, lily, leaves floating in the pond, nor were there shadows of greenery tickling the surface of the water. If *balanda* had thoughts of making Jingana billabong, they had gone the wrong way about it, the ant told himself.

As the crowd chanted "Habemus the Rock," the pontiff leaned toward the ant: "Miraculous, quite miraculous." Gabo Djara thought that his host was admiring the *lharang* but it was the water that he praised. "As clear as tears." The host marveled: "That water comes from melting snow. Europe is free of snow at last." He believed that instead of frosty winters the world would in future know only monsoons which would make plants and humans thrive. As the crowd around chanted "Habemus, the Rock," the host lifted his rod again, muttering, "Miraculous . . ."

The whites hold odd ceremonies, thought the ant, as he clung to the rod.

Chapter 19

WHILE searching for his lost country, Gabo Djara was snatched by a storm which had borne him away into a strange world. Dumped on a lonely road and struggling to catch his breath, the ant tried to stretch out his feelers but both felt numb. All around stretched a long plain of gibbers swept by an icy wind and without the green of one tree to be seen. The ant feared that he might have drifted into some land where plants had long forgotten how to grow. Scorched stumps still stood about but these were covered with a layer of ice that prevented Gabo Djara from crawling into cracks in the wood in search of food and shelter. Having never experienced winter before, he wondered how one might survive in such a country. Though neither man nor spirit were to be seen, Gabo Djara pictured, in his mind, Sir Rock-Pile, and that *balanda* sat on a billowing cloud rising in a mushroom shape, sky high.

A sword flashed through the air, swishing and glittering, then stopped; Gabo Djara stared, mesmerized, at the gleaming metal poised within striking distance of his neck. The ant waited for death, but the blade moved only very slowly forward and gently prodded the lower part of his thorax so that Gabo Djara's front legs rested on the metal. Seeing no apparent harm, the ant then clung, struggled, and finally succeeded in pulling the rest of his body from the frozen dust. He had no strength to climb further; a layer of dirt covered his body, two of his legs felt loose, dangling about as though independent of his trunk, and his empty abdomen felt as light as a shrunken bubble.

The blade rose and Gabo Djara slid down the incline to land on the swordsman's hand, preparing to run in search of shelter but . . . why bother? Life could hardly become worse; the ant could not remember his last meal, and his long tumble through the storm had shaken any remaining fragments from his crop.

"Where are you off to?" The warrior who sounded stern but not so harsh as the ant had feared, appeared to be neither white nor black. He wore a pair of earrings and a beard which sprouted from the end of his chin. "Turn and face your captor, Genghis Khan!" The name meant nothing to Gabo Djara, but the man had the look of a Macassan—the people from far to the north who, centuries ago, had crossed the water to Namanama and there roamed the shore in search of slugs. From the edge of the escarpment, Gabo Djara had watched the vessels sail in and out of the bay, riding before the wind like monsoon clouds . . . yet the boatmen had never ventured inland; they did not quarry the rocks and drag them away. "I'm leading my hordes to free the world from the ice—would you like to ride with me?" asked the warrior. Gabo Djara could not guess how far he had drifted from his country, but hoped that the warrior might be heading toward Namanama. The ant still saw Sir Rock-Pile sitting on the mushroom cloud that he imagined was an immense willy-willy risen from the dust-shrouded land.

A speck of sand, which had been tucked in the gap between the ant's thorax and his abdomen, fell. As it touched the man's palm it grew immediately into a pebble. It came from the cave at Jingana billabong, and if he had succeeded in carrying it to Bralgu, Gabo Djara would have used the sample to breathe life back into his tribesmen when Namanama once more became their own. "Of what use is a pebble, little stranger? Man cannot eat rocks; he does not even fight with them any longer."

A witness to the scene—a man whose whole bearing was that of impenetrable calm—came forward. As the man leaned over, the ant felt a bond of communication spring between them and heard him whisper, "Master, whites grind the stone to extract evil—a bag of dust which could break the whole world into fragments."

"Where is your country, little ant?"

Gabo Djara struggled along the sleeve of the silken robe, hoping that if he could point the horizon in the right direction the Serene Man could tell his master of the place called Namanama. Would the country still be there? The icy winter might have descended on it, too, wiping out the plants. The water in the billabong might have gone rock-hard . . . and yet . . . he must remember that the whites may have already ground the country into dust. Dust hardens with the frost, too, he told himself.

The warrior took a crumb in the tips of his fingers and placed it on his sleeve. The food had a familiar smell, and though it tasted unusual, Gabo Djara filled his crop, then brushed away the dust which begrimed his body. At last, the gritty coating gone, the ant could stretch out his feelers and regain control of all his limbs.

The warrior rode up on a great beast, the like of which Gabo Djara had never seen, or heard of, before. The animal had a bushy mane, which divided the wind at each bound of the powerful legs, and a long head which swayed and jerked as though it were part of the vicious dragon, talked of by the Macassan boatmen. Following the great warrior and his beast came a horde of the same beasts, ridden by lesser warriors. The thunder of hooves echoed like a storm.

Gabo Djara assumed the animal to be the warriors' totem—and a valuable one, since it also carried him about—and wondered how the power of the two would compare to that of the white man and his machines. The hordes rode day and night and neither beast nor man seemed to grow tired. They halted suddenly at a huge hole which had been blasted in the ground before the frost had set in. The ant thought that should there be water at the bottom of the crater, the warrior might use the site to set up his camp. The men who had descended into the crater climbed back without water but with something that looked like a frozen stump which they placed on one of the beasts and covered with a rug. Gabo Djara hoped this was their way to thaw firewood as he longed for a good campfire that would warm his body and help bring back strength to his cramped limbs. There was not to be a fire, however, for the ant soon realized that the stump was not wood but a dingo. As the animal came back to life, it tried to shake its ears and scrape away the frost, but its limbs were still too stiff. Gabo Djara immediately forgot about the cold. Seeing a soul from his country, he felt a warmth such as he had not known for a long time. The dingo stumbled about, unsure of both the ground and its own stiff limbs; it tried to lift a leg and pee, but was unable to stand on its remaining limbs and over-balanced. "He might make a good hunting dog." Genghis Khan hoped that an animal coming from the wild would know how to track well . . . Gabo Djara hoped that, too; the dingo, a survivor when much else in the country had been wiped out by the nuclear blasts, would surely remain faithful to the warriors who rescued him. The ant saw Sir Rock-Pile again sitting on the willy-willy cloud; next to him sat a man dressed in military fatigues. "We shall win this star war, take my word for it," the ant thought he heard the man say. It was the general.

It hailed when they rode again, and with the hail came a cold wind. The ant's limbs grew stiff and his feelers began to droop as, with ebbing spirits, he clung grimly to the soft silk in constant fear of blowing off. One of the warrior's fingers lifted Gabo Djara, drawing him upward and tucked the shivering little body among the scattered hairs of his beard.

Warm again, Gabo Djara fell to wondering if he could persuade the warrior to return him to Namanama, traveling as a guest of the spirit world. The totem beast was galloping even faster, moving across the earth like a shooting star, and the ant felt content, both with pleasure in the ride and with the hope that the warrior might be persuaded to go his way. If anyone in the world could drive away the white man and his machine, it must be the warrior and his magnificent totem. Ahead of the hordes galloped the dingo; the animal must have caught the scent of his country in the air and headed, panting, across the plain. Halting now and then as it glimpsed a mushrooming willy-willy springing up in the far distance, the dingo would howl as if trying to warn that the *balanda* were about and had plunged the world into sand and dust and ice. Looking toward the horizon, the ant again saw two white men on top of the willy-willy, though they appeared closer now, and the general could be heard telling Sir Rock-Pile that stars are made of boulders. Though the old soldier was blind and bald, he planned that as soon as the sky was conquered, he and sir Rock-Pile would settle down to the business of grinding stellar rocks. Gabo Djara did not have time to think how the world would look without stars. With his head buried among the hairs of the warrior's beard, he sent his thoughts to the tribal country, far though it might be. Marngit must be warned that the visitor was coming so that the medicine man could put on his *djamar*, his headdress, and gather the tribesmen for the

ceremony of welcome. The men would need to catch barramundi, or to spear a *barg*, a kangaroo, to make a fine feast.
The ant could conjure up the scene in exact detail. The medicine man with his dilly bag full of *lida*, the ceremonial objects . . . the tribal elders, squatting by the billabong, their bodies
malnar—stained and decorated with *bulg*, tufts of white cotton . . . the men chanting "*ja, ja, ja*", evoking the spirits. One
man would beat a large palm frond against the *ubar*, the log,
and from behind the pandanus grove, female voices singing
"*gaidba, gaidba*" would rise. In Gabo Djara's imagination it looked
as though the spirits were rising and would soon stir the
country into new life, but . . . the picture became blurred. A
tremor shook the escarpment, booming over the billabong;
the silhouetted summit of Mogo rearing against the sky burst
and its belly gushed a mass of rocks which, in a storm cloud
of dust, drenched the country in a shower of stones. The earth
jerked again, twitching like a dying snake, then subsided as
Gabo Djara's dream faded. The mushroom willy-willy remained on the horizon, still spinning upward with the *balanda*
sitting on it. Lifting his head and peering through the sparse
hair of the warrior's beard, the ant commanded and excellent
view of the vast dusty plain now revealed below the willy-
willy. A few boulders remained, scattered in groups across
the open ground and bearing deep scars as if from some
mortal battle. Perhaps the rocks had not been quarried from
the earth but gnawed by immense jaws and, proving too tough
for the steel teeth, had been spat out. A sprawl of dust and
freshly dug earth, the land seemed like an immense cadaver
awaiting a decent burial. The ant looked to the dingo. Poor
Namanama—our country ground to dust. The dingo howled,
more plaintively than before.

As the warrior's beast galloped on, Gabo Djara wondered
if a country remained to which he might return.

My wife Jogu is right: however tough the rocks are, they crumble eventually into dust, leaving behind a patch of sand. Plants are the only ones to be reborn—after all, they hold the soul of man.

Some days ago Yudu showed me the stone head of an old spear he found at the shore. "The counter clacks on it." He expected there would be a quarry somewhere in the bush from which the tribe had been able to obtain the tools. I tried to convince him again that the tools are traded from one tribe to another. The stone could be from Mount Wawalag, or even from the other side of Australia. "Rocks do not rot," I told him. Humans rot, though. Yudu is not fit to search through the craggy Mogo Ranges. It takes years for man to recover from the Rot, if he ever does— fortunately for the mountain. During the monsoon rain, not long after I fled to Namanama, a hillside had slid down leaving behind bare rocks. No man eaten by radiation for years could be mistaken as to how uranium looks. The hill that slid remained bare: the plants did not like it in spite of good rain and sun. A patch of lichens appeared eventually, for they seem to be less particular about what they grow on. Discarded leaves and branches brought by the wind covered the bare rocks and, before long, stretching vines wandered over them. Plants are good at healing wounds of the earth as well as those of humans. As the monsoons went by, the bare hillside had sunk into the green canopy of the mountain.

The day Jogu was to give birth, I often stared at the mountain Mogo but felt unable to pinpoint where the eroded hill stood. It should not trouble me, I thought, and cursed myself for thinking of rocks more than Jogu. Jogu, being from Dingo country, did not have a mother to help her but some local women came, led by Alba. They brought munbi, fruit of styptic tree to be crushed and soaked in a bailer shell. Soon after, a child, a girl, was born. Alba pinched up the soaked munbi, and holding it on the end of a twig, chanted with the women following her:

> Humans grow like trees
> in country of the Wawalags
> people grow like leaves

After the fruit on the twig was placed inside the womb, the afterbirth blood ceased and it was not long before Jogu began to move about again. We called the girl Da for being born under the gum tree. It is believed that as she grows the da will keep an eye on her which, for a tall stringybark reaching up for the sky, is not hard to do.

That day Alba told me that another message had arrived from my brother: "Trees have strength greater than humans." He had learned that the plants were going to cure me. Alba asked me if I remembered the story of mogo monster who tried to eat Namanama and died from feasting on the boulders. "Now that you are about to recover you might be thinking of it."

I expected that she, too, must know that uranium rocks are in the hills. Although Yudu might never find them, there will be many others yet to come, more vigorous and poised for looting. No mountain, tree, or man could hold them.

I sent a message to Sir Rock-Pile: "I have struck it rich, come for it." There was little else for man or spirit to do in the name of trees.

Chapter 20

SOME hope rose at last; too much to expect, though, that all the Namanama wounds would be healed and for the boulders to grow back out of the dust again. However, when the leaders of the feuding world sit down to talk, no man should be out harvesting wrath. Gabo Djara crawled along a concrete corridor against a strong draft. He had to cling hard to the slab under him so as not to be blown off: what does the white man's boss look like? he wondered. No black soul was able to tell that. The whites, all those the ant met, seldom spoke about their spirit master and if he had not seen, at Namanama, the Sister addressing her boss, he would have believed that the white man's world is without one.

How good of the Sister to lead me. Gabo Djara watched the woman some distance ahead of him, only a shadow of her seen on the concrete wall, as she hurried forward swinging her Red Cross bag. She had pleaded with him for years: "Come and see Him. Only the Lord can stop those wild men pillaging your country." She came to see the ant night after night and often wept, "Please do come. He can tell even the devil to stop harming others." The tears rolled down the pale spotty face. She told him that only God knew how she and Recluse had worshiped the plants. Along the corridor drifted fragments of dust. Gabo Djara raised both his feelers against the air current—the smell of ground boulders lingered in the air, the scent humans would hardly detect, but being immortal, he felt it as part of his body, even though it was a half-world away.

The corridor forked. There was no need to worry which way to follow. The woman in front of him now looked much smaller than when he had seen her made into the monument with which the pontiff honored her long ago. A wild storm had partly torn her clothing, exposing one of her shoulders. She persuaded the ant to come. Though he had no more hope than seeing one more white face, Gabo Djara expected nevertheless that while the boss of the white man's world talked to him, his followers would lay down their tools and as soon as the machines stopped grinding boulders, the country would have time to catch its breath.

The rough concrete slab made a good surface for gripping, though not very comfortable to crawl for long. The tips of Gabo Djara's claws began wearing off. Never before had he crawled so long over concrete and he wanted this trip to be the last. He kept going for a while, swung one of his front legs, and, pressing his claw to his abdomen, felt the burned surface of the partly worn skin. It shouldn't be long now, he hoped. How should he address the man he was about to meet? The Sister calls him Lord . . . My Lord; her voice always sounded pleading. Being immortal, however, he did not need to beg or plead but talk as he would to any man who, if not of the same color skin, was at least close to his spiritual ranking. The ant asked if Recluse would be there when he met God. Perhaps he should, as the man who led the whites to Namanama, though not in malice.

The scent in the air, not of the dust alone but something more acid as well, grew stronger, tickling both his feelers. Gabo Djara reared up but nothing else was felt or seen about. The concrete walls stretched endlessly, like the depth of a cave. Perhaps the whites were luring him into a trap. They do it with smell, he remembered so well from his country—he was not sure how. The scent came faster. Yes, it is the white man's medicine from the Red Cross bag. Perhaps the Sister feared he might be lost if he lagged too far behind and left a drop or two from her bottle to help him track her. He had smelled the same scent at Namanama when the Sister treated a young girl who had had half of her arm bitten off by a crocodile, and heard the white woman telling Marngit that the smelly stuff was full of magic and could drive away many curses. That must have been before the plants won her over; Marngit had seen to that. The medicine man helped Recluse to believe in the plants, too, for better or for worse. The ant reminded himself that the whites had invaded Dingo country long before Recluse fled to the bush and that no soul could have saved Namanama. Whatever happened in the bush, I will be polite to the man I am to meet, thought Gabo Djara while strolling along the corridor again, not so much out of respect but for the sake of the Sister and Marngit. The two have stretched their hopes more than humans will ever endeavor to heal the wounds in tribal souls; they did even more—they became indispensable friends in the crumbling world around them.

The light in the tunnel must have changed, for the Sister looked much clearer now. She held half a coconut shell full of water—Gabo Djara saw her spill some of it. Has somebody been wounded? he thought, for earlier he had seen her carrying her bag and the drink only when the curse struck. The ant hastened, trying to catch up with the shadow on the wall.

Why does the white man's boss, God or Jesus, whatever his name, have to live so far off? he asked later. It is too distant for a spirit to reach him, let alone a man. Jingana Cave at Namanama is deep under the ground, too, but placed no further than a voice away from the outside world. There, even the sun, in late afternoon when it is about to perch on the edge of the pandanus forest, finds its way in through a gap between the boulders to throw its light for a while on a Green Ant of a human size painted on the stone wall. The whites organized their sacred world differently—Gabo Djara was going to say something more, but found it unwise to think unfavorably of a host whose home he was entering.

The scent left behind for him to follow weakened while the smell of Namanama, still lingering around, grew stronger. Gabo Djara assumed that the smell came from the specks of dust gathered in the Red Cross bag, and he quickened his walk. When retiring, as the humans do finally, would the Sister go back to her old world or stay in Namanama? Her shadow was hardly traceable on the wall—she, too, must feel worn out after the long journey and the ant hoped that her boss might come forward to meet them halfway. Immortals, whatever their color, remain kind. Perhaps she would have stayed with the tribal people for good and forgotten about the world she came from, but she had to be nice to her old master for sending her the bottles of highly scented liquid so that she could fight whatever curse comes about. Once she told Marngit while giving him a cup of tea: "Let's share this humble world of ours." Was it before or after she grew to believe in the plants? The ant was uncertain, though he recalled that the first *balanda* to have faith in plants was actually Rotar while he lived with the Dingo People at Mount Wawalag. Rotar had a black soul, though, and he never spoke about the Lord. Gabo Djara wished that Rotar would come to the meeting; he was so much wiser than his brother Recluse.

The distance between the Sister and him narrowed suddenly. At first Gabo Djara thought they must be getting closer to God's den and she wanted to instruct him about protocol. However, a moment later, he noticed that the Sister was bent down to help a wounded man, supporting his head with one of her arms while with the other she held the shell with the water against his mouth. The face of the tribesman seemed flattened, and, covered with a heavy layer of dust, it looked like a lump of earth. The drops of water washed the dust from his mouth and his lips moved—Marngit! The medicine man lay half sunk in dust with a chain tied to both his wrists. The patch of damp dust marked the wounds scattered on his strangled body. Gabo Djara hurried closer to see his man, if not able to bring much comfort, at least to share his pain, but the scene drifted ahead of him with the water still spilling from the shell as Marngit's body jerked forward irregularly.

Gabo Djara assumed that Marngit was also being taken to see God and felt happy to have someone around who had witnessed so much pain. He expected the Sister to say some words to her master on behalf of all the blacks. Having three voices to fight for Namanama, a hope rose at last that He, the Lord, in spite of his color, could not but be just.

The scene of the concrete wall enlarged. Gabo Djara watched Marngit's body being dragged along and, after each jerk forward, the ant felt his own limbs struck by the pain. The chain holding the medicine man's wrists was hooked to the back of a bulldozer, and as the machine rumbled ahead, it left a trail of dust from which the black body emerged only now and then. The ant realized that the whole scene was mirrored on the wall from some unknown distance and as it drifted off it took away both of his friends.

Dark set in the tunnel again. Gabo Djara asked once more why the white man's spirit boss had to live so far away; the ant felt worn out and distressed, even though he had not reached him yet.

However depressed Gabo Djara felt during the journey, as

soon as he reached God's den his exhausted body bloomed into life again. Knowing well that looking humble would denigrate his immortal status, he walked high on all of his six legs while his feelers swayed in the air, stretched to the limit. "You will burn in hell!" A loud voice shattered the silence.

Gabo Djara looked around—he had walked into what looked to be a depot made from concrete; no man or spirit was about but only stacks of drums. Had he turned up at the wrong place? "Your soul will melt in the flame. I will . . ." From the top of one drum, through the small opening, a white-bearded head on a long neck sprang out; a pair of wide open fair eyes glanced down to the floor. "Pardon me. I thought it was one of the guards sneaking in again."

Gabo Djara stepped forward to have a better look at his host; he had never met a man or spirit before that lived in a metal drum. "They disturb you, I gather."

"They often come to check if I have spirited away." His host's face had a cylindrical shape, no wider than the opening of the drum. He looked at the ant again. "Lucky you are disguised in that tiny insect shape. You must have dodged all their detection gadgets."

We're immortals, Gabo Djara was going to say, but restrained himself. He had never heard before that a human or a man-made machine could subject a spirit.

The host must have guessed his thoughts. "We do not know any longer where their world ends and ours begins. Please keep your feelers down—they might see them on the screen." He spoke to the ant of the rebellion in progress in which some disloyal subject waged war against stars.

Gabo Djara assumed it must be some kind of white man's ritual to entertain a visitor while sitting in a large metal drum, and since both of them were equally immortal, he thought it appropriate if he also took the same position. Once seated, with his abdomen inside and his head out of the drum, the meeting could assume a businesslike air.

The white face watched the ant struggling to crawl up the metal container. "They make them of stainless steel, too smooth to grip."

The drums were marked "$U_3 O_8$—Perilous." Gabo Djara struggled up the line of dribbled paint, reached the first letter, and crawled sideways to the end of the sign. He looked around, measuring the distance to the top of the drum, then brought the claw of one of his front legs against his jaws and extracted a drop of saliva. A moment later, with the leg stretched upward, the paw stuck to the metal surface and he dragged his body on, climbing slowly to the edge. "They'll not trap you easily," he was told when he reached the top of the drum. The smell of Namanama titillated both his feelers; the ant had felt it on his way up but thought that it came from his own conscience as a constant reminder of the plight of his people: I will speak soon, he promised.

The white head on its long neck tilted toward Gabo Djara: "How good of you to come. After those war-hungry mongrels rebelled, hardly anyone calls on me any longer."

"You had so many worshipers." The ant crawled slowly around the brim looking for the opening.

"A kick from a jackboot—that is what you get from them here." The voice of his host sounded like a heavy shoe slamming against the drum, but it soon mellowed into a friendly whisper. "The Sister told me all about you. Make yourself at home here."

Gabo Djara glanced at his host's neck to determine the position of the small opening from which it had sprung; it sat at the edge of the brim but the round shape of the metal container meant that he had to crawl around till he could step on it. His feelers twitched again and he lowered both of them. As soon as he positioned himself he had to talk to his host about the tribal people. At Namanama the Sister often spoke of her boss and how he created the world in a mere six days. It felt hot in the concrete bunker; Gabo Djara covered only a small portion of the brim when he stopped for a rest, stretching out his limbs. Not far away a small opening through the thick wall brought fresh air from the outside and with it came light as well. Nice den you have here, the ant signaled out. Your people made you a nice, cozy place—it must be warm during the winter.

His host grimaced. "They built this to store power, not for my comfort. They stock the dust from the crushed rocks here— the loot gathered from all over the world."

On the mention of the rocks the ant's feelers twitched again, though much stronger now. I have to talk to him soon, Gabo Djara reminded himself. He gathered that his host never told the believers that it was only the white man's world that he mastered in those six days. Thus the whites assumed that the whole earth was given to them by their spiritual master and that they had inherited the right to blast it to the last boulder.

A metallic click was heard in the lock, and the door in the bunker burst open. Gabo Djara slid his body behind the brim but kept his head high enough to peep over the edge. He expected to see a human but instead entered a monster; it was hard to tell if it was a bird or a beast. It had a head of an eagle which looked too large even for a bull's neck to support it. Plates of armor covered his torso and out of them sprung a pair of heavy metal plates flapping clumsily as the monster walked about. It moved on a pair of legs covered with floppy metallic feathers. The monster walked around counting the drums in the bunker. This must be the guard, Gabo Djara thought, and assumed it to be a close relative of the monsters he had met earlier. Although hounded during the earlier encounters, Gabo Djara's fear was now greater, for he must worry not only about his host but about his world as well.

The monster came to the drum of the host and shook it with several kicks of his foot. "Don't try anything foolish. We have enough stuff stocked here to blow up the whole universe many times over." As the words mixed with the drumming of the metal echoed in the bunker, Gabo Djara noticed that each monster's foot branched into four claws like birds, each of which, including the rear one, had a jackboot on.

"You shall burn in hell!" cursed his host.

"When out of service we're dumped for scrap metal." The voice sounded too distorted and overamplified to be human. While walking, the monster limped, as though a part of one leg had been worn more than the other. It stood for a while at a small panel fiddling with the instruments to record the inspection visit and, before leaving it, kicked the drum again. "Stay quiet, we have a ceremony outside. If we're troubled I'll put you in the reactor—no immortal could survive that furnace." The lock of the door snapped behind the monster.

When they rose again, both feelers itched; the scent of Namanama grew even stronger, urging the ant to talk before he could find the opening, and take the ritual position. Suddenly it dawned on him, however, that complaining about his plundered country to a man who had just lost the whole world might sound selfish. "They're hard on you as well," he said instead.

"The devils took over completely. A drum of this metallic dirt counts for more to them than all my commandments."

Gabo Djara's voice rose slightly: "Fight your way back."

"They have bottled me in; couldn't you see. They have trapped me inside the container, I cannot get my shoulders out. It's like sticking your finger through a bottle neck."

Gabo Djara never drank from a bottle but only coconut shells. "What about your followers?"

"They conned me into this."

The ant was going to mention the pontiff; the man looked polite, and though he did not do much to help the tribal cause, he seemed more faithful to his master than other whites. Instead of saying anything, however, Gabo Djara crawled on, past a part of the brim, and came to the opening at last. The lid was screwed off, though not removed, and had left a small gap—the ant poked in one of his feelers and was struck by the overwhelming smell of Namanama.

"Don't get inside; the devil'll trap you, too."

"What do they keep in there?"

"The rock dust—'yellow cake,' they call it."

"They eat the stuff?"

The host grimaced. "They feed on it, yes; growing so addicted—there might soon be no boulders left to grind."

Saddened by the sight of the remains of his country, Gabo Djara was still for a while and then looked away. Through the opening in the bunker wall the compound outside could be seen surrounded by concrete towers looking like a mountain of boulders. On one of them a flag flapped in the breeze. What do the whites have to celebrate? asked the ant, staring at the leaden sky behind the flag. A sound rumbled; he thought the clouds might be gathering on the horizon to storm the place but, as he soon learned, the noise rose from the ground. In one part of the compound stood a group of men; the ant moved closer to the opening . . . yes, they were all there, ceremonially dressed in dark suits, the men he had encountered, not for his own liking, but in their lust for the rocks. The men stood on a small platform, stiffly—Specs (holding a large picture of Madame Curie and Recluse together in one frame), Pontiff, Sir Rock-Pile, Sheik $-i, the blind general, and others, like a bunch of pillars molded out of concrete.

A bulldozer driven by the eagle-monster rattled past the platform. The men raised a hand each, with two fingers stretched out to make a V sign. In front of them, Marngit's body, dragged by the machine, dangled over the ground. In one of his hands the medicine man still held a piece of the broken coconut shell, swinging it in front of the white faces as though to tell them there was still some life in the strangled body to struggle with. What a bunch. Gabo Djara watched the line of men, feeling that the lust for loot had grown on the white faces for so long that it had finally hardened into some malevolent force. Now even the spirit world was powerless to challenge it.

"They brought a new consignment again," said the host. "You ought to leave soon—they might trap you, too."

"What about you?"

"Can you chew steel?"

Gabo Djara wished he could, not so that he could make the hole in the drum, but to cut the chain, eat the bulldozer and every tool the whites have made to crush the soul of man.

The host's head tilted forward: "You can paint; that'll help." The ant was shown several drums that had different codes— a letter and a two-figured number—though he failed to grasp at first how those could affect the faith of the spirit boss of the white man's world. "They're the rejects, assigned for disposal," whispered the host. "Once dumped, the steel rusts fast. Everything the man makes, crumbles finally. 'Earth to earth,' we often say."

On a bench near the doorway lay a tray. Gabo Djara had to crawl there, dip one of his front legs into the paint, and walk back across the floor, with his colored limb held up in the air, to brush it finally against the side of the host's drum. It took many trips to make a single number, but for the ant the hard work meant a challenge and he struggled to see the end of the task, just as he would do for his own kind. He stopped only once, after the lump of the paint on his claw had begun to dry and the leg got stuck to the surface of the drum. He waited for a while to gather new strength and disengage his limb. The host looked down on him from above: "When freed, I'll come to see you."

If there is anything of my country left by then, he thought. However, instead of troubling the host with his own worries, the ant gestured with one of his feelers: "Will you make the world again in six days?"

"I might. Next time, though, I must be more selective about the species I choose."

Gabo Djara had only a few final patches to add to the number and complete the code when the door opened. The jackboots of the eagle-monster stumped across the floor, treading on the limb with the lump of paint. The ant tried to free himself but, losing hope, he soon swung back to reach shelter in a depression between the heel and the sole. I will wait for more strength or *dal*, the magic to break free, he told himself.

PART
THREE

Chapter 21

GABO DJARA could have chosen no more appropriate time to arrive; the table was set, in readiness for an early morning feast, and the servants had just withdrawn, leaving behind them a mound of food, which sent a tempting savory smell wafting on the morning air. It seemed that the time had come, at last, for the ant to fill his crop, though the meal might be one he would regret for the rest of his life.

Gabo Djara strolled across the white tablecloth among embroidered patterns of the Seal of the States, then, having negotiated the saucer, he assaulted a small cup and headed upward. All of the ant's legs scrabbled to gain a grip on the glazed surface of the china, but they were unable to take hold, and his body slid back into the saucer. Angrily Gabo Djara tried again to climb; in the bush he had scampered up the tallest gum trees and ambled to the top of a boulder overlooking the whole country, yet this paltry cup gave no foothold.

At the end of the table sat the President reading the morning newspaper; Gabo Djara took a running leap on to the edge of the sports page and made his way upward. The head mumbled as he read, breathing noisily and clearing his throat, but the ant was unworried at the prospect of being blown off his perch, for there could be no better place to land than in a dish of food. What a fine way that would be to die. One corner of the "Amusements" page dropped over the table and Gabo Djara, holding on to one leg, lowered his body and stretched out, trying vainly to reach the cup from above. Only a fraction short of his objective, the ant bounced about, hoping his weight might lower the page a little. But an empty crop and flat abdomen weigh nearly nothing, the paper did not budge and the cup stayed out of reach.

Opposite the President sat the Good Lady holding an open magazine, on the cover page of which appeared Curie and Recluse. "They pushed us into the Nuclear Age before the world was mature enough for it . . ." It was uncertain if she was talking or reading aloud.

The President mumbled, "They talk a lot about them lately."

Madame Curie was depicted with her rose. It must have been an old picture, taken perhaps not long after she had planted the bush, for it looked small and had but one bloom, a dull white. "Why did she do it?" The ant felt uncertain whether the Good Lady referred to the Madame's scientific discovery or the rose bush she had planted. That hardly mattered now. He had begun to crawl and make a fresh attempt to reach the food when the man flicked his finger against the opposite side of the page: "Had it not been for her and good old Einstein, we could never have had star wars." The ant fell down on a boiled egg and while the President and the Good Lady giggled, Gabo Djara could find nothing to laugh about. The egg was as hot as a sunbaked boulder and the ant hurried his burning feet to the rim of the egg cup, a circuit of which proved that the food was not only hot, it was unaccessible inside its ant-proof shell. A damp crumb flew from the hostess's mouth, landing on the cloth near the cup, and though Gabo Djara was tempted to rush and devour it, he remembered previous tricks played by the humans, and left the morsel untouched.

The Good Lady had another look at the magazine cover and asked her husband to see that a rose in their garden is named after Curie. "It would help restore the morale of women." The President thought differently, in a time of star wars, inflation, and broken-down computers, white roses are unpopular: "We have to restrain ourselves, my dear—there's that dreadful Diridiri about," he apologized. The Good Lady wanted to know if a breakthrough in combating the phantom disease was likely, but was told again that the subject was inappropriate for the breakfast table.

Though out of reach of the food, the ant enjoyed a good view from the egg cup and the air carried such a strong scent of fried bacon that it was nearly a meal in itself. The smell of Namanama seemed somewhere about, too, but how Gabo Djara could not imagine, for the cloth with the Seals of State appeared spotlessly clean and, anyway, the tribal country was surely too far distant for even a fragment of its dust to reach the table. The Good Lady thought that Recluse could be Curie's son, for in the photograph they looked as though they were posing for a family album: "Could we have a rose named after him, then?" The President grinned at the suggestion; though Recluse had been credited with the splitting of the atom, the man remained a mystery—"the Dark Horse of science or Trojan Horse, he might well be." The President complained that Recluse had mystified the computers and that no machine was able to tell why he gave away the richest deposit of uranium for nothing. "The mountain was worth its weight in gold." A mountain like that, he thought, had made the star war possible.

The hostess preferred to talk about Diridiri instead of star wars. She had heard rumors that Recluse might be the only scientist who could come up with the cure for the disease, and if he should fail, she warned her husband, "You could be the President of a nation of women deprived of pubic hair." On being told again that the topic was inappropriate, she said, "You know that we are running out of yellow cake, don't you?"

The host mumbled into his newspaper, but Gabo Djara was distracted from the family chat by his own concerns; his right feeler was itching again. The ant's thoughts flew to Namanama, trying to recall the familiar faces of men and spirits, but his country, far away, seemed steeped in shadow. If his country-men could only find his way here, the overflowing plates there on the snowy cloth held enough food for the whole tribe.

"Just tell me what we are going to serve at Sir Rock-Pile's state dinner if those yellow cakes don't turn up." The hostess sounded peevish.

The President was uncertain whether Sir Rock-Pile would turn up for the dinner. He had been invited long before the star war broke out and there had been some rumors that he was not around any longer. "In his field of endeavor, people do die unexpectedly." The hostess wanted to know if Sir Rock-Pile would be suffering from Diridiri, which she as-sumed was very contagious. "Shouldn't you find out?"

The President said vaguely, "One does not ask a guest if he is dead or alive." Lifting his eyes from the newspaper, he suggested that the dinner should go as planned and assured her that the consignment of yellow cake would arrive on time.

"Well, it hasn't arrived yet, has it?"

"The ships left Wilberforce Gulf weeks ago. They shouldn't be long now, dear."

Trekking across the cloth again, Gabo Djara came upon a fragment of food lodged in the serrated edge of a knife, and though he gripped the crumb tightly and dragged it with all his strength, it was firmly caught among the metal teeth and gave no sign of shifting. The knife rose in the man's hand,

and the ant, still clinging to the food, gained a view—out of the dining room window—of a gloomy day with a flower garden wrapped in a misty haze.

The Good Lady read aloud a paragraph from the magazine which told how Recluse had discovered a new healing power which had been passed on to him by a tribal witchdoctor from Wilberforce Gulf. She told her husband that a breakthrough in curing Diridiri would come soon, for it was said that the natives have known it for generations. "He'll help us," she thought. Recluse could be a new messiah who was entrusted with a magic remedy which would save the human race by making it possible for people to have intercourse again. Excited, the Good Lady reached another paragraph which was actually an extract from his diary and which said that plants are close relatives of man and would bring a cure when it was needed. "That man's vegetarian," she told her husband.

The President still held the knife in the air: "Perhaps you mean 'herbalist', my dear?"

The hostess sounded offended. "I wish we could have him to dinner instead of that mining tycoon—if that tycoon is alive at all." She warned her husband that the enemy had struck below the belt and there would be no more newborn children. "Certainly not from bald mothers. Please let's have Mr. Recluse to dinner."

The knife swayed: "Both the FBI and CIA have files on him." The host explained that it would be most improper to invite a Trojan horse to a State dinner. As for Diridiri, he suggested that a "Bald is Beautiful" promotion campaign would be instigated soon. The knife, clattering against the plate, sliced off a chunk of bacon and Gabo Djara narrowly escaped amputation. He skidded to safety across the greasy surface of the plate. "Here, you're not getting a free meal—not from my table." The knife slid under the ant and flicked him off the plate, headfirst into the butter dish where the soft mush cushioned his fall, but also imprisoned one of his feelers. Gabo

191

Djara tried to free himself, but soon realized that if he was in too much of a hurry he might well emerge a limb short, so he decided he must wait, and hope that the stuff in which he was bogged would soon melt. The Good Lady's knife scraped at the butter, coming within a whisker's breadth of the ant's abdomen and then bulldozing him along in front of the blade. For an instant it seemed as if Gabo Djara would be consumed, but the woman noticed him in time and shook her hand, catching the edge of the cup with her knife. As it tipped over, Gabo Djara was plunged into the tide of white coffee which swept across the tablecloth. The liquid was warmer than any puddle the ant had forded in the rocks after the monsoonal rains and it tasted rather nasty. Its scent was that of Namanama, however, and though it was probably not strong enough for the humans to notice, the ant savored it, and gazed long at the particles of his country scattered across the cloth.

The Good Lady proffered a plate of food. "The last of the yellow cakes. Would you like one?" she asked, then, noticing the ant making his way out of the coffee pool, she seized her fork, ready to pin him against the seal.

Outside a storm had risen and raged among the roses when Dodoro came tumbling through the air to crash against the window, but instead of falling, the bird stayed suspended against the glass with its wings outstretched. Gabo Djara squeezed between two fork prongs and dashed to shelter under a saucer rim; the pigeon was still pressed to the window and the ant wondered—if he were able to carry a crumb from the table across the floor—if a small crack might be found through which he might crawl. Even in the best-built houses, a fissure might be expected. Dodoro ate seeds usually, but none appeared on this white man's table. A tempting crumb, lightly tinged with the oxide color of yellow cake, smelled of Namanama rocks now pounded into dust, and birds know better than humans—they do not eat boulders—so there was no sense in dragging that to the pigeon.

Diridiri still lingered in the Good Lady's mind. "They suggest in the article here that Recluse might have the cure already but is waiting to be asked formally to save the world."

The President held firm that one should not trust a Trojan horse.

The Good Lady insisted. "He has split the atom, you know. Without this we will all be in the dark—it says here." She felt curious about Recluse but the President was not able to do much about his whereabouts. According to him, the man had vanished from the Australian bush after rejecting a reward for his discovery of uranium at Wilberforce Gulf; the CIA claimed that Recluse had died due to the same hazardous radiation which he had claimed to cure. The President noted, however, that the death was neither confirmed nor denied by the spiritual world of the natives from Wilberforce Gulf.

As Gabo Djara emerged from hiding, a large drop of honey plopped on the cloth in front of him. Even though it might have been a trap, the sweet scent was irresistible and before the ant could reconsider, the first mouthful was sliding down his thorax. The smell of Namanama was strong, but the sweetness was so tempting that even the fear that it might be his last meal was not sufficient to deter him.

The hostess chuckled: "The greedy thing. Surely he will burst."

Outside, the storm had stripped the roses and now flung the tattered leaves and petals against the window. The daylight was being smothered by clouds that had clotted together over the earth. A flurry of wind again blew fragments of green and red against the glass where, this time, they clung clustered on the pane.

The President turned to the window: "It's so dark. Quite suddenly it's dark—this is ridiculous."

"There was no storm forecast, was there?"

A man walked into the room and, bending low, whispered in his master's ear. Gabo Djara did not bother to lift a feeler to catch the words, for he had recognized the Usher immediately as he appeared in the doorway. He had already guessed that whatever was said might be glad news for the whites, but would bode no good for the black man, or for his spirit. The ant lapped more honey and then, while cleaning the stickiness from his jaws, glanced toward the window, wondering if Dodoro would like a share. Plunging the bristly part of his legs into the food, Gabo Djara loaded himself with honey and, walking with difficulty, began a journey toward the window. As he drew nearer, however, it became obvious that the shreds of green plastered upon the glass were not crushed leaves but a mass of ants swarmed and clinging one to another. Some had died and loosened their hold on the cluster, but, being weightless as well as lifeless, they did not fall; they floated as airborne satellites around their living companions.

"Have you won the star war?" asked the Good Lady after the Usher left.

"The convoy with yellow cake from Wilberforce Gulf has been ambushed, lost at sea."

"Now, the blooming pirates will eat the lot, I suppose. What am I going to serve for dinner?"

The President told her that the pirates might well be extra-terrestrials: "We're at star war, mind you."

Gabo Djara was sidetracked from his journey by a whole spoonful of honey piled on the table, irresistibly tempting and so sweet that he regretted being able to eat only one cropful. The mouthfuls kept sliding down, but more slowly, until finally he could eat no more. The ant's abdomen was so tightly stuffed that it had expanded into a huge green balloon that no longer felt like a part of his body. When he tried to move, all six legs gripping the table and every ounce of strength mustered, Gabo Djara could hardly shift his swollen body.

The Good Lady grew impatient: "Well, what did that Usher have to say about Diridiri?"

"Our man at Wilberforce Gulf has seen a native much like Recluse; almost identical, he claims."

The face of the Good Lady brightened. "See that he's invited for dinner." She thought that Recluse might indeed have died but been reincarnated as a native, so he would have access to the healing power.

The President apologized: "He disappeared in the bush, I'm afraid."

Outside the glass, the weightless skins were still huddled. The ant stretched his honey-covered legs toward them, but the window seemed far, far away—too far for Gabo Djara until his abdomen had subsided to a more portable size, and how long that would take, Gabo Djara could not remember; so many years had gone by since he had last held a full crop. It was even possible that by the time his body had become small enough to move once more, few of his countrymen would still be alive and waiting for a meal.

A glass, piloted by the Good Lady, came down over Gabo Djara, trapping him inside. "I think he will look just perfect on Sir Rock-Pile's plate, don't you?"

From inside the glass prison the window seemed even more distant. The storm, still lashing the rose garden, clawed the last of the ant-clusters from the shadowy pane. It seemed that he was to be left alone again; Gabo Djara fervently wished that he were a part of the storm-tossed swarm and sharing their fate, for to be ground into dust and scattered over a foreign countryside seemed a more pleasant fate than being served up on a white man's dinner plate.

Chapter 22

THE whites had a strange way of holding *magarada*, the peace-making ceremony. Gabo Djara was in the process of attending this ritual and feared that he might be pounded into dust like Namanama, before he had learned all about it.

The ant had been brought to the gathering in a discarded pin-box and tipped out on to a round table. Lucky he was out at last! The small container had not been completely emptied and, while inside, his skin had been constantly pricked by two small needles. As soon as he emerged, Gabo Djara looked around for a way to show his gratitude. Opposite him a pair of human eyes, hard and fixed, gazed through heavy spectacles. The man behind them lifted his fist and smashed it down on the wooden surface. "Mankind wants peace."

He had a strongly accented voice, and although it sounded unfamiliar, Gabo Djara thought of Specs in disguise. The ant was shocked that his enemy had not passed away, but was still moving about shouting tempestuously. Behind Specs stood Yudu striking the pick handle against his open palm. He, too, thought that mankind deserved peace and muttered, "Let's break the Phantom's neck."

"This planet needs peace, you creepy pest." The malletlike fist slammed down again, forcing the ant's body to jump from the table surface.

What are they after? Around his gut Gabo Djara felt a light metal shell, with the edge curled around the narrow passage between the thorax and the abdomen. Perhaps the whites wanted to dress him, covering the lower part of his body; that hardly worried the ant, but he suspected that the shell could signify a more sinister purpose than simply to cover his bare belly. Though weighed down, the ant was still able to move by dragging the armor with him; however, as soon as his feelers stretched out, indicating the course he would take, the fist pounded in front of him: "The peace!"

Rightly or wrongly Gabo Djara assumed that Specs blamed him for something: he paused, trying to remember if he or his flock might ever have done anything to harm the whites or trodden over . . . no, they could not have done that; it was impossible to bite the whites and their tough metal beasts. The *balanda* wear clothes and at night sleep in locked huts. Only the stuff that they swallowed—loads of food, cartons of drink, and clouds of smoke—could hurt them, in the same way that rust catches up with their machines soon after they are bogged in monsoon mud; but neither the black man nor his spirits had power to control how the whites lived. "Malignant little beast—mankind has had enough of you!" Specs pressed his thumb down on the ant's thorax and pinned him against the table. Gabo Djara tried to lift his abdomen and, swinging back the lower part of his body to sting the white man's skin, ah . . . yes, that is it, they have cupped the metal shell there to keep him harmless. For a moment he lay still, overcome by feelings of despair. Even the last little weapon left to him to fight against the white man and his machines had to be stolen.

The whites must have feared Jambawal and Ngaliur and are probably uneasy about Recluse, too; they would know by now that the white man has defected to our world. The tip of the right feeler itched, not strongly enough to bring the message from Dodoro, but strong enough to revive his strength to soldier on. Gabo Djara gripped with all six legs, squeezed out from under the thumb, and fled from the white man's grasp. Around him the surface of the polished table looked like a bare plain stripped of bush, with not a single sliver of grass or a leaf to hide under. He imagined he was crawling across his Namanama, flat and bare as a blade. The weight of the shell on his abdomen wore him out quickly, and Gabo Djara wondered if he would ever reach shade or a water hole. The country looked reshaped now. It lay ugly and flat from one foot of the sky to the other, and he doubted that if all the tracks in his lifetime were strung together, they would stretch far enough to match the distance.

Above loomed a heavy iron weight held in a white hand; Gabo Djara had no time to notice Specs again, but heard a man's voice imitating the sound of an aircraft. The hand closed on the iron, and as the fingers spread open, the weight slammed on to the surface, clamping the right feeler. "Shall we talk about peace?" Gabo Djara felt Specs' breath on his skin and wondered . . . could the whites have mistaken him for someone else? He could not recall a time when either he or any of his fellows had knocked down a tree or drained a water hole. Over the years, with the end of each Dry season, the tribesmen would gather for the long ceremony, bring out ubar and other lida—ritual objects—to call Jingana to bring the rain and with it new life to the withered country.

"Malignant beast, peace! We'll all perish otherwise."

The whites must be in pain from swallowing the boulders.

No man or beast could eat a whole country and get away with it. Did Recluse tell them about Mogo, the monstrous crocodile? Maybe he did not, for, in the world he came from, the hunters would never believe what the hunted one has to say. Life is different in the bush, though there, too, trouble strikes now and then. Gabo Djara remembered how each year Dodoro had to recall how badly Namanama had been gripped by drought. The pigeon lived on the sandstone plateau beyond Mount Mogo, a country full of pitiless sun. As the days of hot weather stretched out toward the end of the season, the last of the water holes dried up and the struggling trees dropped their leaves off to last it through. Dodoro had to come down to the foot of the mountain; the billabong always had water, enough to provide for all the flocks of birds and animals from the bush. The pigeon hung around the escarpment and cooed every morning, warning Marngit and the tribal elders how hard the country was struck by the pitiless sun and how they had better do something, and see to it quick! "We don't want to perish—malignant pest!" cried the white voice.

Gabo Djara thought for the moment that his ancestor Jambawal must be closing in on them, but reminded himself that the *balanda* were not likely to be hit by the Thunder Man. Like the beast, man, too, could die from eating too much and if you swallow a whole country there is no way out of the trouble. Yudu brought another weight, struggling to hold it. He placed the iron on the table in front of his boss. "Shouldn't we try a boulder? It might flatten the little devil." He, too, felt determined not to perish. No one ever threw a stone at the pigeon or shouted in anger. Like Gabo Djara, she, too, had come from the Dreaming and had lived in the country ever since. When in the ancestral time Mogo began to eat Namanama, she was an uninitiated girl. The monster saw her while she was out gathering *gugu*, yams, on the plain below the escarpment. Being young, she ran fast through the mangrove forest and sneaked inside the cave above the billabong. The monster had to eat boulders to make his way inside the shelter, and by the time he caught up with Dodoro his tummy was already full. It was wiser to make love than take food on an already burdened belly. Mogo had no woman of his own and thought that Dodoro would bear him children—a clutch of little crocodiles; they would crawl from the cave into the water and learn to live on rocks and follow him about as he kept on eating Namanama. Beasts, like humans, have tribes of their own: when living in the cave Mogo had rolled heavy boulders over the entrance and kept Dodoro inside. He left a gap between the rocks big enough only for the little crocodiles to crawl out and join him. Dodoro did not like to bear little monsters which were to eat her country; inside the cave she found lharang, the bush, had been swept in ahead of the boulders. She ate the leaves at first, but when they ran out she turned to the bark. Apart from the remedy against unwanted birth, there was hardly anything else to eat in the cave. Stricken by hunger, Dodoro shrank from a human into a pigeon; she cooed for help. Her call was heard by Waran, at Mount Wawalag in the neighboring tribal country, and he hurried to Namanama. No dingo could move boulders. But Waran had a tough penis and, forcing it against the rocks, he thrust a hole through and freed Dodoro. Once free, the pigeon went to live in trees, where she has been ever since and is the ancestor of both the Green Ant and Dingo People. Though Dodoro stays away from swampy mangroves and lives inland beyond the escarpment, she comes down during the Dry to the billabong to drink and call for the rain.

Gabo Djara was still thinking about Dodoro and the monster when the weight came down from the air, flattening the right feeler and one front leg. With the country ground to dust, do the spirits' ancestors die, too? "Don't harass the world— we must live!" The white man sounded distant; Gabo Djara wondered if Sister had told her people about the ceremony held at the end of each Dry to ensure that the rain comes and returns life to Namanama. She could have been shown it by Marngit's wives; the women also took part in *barura*—the festivities. They grouped in the main camp and formed a circle while each held on to a bark string. From the bush would float the sound of *ubar*, *didjeridu*, and *bilma* together with men's voices: "*Ja, ja, ja.*" The women would begin to dance, lifting the dust with their bare feet and calling "*Gaidba, gaidba*," the voices bouncing back from the fringe of the pandanus forest, and floating across the bush to the men's camp. If the life cycle is to be renewed for a year, it must begin, as with everything else, with a pair of kangaroos, mating dingoes, or two frogs riding on one another—the earth is not different. Jingana, the mother of all life in the country, will come only on calls from men, but the women have to voice their consent.

"Recluse . . . whereabouts is he now?"

How is it that Recluse did not tell the whites the story of Mogo? He and the Sister learned about our ancestors and the plants of the country and knew how to heal humans.

Another weight slammed down. "We don't want to perish."

To halt the pain Gabo Djara beamed his mind to Namanama again. The sound of *ubar* accompanied by the howling of the dingo echoed for days across the plain below the escarpment. A serpentlike line of men, the bodies of each stained with *malnar* and covered with *bulg*, tufts of white cotton, winds its way slowly. Part of the column rises while another sags down— the men prop up on their toes to show the undulating movement of Jingana. The serpent arches, then her head stretches up to lick the sky with her *djeno*, forked tongue. "*Ja, ja, ja*" echoes across the country. The men hiss to tell of the whistling wind coming ahead of the drifting clouds. The storm later lashes against the lifted head of the serpent as she, accompanied by Jambawal and Ngaliur, makes her way across Namanama. Along the line of the procession walks Marngit wearing a djamar, a tall headdress made of straw and covered with cockatoo's feathers. He holds . . . no, it is not Marngit, the tribe has a new healer, a young face almost sunk into the headdress. The boy holds a stone, the same as all the others from the mountain, but smoother and partly worn from being touched by human hands since . . . not the time of which a man alone could remember, but far beyond it—the time of the spirits. The stone is part of Jingana's flesh, the same as everything else in Namanama. Each man in the procession has to touch the stone and needs to bend to reach it, for the healer is not fully grown yet. Not a soul complains, though. As the stone is touched, each man calls out "Ja, ja, ja" to tell that he, too—like all his ancestors—has made love to Jingana, the mother of the country. At the tail of the procession limps a dingo. Good old Waran, he is still about. Who is that young healer? Gabo Djara tried to recall the face.

Specs whistled to imitate the sound of a jet-fighter on a raid, and another weight banged on the table. "You and Recluse plotted all this—lead me to him."

Gabo Djara wondered if the balanda would ever be able to believe in the plants. When people grow on rocks and lust for them they could see nothing else. Man turns into a tree, if he believes in one, but to think of it, the whites would be just as horrified of the idea as they would be of death.

The weight pounded from the air again: "Creepy devil, you have brainwashed our man."

As the festivities drew to an end, the men sat astride a pandanus log with their minds on Jingana. They walked over strips of flat land stretching along the foot of the escarpment and the women followed behind. "Ja, ja, ja"—"Gaidba, gaidba." The voices resounded from the walls of the mountain and spread out over the mangrove forest to float to the open sea, and travel toward the line where the sky meets the land—the sleeping place of the spirits. That new healer looks young, must have been born after Recluse came to Namanama; he looks well groomed.

"Peace! We'll pound you into dust!"

By the time the man reaches Billabong the sun is already down and perching on the dark line of the mangrove forest. On the far sky appears a cloud spattered with red color to tell of Jingana giving birth to the country again. On the ground near Billabong a big fire is lit to dance around and shout bright words toward the sky to hail the mother as she comes home. Then, as the chanting floats away, the men and women, every tribal soul, rush into the billabong for a bath. Tomorrow or in the days to come the seeds of new plants and grass will shoot out from the reborn land. The humans, they are much slower and it takes many months after the ritual bath for the children to be born. The new healer must be worn out, looks pale ... no, his skin always looks like that. Gabo Djara tried to recall what name had been given to Recluse's son; the youth looks ... good old Marngit must have seen to it that the lad grows into a good healer.

The weight bangs on the table, flattening the ant's limbs. "Peace!"

The white man cries again that he does not want to perish. Gabo Djara looked into the core of the eyes behind the heavy spectacles. How do the whites and their saints breed—with machines, perhaps? Now and then they drag the metal beasts into their camp ... No, balanda live in houses, they often gather in churches, factories, banks, and auditoriums, and wherever they are together they worship the metal beasts and make love to them. The machine needs no lharang to feed on, but drinks petrol and with a bellyful of it roams over the country. Gabo Djara was curious; if you cross a balanda with a machine, what will be born—perhaps only dust and sand, but what good can that be to anyone?

"Peace!" Balanda asked about Recluse again. The ant thought

even if he told the truth, it would be of no value to his captors. When in the bush white man seldom knows one tree from another and when you crush them into dust it matters little from whose soul they have grown. As the white man yelled again, Gabo Djara reminded himself of Marngit telling Recluse how monstrous Mogo died from eating half of Namanama. Although his country is ground into dust again, the ant hoped that Dodoro would turn up and coo for rain. When it comes, new plants will sprout. The trees have a much longer memory than humans; they will never forget how to grow, the ant told himself as he tried once more to hear Dodoro and Marngit calling for rain.

Chapter 23

THE whites were gathered, ceremonially dressed and grim-faced as if mourning one of their dear fellows who had passed away, and the fear that black spirits might hound his soul and pound his bones into white powder had drawn his clan together. What are *balanda* up to now? wondered Gabo Djara as he tiptoed across the orator's table, trying to avoid the slip-stream of the powerful human voice. The speaker had leaned far forward, his mouth wide with the passion of his discourse and one cough, or a gust of excitement, might blast the ant off the smooth tabletop.

"I hold, in two fingers, the substance of peace." The voice quavered with emotion and the hand stretched toward the audience, trembled over the lectern like the tongue of an iguana. As they trickled from fingers to hollowed palm, a few particles of yellow dust escaped onto the polished wood below. "This is the essence of a boulder from Wilberforce Gulf; it will bring us prosperity and peace for generations to come."

The orator paused to sip water from a glass and, after clearing his throat, explained that mankind will be indebted to the man who gave a whole mountain for the sake of peace. Had they not met before, Gabo Djara might have thought Specs the sincere advocate of a cult to which he was personally committed, but knowing the man, the ant was aware that this *balanda* used his voice only to mouth words on behalf of his master. From the end of the lectern Gabo Djara could see Sir Rock-Pile—high on a pedestal and only a hand-span away, his red sash adding an impressive splash of color to the scene. Perhaps it was dust gathered on the silk which made it droop or could it be that lassitude common to humans and spirits alike, which comes when the edge of life is reached and the downward spiral seems inevitable.

"As we reduce boulders into specks, man—whatever the color his skin—shrinks, too; in the eyes of nature, we're equal." Specs spoke of the mountain again as being "worth its weight in gold" and destined to bring peace, but the ant's mind was on Sir Rock-Pile, who had aged and seemed to be covered with a layer of . . . Gabo Djara could not tell whether it was lichen or soot. Here and there patches of moss had dried and it hung down, partly peeling and revealing blotches of blood-less flesh beneath. Above these spread a strip of lichen, yellow as though a rotten egg had splattered against the rough surface. Gabo Djara felt an urge to creep inside a clump of that moss and he measured the intervening distance. To reach the rock he would have to climb down to the floor and then crawl up the pedestal; the ant stretched out both feelers, searching for the safest descent. It dawned on Gabo Djara that Specs was speaking of Recluse. "He lived in two worlds, the black and the white, and steered both of them toward progress." According to Specs, Recluse had come partly from a tribal back-ground, but had been fostered by a white family. He hedged about the color of his skin, but explained that the soul of man matters, not his face. As he spoke, Specs leaned on a stout stick, to support his feeble body. The piece of wood seemed familiar . . . Gabo Djara recognized a *didjeridu*, cut from a hollow sapling, stained with *malnar* and entwined by Jingana, painted in white, holding her head high to hear Namanama in the long, drawn-out sound of the pipe blown by Marngit. "We are honored to be here to join your gallery of laureates." Specs looked at the row of framed faces on the auditorium wall, faces stiff and cold like *waranu*, mortuary poles. Above them loomed an enlarged picture of a bearded man which the ant had seen before on the packs of gelignite when the whites had first arrived at Namanama. The speaker bowed to the bearded face to thank him for giving the world explosives. "Without them no man could have flattened the mountains." After paying tribute to the old Foundation Principal, Specs returned to the script, and read that at the news of the splitting of the atom, years ago, no one would have thought that the man behind it might be a half-caste native from Wilberforce Gulf. Specs pulled out a paper from his folder, purportedly a written confession from Sister Alba admitting that when in the bush she had had an affair with the tribal healer which, according to local custom, was merely an act of courtesy. Though she took precautions by using *lharang*, the native contraceptive had let her down, and thus Recluse was born. The ant was about to crawl down, but halted at the edge of the lectern and glanced at the speaker. What was the trickster up to now? In the bush, Sister had entered the tribe and had become a member of Marngit's enlarged family, "become one of his women" is how the *balanda* would see it. Now the whites assumed more than that. As Gabo Djara descended from the lectern he could hear Specs rustling his papers. He expressed his thanks to the library of the Holy C for making a transcript of Sister Alba's confession available. "Truth is our inheritance from God." It bemused Gabo Djara to hear about God and for a moment he wondered if the old white man boss had been freed from the metal drum. If he ever makes his way out and is to be heard he might clear the names of Sister, Rotar, and Recluse, but by then their souls, as the soul of every tribal man, would be ground into the dust.

As he read the paper, Specs constantly rapped the *didjeridu* against the floor. Each time the pipe struck, a few ants were shaken from the hollow sapling and rolled to the ground, immediately running off in search of shelter. From the brief-case under the table, the long snout of an anteater poked, snuffled, and cleared the whole area, before retreating into its hideout, to await another strike of the pipe. Above on the lectern the paper rustled again as Specs praised Recluse for helping to split the atom. However, being drawn back to his native land, he gave up his bright scientific career to help his paternal people in the bush. "In the eyes of God and Science we are all equal." The *didjeridu* struck against the floor again. Gabo Djara wondered about Marngit. Did they have him too? Or only his *didjeridu*? The ant crept back to the orator's table seeking sanctuary, then with closed eyes he directed his mind toward Namanama. Ahhh, Marngit was there still, but more spirit now than human; grown to the size of a cloud, he walked across the country, to the far horizon, his feet seldom touching the ground but when they did, the craggy tops of mountains burst apart. The pipe was heard striking against the floor once more as Specs read that when back in the bush Recluse had set his mind on emancipating tribal man. According to him, the natives of Wilberforce Gulf had known of no progress since the Ice Age. They subscribe to the cult of rocks and plants. "It is a mortal sin to chop a tree or chip a boulder." Specs explained that this changed after Recluse, to whom he referred as a new messiah, returned from the white man's world and set his mind to freeing his people from their dra-conian customs. Being a man of science and progress, he turned to Sir Rock-Pile for help.

For a moment Gabo Djara saw Namanama. It looked like an immense claypan: Mogo mountain had swelled into clouds of dust and smothered the sky. From the cloud appeared *djamar*, floating through the misty air, looking tattered, with the parrot's feathers fast breaking away. Yet Gabo Djara knew that *djamar* belonged to Barg, the young healer in Namanama. The headdress fell to the ground, and as the ant watched it resting in the middle of the immense claypan, dust gathered over it and soon swallowed the precious old garment.

The orator read from his paper that no tribal phantom could stand out against progress forever; he exhibited a flask which looked much like an empty whiskey bottle the ant had seen at Yudu's hut when the whites arrived at Namanama. "Here are some of our black brothers freed from their Stone Age enchantment." Specs struck against the glass to shake some of the ants out. Would there be anyone still alive? No soul rolled out, but inside the glass Gabo Djara could see a feeler move. The white man shook the flask, explaining that after being emancipated the bush people remain shy—this would be inherited by descending generations. The feeler moved again as inside the flask the ant clung to the glass. Would that be . . . yes, it must be Barg, the new healer. Gabo Djara could see tribal marks incised on his torso. The skin still looked smeared with *malnar* from the last ceremony, although the painted tribal design seemed blurred when seen through the glass. Gathered around Barg were other captives, not all ceremonially dressed, for some of them must have been uninitiated and young before being bottled up by the whites. The people held still against the glass—no limb moved now. Gabo Djara told himself that his countrymen would soon become just a stain on the glass and the echo of a chant floating through the misty air over Namanama. As time goes by, they will become a story of the trapped tribe told forever in the spirit world which only the black man attains.

Specs explained that the inmates were happy in their dwelling and apologized for none of them being willing to venture out. "They're shy. A whole tribe of them is accommodated in the flask, thanks to scientific and social progress." The orator leaned one elbow on the lectern and, rather than be squashed, Gabo Djara gripped the sleeve and crawled towards Specs' shoulders. The white man looked in the script, praising Recluse again as the messiah of his people. He went to some lengths to explain how Recluse had waited impatiently to inherit the position of tribal healer from his father, then led his people out of darkness. He taught them two new words: "progress" and "peace." It intrigued Gabo Djara to hear what was told about a man who he had known very well from the bush. In the *balanda*'s world, they can turn you from white into black when it suits them. Poor old Recluse, he had fled to the bush from the white man's world to lick his mortal wounds in peace. They had followed him, wrecked his home, and stolen his new country, and now they were after his soul as well. Reaching the man's neck, the ant scaled the collar and struggled further upward to an open field of bare skin. The bald pate was little different from the Mogo Plateau, but the view from the top was an unfamiliar scene. He gazed for a while at the row of laureates on the wall and wondered who they were about to initiate now—perhaps Specs. While talking about peace and progress he had often looked at the large picture on the wall, complimenting the bearded man for discovering explosives which made possible the flattening of the mountains. The ant had learned that the bearded man's name was Nobel and, as he mentioned him frequently, it sounded as though Specs was pleading to be accepted as a new laureate. Looking again at the row, Gabo Djara suddenly recognized the familiar face of a woman posing beside a white rose bush. Did she start the Nuclear Rot? The face of the woman looked as innocent as the rose she touched. According to Sister she could be innocent indeed. For a long time before Madame Curie, the *balanda* had gone about blasting the rocks and ravaging the forest. The whites believed in grains of sand and not in plants. The ant remembered Sister telling Marngit once: "In a world where *lharang* is a sin instead of a remedy, no single woman could do much." The ant stared for a while at the empty frame hung next to Madame Curie on the wall and saw a fluttering shadow—it must be Specs, and the whites were here to initiate him.

The *didjeridu* pounded several more times upon the floor, the hollow sound rebounding against the walls as Specs leaned over the lectern and held up the bottle: "You will notice that there is not a single complaint from the inmates. Their silence is a mute appreciation of their new freedom." Gabo Djara closed his eyes: from an eddying cloud burst a shower of stones which scattered across the open fields and sky. With it emerged *djamar* again; no cockatoo feathers held any longer to the pandanus frame of the headdress. The sacred ornament hovered awhile in the fringe of the dust cloud, as if unable either to fly further or fall through the turbulent mist. The mountain rocked again, jerking the *djamar* upward like a kite, and a second later a cloud of dust filled the sky as a new wave of bursting rocks spewed upward.

"I wish good old Nobel could be here—and all those laureates honored for their contribution to peace—to share this moving experience of social development."

Only one black face hung among the white ones lining the wall and that one was barbered and collared in identical fashion to the others. How many hatchets or boxes of matches had the white men given for that black soul? Gabo Djara wished that he had met the man before, so that he could have taught him to make the stone axe and to strike fire by rubbing *dudji*, the wooden sticks. Had the black man learned the old ways, he could have gone to the spirit world with the rest of his tribesmen, instead of consorting with the *balanda*. Jesus might hand him a cup of tea and lumps of sugar, but his face would never grow white.

The orator held a crumb between his fingers and let it slide through the neck of the bottle: "Only a scrap of food is needed now to nourish the whole tribe." A stone-headed spear flew from the cloud and as Gabo Djara watched it aim toward Specs, he sensed that the time had at last come for the men and spirits to strike. The ant clung to the human skin and stung . . . and stung. The orator lashed at his bald head, then rubbed his palm against the rapidly swelling weal. The ant, flung forcefully to the lectern, lay bruised and crushed, looking more like a knot of black cotton than an insect. Gabo Djara dragged himself to shelter behind a small box, wondering, if he survived, whether he would ever sort out his tangled limbs and feelers. Specs seemed to forget quickly about the sting and gazed in admiration at the bottle again: "One piece of yellow cake would last a whole generation." On the empty frame on the wall the shadow fluttered again, but no picture appeared yet.

The ant freed two front legs and, gripping the small dark box, tried to raise his stiff body erect. The damaged feelers could not stretch far enough to explore any great distance so, deprived of his main sensory device, Gabo Djara slid over the edge of the open box and rolled onto the dark velvet within. The ant had never before experienced anything so soft, and immediately wary, he tried to force one of his feelers into action in case the pleasure concealed a trap. As his front legs reached the rim of a small disk, Gabo Djara thought at first he had encountered a large coin, but crawling across Pro Pace et Fraternite Gentium (for peace and brotherhood), the ant realized that it was not metal under his feet, but a medal which had been chiseled from one of Namanama's rocks. The scent of malnar lingered in the velvet, and the ant struggled to wrench open the other feeler so that he could explore and perhaps discover a trace of his marain painting. Later, when he poked his head out to glance for a moment, he saw Barg in the frame next to Madame Curie. The man had his face smeared with malnar and covered with the tribal designs, just as he had looked at the time of his initiation. Though the painted skin partly concealed his real age, his shy adolescent manner gave it away. Why the *balanda* had tried to pass him off as his father, the ant could not tell. Specs apologized for Recluse being absent and explained that it was an honor to appear at the gathering on his behalf. As the white hand lifted the medal, Gabo Djara rolled back into the soft velvet. He thought, at first, of running, but the dark cloth gave good cover and it seemed that the best way to save his skin was to lie hidden and to pretend that he had gone. Overhead, a finger tipped the lid, which slammed down, bringing sudden and complete dark and silence. The storm of clapping and cheering from the auditorium was cut short, and though Gabo Djara strained to hear the *didjeridu* thumping the floor by the lectern, it was in vain, for that sound, too, had been smothered when the jaws of the velvet trap snapped shut.

Chapter 24

SILENCE had returned, disturbed only by the scratching of a pen ploughing across a field of plain paper. The furrows of words were made with the speed of one who must sow his seed before the breaking of a threatening storm.

Gabo Djara watched the pen's tracing unnoticed until he put himself in its path and stretched out both feelers, seeking attention. A line of written words lay across the sheet above, and the human hand dropped quickly below him to begin anew, but though the tip of the pen passed close to the ant's abdomen, it did not pause. Caught there between the lines, Gabo Djara made a dash across the fresh ink toward the blank part of the paper, fearing that he might become entangled amongst the words.

"Keep out of my way, there. I'm in a hurry to finish this 'manifesto'."

The writer's hand hovered over the ant and then, with the tip of the pen, moved him carefully away.

"Where do you come from?" The writer's face was framed by a generous growth of floppy hair and a frizzy beard much the same as any bushman's. Gabo Djara wondered why he hadn't already heard about such a man who appeared more gentle and kind than other whites. The ant wondered how to introduce himself, or if that was necessary, for after wandering half across the world, perhaps he had left some trace, which, if it was not in words or books, might be in dreams creeping into the minds of those whites less inclined to crush the rocks and melt the dust into machines, coins, and medals.

The writer's index finger pinned one of Gabo Djara's feelers against the paper. "You're one of the proletariat, I assume?" While being held with the host's finger against the paper, the ant was told that the white mans world is divided in two groups—workers and bosses. Both are of the same skin, though their faith often differs; you can distinguish one from another, for the workers wear blue collars and the bosses wear white. The workers labor much harder and, when perspiring, their collar grows dark with sweat. The host's face brightened: "You see, we might be relatives after all." Still holding Gabo Djara under his finger, he explained that the bosses have their collars cleaned twice daily and they wash their hands before each meal, so their palms are smooth. One should not be tricked by that. "You don't wash your hands when there is nothing to eat. Even the spoon the worker uses is not his."

The ant thought to tell the writer that the people at Namanama wear no collars and are not divided by the color of their finery. During monsoons the rain washes their skin often, but with a drought about, there is a single water hole for the whole clan and you have to share it with animals and birds—the pool is held sacred, no soul dares to wash in it. When drinking, the people lean over the waterhole like dingoes and they don't know about spoons. Man owns *gara*, the stone spearhead, however; he owns a piece of wood with which to launch the tool and a *murga*, dilly bag. In the bush, man carries with him a boomerang and *galpar*, stone axe. You need to own no more when the country is your tribal mother—it cares not only for you but for animals and trees.

The host lifted his finger from the paper. "Would you like a cup of kosher tea and a yellow cake?"

The ant's eyes bulged.

The host apologized. "The cake is very nourishing and popular—either be in the game or stay odd man out." He explained that many of his followers feed on the cake.

Though the *balanda* seemed to be divided by the color of the collar they wore, Gabo Djara had difficulty in distinguishing one white man from another and assumed that all were of a single clan. He had often pondered over why some of them were poised ready to pound his mother country into dust, and others hardly knew that he lived. The writer's eye measured him, perhaps determining the color of his skin, or the shape of the abdomen. Gabo Djara's crop had held no food for many days and the shrinking green body sagged, and though he was embarrassed to present himself in such a humble state, the ant knew that to appear in better condition would be dishonest.

The writer picked up Gabo Djara by one feeler and placed him on his palm: "Have we met? At a gathering of The International, perhaps?"

Never before had Gabo Djara been away from Namanama—the black man always stays where his soul belongs, as do the trees and animals. The writer told the ant that he had met a man from Wilberforce Gulf who had recently defected to the Blue Collar side and had joined the struggle to see that all people should own the spoon they eat from and have water to wash their hands before a meal. "A three-course meal— we should settle for nothing less." The writer explained that according to his friend who defected, there are uncharted mountains in the Australian bush packed with precious metals to provide a spoon for every living man, perhaps a knife and fork also, if there are enough boulders to make them from. Gabo Djara did not mind what utensils *balanda* ate with, but he felt that the mountains were his and he objected strongly to the rocks from Namanama ending up on the white man's table either as cutlery or yellow cake. The ant lifted one of his feelers to object, but the writer mistook this for a sign of solidarity. "United we stand!" he shouted his creed. Later, while sipping his kosher tea, he stroked the ant's feelers gently, complimenting him on being a hard worker and a proletarian. Gabo Djara was told how his own country was owned by absent landlords. According to the writer's informer, whom he called Defector, these landlords dwell in the spirit world and do not depend on food or water. As the writer urged Gabo Djara to rise against oppression, his hand moved, bringing the ant to the fringe of his bushy beard. "Namanama, the country, belongs to you. United we stand." Gabo Djara lifted both feelers. Does this *balanda* know that I am the spirit master of my tribe? Why would the people of Namanama struggle against the ancestors who gave them the land? The black man has been his own boss since Namanama was first shaped, with no one but the spirits to tell him how to live—and those *djang*, those ancestors, demanded nothing in return for so much, nothing . . . for the land, for *galpar*, the stone axe, for trees under which to shelter, for good rain to bring the country to life at the end of each Dry—nothing.

The writer stroked the ant's feelers again: "I shall introduce you to Defector—a decent worker, you might know him from the bush." The writer thought that tribal people had to rub shoulders with the workers, though it would be a while before a man from the bush, who has known nothing but a wooden spear, acquires the skill to employ metal tools effectively. The ant wondered why his tribesmen had to give up their old tools. At Namanama, the people have lived with spears ever since the first black man came into being, and could have gone on that way forever; humans can last as long as rocks if they are only wise enough not to grind the boulders into dust. The writer must have noticed Gabo Djara's objection and his voice mellowed: "I'm afraid it is all written down in my doctrine on progress." The *balanda* assumed that the misunderstanding had been brought about by cultural differences, but as soon as the emancipation was set in train, Defector would be at hand for guidance and advice. Gabo Djara felt at odds with this idea of advice. What more was there that a hunter should know but his land, and the need to keep faith in those who shaped it? The ant looked deep into the writer's eyes in puzzlement. Why had this meeting taken place now, or at all? Had the white man mistaken him for someone else? Gabo Djara crawled to the edge of the palm with both feelers outstretched, probing empty space in search of something ... anything to grip and so make his departure.

The white man muttered something about Defector, then went on saying that the miners sweat more than any other workers. He praised the man who quarried the rocks, claiming that Saint Paul mentioned them in the Scriptures often, then, glancing to the wall behind, he explained that Moses spoke of them, too. On the wall was a mural of an old bearded man with a walking stick whom Gabo Djara had seen before pictured in a book carried in Sister's grasp. The white man's prophet was leading his people across the sea—which looked much smaller in the picture—and had elbowed aside two great walls of water to make a pathway for his tribe. But what were they running away from? Had their country, too, been pounded into dust and they were in search of a new land? The ant stared at the scene; should he have done the same? Gabo Djara knew, however, that with Namanama gone, there was only one path he could follow and that one led to the spirit world, precarious as it might be when pursued by machines. While looking at the mural, the ant was told that now that blue collar workers are entitled to wash their hands before every meal, it has been discovered that there is not enough water to go around: "Here in Europe we have to melt snow; that is why you are here, I gather."

On the wall beside Moses was another picture—that of a man with rolled-up sleeves and raised hammer. His clothing sagged under the weight of sweat, dust, and grease and he reminded Gabo Djara of . . . Yudu! How could that man be here? The white face clouded with anger, and one corner of his lip caught between his teeth as though he, too, were wounded.

"Undoubtedly, you two have met before," said the writer. Gabo Djara realized that the pick handle in balanda's hand was the same as he had seen before, though the hammer looked new. Yudu's hand rose and shaped itself into a fist. With his jaws clenched and his teeth bared in a snarl, the hammer resting on his shoulder and his fist raised high in the air, the man stepped out and marched along the wall! "I want my spoon," he snarled.

Swooping through the air on his host's palm, Gabo Djara became aware that he was witnessing a white man's ritual— an uncommon ceremony dear and precious to these humans . . . perhaps even sacred to them. Should a stranger be allowed to see it? The ant closed his eyes for fear of offending his bearded host. On the wall, the sound of marching feet rose louder, the room trembled, and a pile of plaster slid to the floor. As Gabo Djara peeped out of the corner of his eye, Yudu swung the hammer, smashing the wall where Moses had stood and crumbling the bricks into choking red dust. "I want water! Water!" he yelled. The ant tucked his feelers behind his head to shield them, and clung desperately to the swaying hand. He had no wish to end on the pile of debris.

When the writer stood up, whistling a marching tune and forming a fist with his raised hand, enfolding the ant, Gabo Djara expected to be squashed. He quickly learned, however, that no harm would befall him, for the white palm had not a single blister or even the callused remains of one—and the soft skin pressed silkily against the ant's abdomen. One of the fingers which folded so close was stained with a dark blot of ink, and suffused with an unfamiliar smell. How glad the ant felt that his captor had never held anything more vulgar than a pen or a spoon, to roughen the hand in which he was enclosed.

Crawling, later, across the paper stacked on the table, Gabo Djara learned that he had not emerged from the fist quite unscathed, for one of his feelers dangled uselessly and when he tried to lift it he felt a stab of pain. The picture of Yudu was gone and at the end of the wall where he had marched was a broken opening through which fragments of stormy sky could be seen. The floor was littered with crushed bricks and mortar, one of the larger pieces of which still displayed Moses, but one-eyed now and very ragged of beard. Gabo Djara shrank from the smell of this unnatural dust, and looking down at the debris, he was grateful that he had not been flung to the floor to be buried there in the same dust as the white man's prophet.

The sound of the scratching pen making its way across the paper filled the air again as Gabo Djara moved discreetly toward the edge of the desk, trying not to distract the writer and pointing his guiding feelers toward the hole in the wall.

"*Das Kapital.*" The writer flung a large volume. The whole weight of the book landed on the top of the ant, crushing him into the dust. "Read it. Everything you ought to know I have written there."

Gabo Djara lay still, the great volume like a heavy boulder pressing down on his helpless body. How many words loomed there, above him? More than all those rocks, trees, and birds at Namanama perhaps—and how, wondered the ant lying in the dust, could a man who had never earned a single blister have written so much about workers. What collar would he wear?

Chapter 25

SOMETHING must have happened to Sir Rock-Pile. Not that there had been any news to that effect, or even any rumors spreading, but the machines had stopped. The world was plunged suddenly into silence, drowning in a sea of dust and making no sign of a struggle to rise again. It seemed that the metal beasts had stopped to give their boss respite, but had themselves run out of breath.

The silence did not worry Gabo Djara. He walked over the pile of shrunken bodies, crept to a piece of broken glass, and, avoiding the sharp edges, crawled to the neck of the bottle. The pit around him was only half full; which had the whites run out of, he wondered, flasks or tribesmen?

The pit, a voice in length and a couple of spears wide, lay inside a fenced compound. At its far end, a cover of weeds had grown over the smashed glass, concealing the dump. It pleased Gabo Djara, at first, to see stems and leaves springing out of the bare dust but only until he realized that the greenery was not rooted in rain-soaked soil, but in the bodies of his tribesmen. In the ditch around him, the refuse was still fresh; no wind came and the air was laden with such a smell of decay that . . . even *goarang*, the anteater, would find it hard to breathe. "Let's get on with the *gad*," whispered Gabo Djara, looking about in the hope that Marngit had gathered the tribal elders for a burial ceremony. How could they assemble, though, if they, too, were in the pit? Will Barg be in the pit? Though the *balanda* had his picture hanging on that auditorium wall, Gabo Djara expected that the young healer would be among his people.

A crashing of smashed glass shattered the silence; two men were scavenging in the dump, though there could surely be nothing of value to salvage. The whites had no interest in discarded bottles, and the handful of shrunken bodies they contained were of no use now. Gabo Djara crawled over the crest of the pile, climbed onto the top of a flask, and came face to face with Yudu and Usher. The men wore bush hats, with rows of corks hanging by strings from the brims to discourage flies. They hardly spoke, undoubtedly not so much out of respect for the dead as to shut out the smell of decomposing. Behind them along the bank of the pit moved the shadow of a dingo. Good old Waran, he is still about; spirits take longer to die than humans. Gabo Djara dodged inside a bottle, hoping to evade the whites. In the bottom of the flask lay a cluster of stiff bodies and, clinging to the corpses, the ant tried to crawl underneath, wondering as he did so if Marngit might be there, or perhaps in one of the other bottles? Spirits do not die easily, though they might fall into such a trance as to seem lifeless. Gabo Djara hoped that if he could find the old medicine man, together they might breathe life into others—into enough tribesmen to stage the *gad*—the burial ceremony. The tramping of boots came closer, the splintering of glass reechoed inside the bottle, and the ant burrowed deeper beneath his shrunken brothers. A long chant and strong *dal*—

powerful magic—might restore those lives but . . . Gabo Djara wondered about the lack of ubar and didjeridu, for without the sound of the hollow pipe and the sacred log the spirits might never hear his chant. Perhaps if. . . The bottle slammed against a metal edge, the glass shattered, and the cluster of ants slid into a bucket.

If I find Barg, should he be buried with the rest?

"Give the bucket a shake, that's right. I'll read the service when it's full to the brim." One of Usher's hands pressed a handkerchief against his mouth, while the other clutched a book.

The bucket swung in Yudu's hand, shaking down the contents, and Gabo Djara pressed closer, as never before, to so many of his countrymen. Most of the bodies were quite stiff; mold had already grown on some, but a few still showed a hint of warmth. A limb or a feeler twitched here and there. As though too weak to grab for life, the insect was only strong enough to signify that the end was near. Gabo Djara dragged himself to the rim of the bucket and looked out, over the pit. Though there seemed to be nothing there but bottles, perhaps the ubar and the didjeridu were somewhere about, for the pipe and the log had never been parted from the tribesmen in all their long history, and so it was likely that they too would have been bulldozed into the ditch. Waran's shadow moved again, passing over the pile of bottles.

Yudu put the bucket down. "They're getting heavy . . . that's enough. Come on, now, get on with the bloody blessing."

The book looked much like the Atomic Act, seen so long ago, except that a cross replaced the words on the cover. Usher held the book over the bucket. He assumed a pious expression and whispered, "You brought nothing to this world and shall take nothing. Ashes to ashes, dust to dust . . ."

Why must they carry on like that? Gabo Djara had no choice in his way of burial, but if he did, the vote would certainly have rejected the Christian style. There was still a hope that

223

the medicine man might appear with the breath of life . . . but what if the *dal* did not work so well on those forced into another faith? Even if it did work, Gabo Djara feared that he and the others might turn up in Jesus' spirit world instead of in their tribal country. If I found him would Barg be any good at breathing life back to those poor souls? He was young when he was initiated. Marngit must have been in a hurry to leave and had little time to teach the boy to be a good healer.

Gabo Djara suddenly realized that there might not be a burial after all. Usher levered up the lid of a large drum and as it clattered to the dust, acidic fumes belched into the air from within. Yudu shook the mass of decomposing bodies in the bucket, picked up a handful of those looking rather less moldy, and threw them into a trough made of insect-proof mesh. What corpses remained were tipped into the ill-smelling drum and stirred with the pick handle. "There, now. They should burn up all right." He breathed heavily, as he mixed the grisly brew. The dingo sat on the pile of bottles watching him.

"What about the ones you've left out?"

"I'll have a go at fattening those up. They'll yield all the more then."

"They all look pretty stiff to me. Can you really do anything with them?"

"I reckon so. Abos die hard, you know."

Gabo Djara lay flat, afraid of showing himself to be any different from the others. Beside him, entangled in the wire mesh, was a small cockatoo feather, dirty and tattered, but still a sign that Marngit might be around, for the medicine man never strayed far from his ceremonial headdress, even though only such a small fragment of it remained. The *dal* would still be stored in the feather and when night fell, and the whites retired to their own world, Marngit should appear; or would Barg come instead?

Usher moved closer to the drum: "I'd better make tracks

to the airport—I don't want to be late for Sir Rock-Pile's funeral. You'll be able to manage on your own?"

The handle stopped spinning. "No man should be on his own here." Behind him, at the approach of the dump lay a battered sign proclaiming URANIUM ENRICHMENT PLANT, but it was uncertain whether this had been discarded or actually erected there.

"Don't spill any of that, will you? Every bucketful makes more yellow cake, remember?"

Yudu stopped, doffed his cork-string hat, and wiped his forehead with a sweep of his arm: "The funeral will be pretty spectacular, so I've heard." His voice quivered and then he admitted to being nervous at being left alone. Usher apologized, but thought that it would be most inappropriate for him, as a state official, not to attend the funeral of the man who in his lifetime fought mountains and changed the shape of the land. He held out the book: "Here . . . you'd better have this; read a sentence or two for each bucketful." He assured Yudu that if there were any tribal phantoms about the good Christian words would chase them away quicker than anything else.

Gabo Djara's left feeler failed to itch and he wondered whether Marngit lay on the pile, or had wandered off into the bush . . . but no . . . Namanama was no longer a country of trees and scrub, just a sea of dust. The ant climbed cautiously to the lip of the bucket and stretched both feelers out to the desolate scene. An immense claypan spread from one foot of the straddled sky to the other without a single rock jutting above the flat bare ground. Marngit would have to travel far in search of a suitable hollow tree to make a didjeridu. And what if there were none left growing? Then he would have to try to heal the country first and when gugu, the yams, began to grow in the ground and bushes sprang from the dust, he could cut a branch and make a djad—a digging stick—with which to gather the food from the soil. Only then would he bring out the tribesmen to start afresh in the country. There was no stone for making *ngambi*, the spear-blade . . . ah, but the rocks could grow again as everything had first grown long ago, at Namanama. Then again . . . yes, it would be best if the rocks did not return, for Gabo Djara reasoned that if the spirits did not make boulders, then the white man would not come in search of them.

Stirring the drum made Yudu sweat profusely. As he halted to wipe his forehead, he suddenly saw the dingo snarling at him. The man swung the pick handle, but the dingo clung with his teeth to the wood and held firm. They wrestled for a while, but the handle broke. Left without a tool, Yudu backed away, kicking the dust in the face of the raging animal. Retreating, *balanda* came to the edge of the pit, then slid down on to the pile of bottles. Gabo Djara found it wiser to keep his eye on the white man's tool rather than on the man himself; he looked over the dusty ground, searching for the two pieces of broken handle. When darkness fell and Marngit came, those two chunks of wood could become *bilma*. Though the clapping sticks might not be stained with *malnar*, and would not sound as they should, joined with the chanting of the medicine man, their message would surely reach the spirit world. Tomorrow, or perhaps the day after, Jambawal would show that he heard and appear in the sky, rolling the clouds from the faraway sea across the mainland; and with him would come Jingana, the mother, to give new life to the country. It dawned on Gabo Djara, however, that Marngit must have hastily initiated Barg as a tribal healer so that he could be free to hasten to the spirit world. While there, Marngit would try to pursue the tribal ancestors to bring help to Namanama—poor old soul, what else was there that the man could do?

Chapter 26

THE bell tolled, distant and unreal.

Its peal had no sharp metallic edge and when heard thus it sounded much like a stick slamming against a carcass. Gabo Djara guessed that the sound was muffled by the flag draped over Sir Rock-Pile and that most of the clamor was forced to vent itself somewhere far away. Much better that way, Gabo Djara thought, for when he had witnessed mourning rituals other than those held at Namanama, he had observed that white men were inclined to overplay their emotions at the expense of dignity. While the *balanda* persisted with their ceremony, the ant, hiding under the flag, dozed off.

No warmth came for Sir Rock-Pile; no patches of moss and lichen clung to his sides. The boulder had undergone another change—become shrunken—and though Gabo Djara was unable to see its color, the shrouded shape suggested a pile of dust . . . hardened dust. Two women were whispering and their words made the ant suspicious that some plot was being hatched. A female hand sneaked under the flag; it held a safety pin. Gabo Djara thought he was to be the prey, and stretched out his feelers looking for an escape route under the flag, but the point of the pin passed him by to gouge at the surface of the mound. "Quite soft, I'm afraid. He's dead all right." The female voice sounded familiar. Would that be the woman in the dingo fur coat? The ant tried to remember. Again the woman pinned the rock. "He snuffed it without paying for my mink—that phantom bug got him, too." The woman sounded content, as though justice had been done.

Gabo Djara smelled a whiff of chalk powder, then realized that the scent came from his memory, not from the air. His feelers caught the smell of dingo fur. Would the woman be still wearing that coat? *Waran* has a tough skin, the garment could outlast *balanda*. Gabo Djara remembered distinctly the day he met the woman at the Stock Exchange and her complaint about the damaged mink, for that was the day he first saw Sir Rock-Pile on his pedestal. That time, a whole generation past for the white man, was for Gabo Djara, who had been around for millennia, scarcely more than yesterday. Had others present on that occasion also come to pay their respects to the deceased? The woman's hand withdrew, leaving a hollow space under the flag where it had sneaked in and out, and the ant crawled along this tunnel until he could peer out. There was little of interest to see, however, only human limbs passing slowly around the pedestal, tiptoeing as though Sir Rock-Pile had dozed off, and the mourners were anxious not to waken him.

Gabo Djara crawled further forward and peeped out from under the flag. He had assumed that the place was an abbey, but no. Against the wall stood a board listing mining stocks, but marked with a red sticker reading "Trading Suspended" and on a platform below two clerks dressed in dark suits stood motionless, with bowed heads. Gabo Djara waited for either man to move, but they stirred only to blink. The gallery opposite was filled with faces that the ant had seen once before, and these, too, were quite still. The man with the binoculars was there and Gabo Djara shrank back for fear that he would be sighted, before he realized that the security man was actually human and, stricken with grief, stood stiff and unseeing.

A long, strange shadow fell across the trading floor, exaggerated by the light from the main entrance. When Gabo Djara raised his eyes he saw a monstrous anteater holding Sir Rock-Pile's lance, and waiting to give the master the Last Rites. The ant held his breath a moment and then cautiously crawled back under cover.

The tolling of the bell quickened, splitting the stale air. A baculus passed by, followed by the mourners, but from under the flag Gabo Djara could only see a white hand clasping the rod. Stretch as he might, he could not see the face of the bearer. A wreath being laid from above pressed the flag down on the lifeless shape that had been Sir Rock-Pile and encircled the ant who leaped backward and began to worry about the cloth which threatened to enshroud him. He thought of making his way out for a moment, but hesitated, uncertain whether he should emerge into that gloomy world of human grief. What good would it do? Should he stay there under the cover . . . but that would be pointless. Gabo Djara decided that he preferred to struggle on and seek a way out rather than to remain and be buried with the white man's pageantry and honor.

By the time the ant had chewed his way out, the band of silver trumpets had played the Last Post and a salvo of gunfire boomed out to set the solemn mood for the procession. As Sir Rock-Pile and the mourner left the Stock Exchange the weather was mild, for though the sky was overcast, there was no hint of rain or storm. It seemed that the spirits, black and white alike, had chosen to stay away.

Where were they taking him? Gabo Djara crawled up the flag. From the top of the mound, he could see that Sir Rock-

Pile, or . . . anyway, whatever remained of him . . . rode on a trailer towed by three bulldozers rattling through the wide, empty streets. Ahead of the machines marched a military band, the beating of their drums and the blare of trumpets competing with the metallic rumble of the caterpillars and winning the admiration of the crowd lining the route. Flanking the trailer marched a guard of honor—men in safety helmets carrying picks, sledgehammers, pneumatic drills, and kegs holding enough gelignite to blast many a mountain out of existence. The men, all dressed in singlets and heavy boots, tramped with noise and vigor, till drops of sweat glistening on their sun-darkened skin began to roll from necks and shoulders down over the slogans tattooed there. Gabo Djara craned his head to read some of them, but at that moment the trailer hit a bump in the road, the ant flew off into the air, and only by clutching at the flag as he passed it on the way down, did he avoid being thrown under the marching feet.

Where were they going with Sir Rock-Pile? Gabo Djara expected that the whites' burial site would be bigger than the cave and Jingana Billabong. There would be no *waramu*, mortuary pole, of course, but a cross instead and maybe the *balandas* would have a bulldozer at the graveside to provide eternal peace and to chase away malignant spirits. The Usher of the Black Rod would organize all that, probably, and call from time to time to pay tribute to the deceased and bring a medal or two to pin on the machine for rumbling well.

Gabo Djara reared up in order to view the procession more clearly. Behind the trailer walked Usher, holding the lance in one hand and a book in the other, followed by other whites, their faces grief-stricken. The Queen, her face partly hidden behind her veil, looked exhausted, though the ant could not tell if this was from sobbing or from the strain of the march. Behind her walked kings, princesses, pontiffs, archbishops— all arrayed in a dazzling display of glitter, color, and decoration—and after them tramped generals, admirals, tycoons,

230

statesmen, many of whom Gabo Djara had met and talked to, though not at his own wish, or for the ultimate benefit of the black men. The ant moved his eyes slowly along the ranks of the procession, remembering as he gazed into each face when and where they had met before. As he searched among the marchers the ant hoped . . . but no, Jesus had not come; perhaps he had not been invited. Both feelers drooped in sadness that someone of similar rank and status to Gabo Djara's own had been ignored.

When a man dies at Namanama, Marngit beats the *ubar* day and night to warn the spirit world to make room for a newcomer. The body is placed in a hollow log, the tree bark stripped, the wood stained with *malnar*, and tribal designs painted so that the spirits can identify the totem from which the deceased has sprung, and know which lingo he speaks. No man is ever lost—alive or dead—if his soul is black; but could the whites promise the same for Sir Rock-Pile?

When he looked at the whites again, Gabo Djara saw that the procession had long since left the streets, and was moving through the countryside. A fanfare of drums and trumpets floated over green paddocks, bounded by low-trimmed hedges; no tall trees stood out, and though a slim sapling showed here and there, against the dull sky, none promised a hollow with room enough for the honored dead. Perhaps they would pound Sir Rock-Pile into dust and scatter the remains over the countryside. That would not be difficult; a few blows with a sledgehammer and the mound under the flag would shatter. Gabo Djara felt uneasy, perched on something that might well be pulverized, but where else to hide? The guard of honor still marched beside the trailer, but the men had exchanged their hammers and picks for a sewer pipe hefted on their shoulders. It was long, and quite wide enough to house every bit of Sir Rock-Pile, but Gabo Djara's roving eyes found no tribal marks upon it but a cross, painted in white over the glazed surface of the tube. It seemed too little to show which country and lingo the deceased shared . . . but why trouble with such thoughts? Sir Rock-Pile was not destined for Namanama and when he reached the white man's spirit world, Jesus—or whoever the *balanda* caretaker might be—would not know how to read tribal signs and messages accompanying the spirit of the dead.

The procession halted. Usher put down the lance and hastily shuffled the pages of the book, perhaps intending to read "ashes to ashes . . ." Or had the whites lost their way, and must now peep inside the book to find the right track to their burial ground? From the procession someone said aloud, "This should be the right way to the nuclear plant, surely." That must be the burial site, thought the ant. At Namanama the burial log would be placed in a rock shelter tucked between the boulders at the foot of Mount Mogo, barely a spear's throw from the billabong, but the spirit of the dead would find his way even if it were far and he blindfolded. Once he has reached the water and seated himself on the bottom of the pool, still hearing the beating of the *ubar* and chanting voices from the camp, Jingana, whether she is wandering the country or sunbathing at the boulders, knows that a man has returned to her. There the spirit will rest, in the peace of the billabong, and await rebirth, for the dead spring to new life with the arrival of the monsoon, and many make a fresh start as trees, birds, fish, and, the luckier ones, as boulders for eternity.

The procession marched on again. Behind the trailer tramped Usher, with his eyes on the open book under his nose. As Gabo Djara watched, he wished that the man might quickly find whatever it was he sought from the pages. The men in singlets breathed heavily under the burden of the sewer pipe; even the bulldozers were showing signs of strain, their rumbling taking on a note of whining complaint. The procession came to a road junction in grayish countryside and took a turn bearing the sign: To Nuclear Plant—No Through Road.

The dusk crept in faster than the whites had anticipated.

As a chill breeze sprang up, the ant gripped the flag tighter and shivered. Surely the ritual must come to an end soon, and hurriedly, if the whites were to find shelter for Sir Rock-Pile before the threatening storm and the night closed in. As the man behind the trailer lifted his eyes from the book, and Gabo Djara glanced skyward, lightning flashed, splitting the clouds, and on the ground below appeared a mountain molded out of concrete. There it is—the burial place, the ant told himself. The towers, much taller now, looked like pillars supporting the leaden sky and a flag at half mast still flapped on one of them. Yes, that was the place he had visited before—the ant stared toward the concrete towers, trying to recognize the bunker. Would God still be there? Gabo Djara suspected that the white man's spirit boss might have escaped from the drum but not for long. In a world where mountains are baked into cakes, every single soul will be cremated while the immortals are brought in to fuel the oven.

Above the concrete towers the lightning flashed again. Jambawal! Yes, the Thunder Man is here at last. The earth, struck by the lightning, jerked like a mortally stricken snake. Though so far away from Namanama, Gabo Djara felt some comfort in all his despair that the mighty ancestor had come to see him at the white man's burial site.

Chapter 27

AT last it seemed that the world had come to rest.

Gabo Djara drifted long a narrow tube, in a space which seemed packed with some foreign liquid, and although he unfurled all six legs in an effort to hold on to the surface, an irresistible force propelled him onward. What trick had the whites come up with now? Before being shoved within, Gabo Djara had been dressed in striped pajamas; the first clothing he had ever worn, either of this design and shape, or of the basic cloth strip model given by the whites to tribesmen to drape about their waists. Now, however, before the ant could refuse, the loose uniform was put on, and he was pushed inside the chamber which at first seemed to be a baking oven.

There was no sound; immediately around him the ant sensed a hard metal core and beyond that the presence of a thick wall—a whole mountain molded out of concrete to contain him. Gabo Djara marveled that the whites had troubled so much to build him such a shelter. A hollow log would have been a warm enough place for retirement and if the country could no longer yield a suitable tree . . . why, even a sewer pipe could provide a refuge in which to rest and await rebirth.

Though alone, Gabo Djara did not feel solitary, for he felt that outside the metal core Jambawal hovered above the concrete towers, in the shape of a cloud. No larpan showed yet, but the ancestor was fast changing into a dark turbulent mass, laden with tempest and anger.

Drifting, Gabo Djara was carried into a chamber, where the warm surrounding liquid began to grow hotter. A slight itching flickered at the tip of his abdomen and the ant swung one of his legs backward to scratch, but the limb fell short of the irritating spot. Gabo Djara struggled, trying to grip the surface of the chamber and rub his skin against the metal, but the drift forced him away, and he tumbled onward through the swirling liquid. The abdomen began to swell, suddenly, and before he could determine the size and shape of his expanding body, the ant felt as though he was trailing a balloon behind him. He could not recognize the new shape of that part of his body, except that it felt weightless, like a bubble, and seemed to be at the will of the drifting current. Gabo Djara stretched all of his six legs and made another effort to cling to the interior of the chamber, but the size of his body, thorax, head, and limbs were only a speck compared to the abdomen, and the irresistible fluid force was drifting away with it.

The liquid from the chamber flowed through a tube wide enough for the ant's head and thorax to pass but not the abdomen; it plugged the passage, the flow stopped, and it seemed as though the outside world did the same, holding its breath.

The whites have trapped me at last. Behind him Gabo Djara felt the melting metal and in front stood a passage too narrow to squeeze through. At some vague distance, workers rattled tools, sending sharp metallic sounds echoing through the network of pipes. Would they reach him? The ant wondered whether the whites were trying to save him or the machine, but whatever their purpose, it seemed to be beyond their reach.

"It could cause a meltdown, you know." The voice sounded like that of Yudu, but faint—perhaps weakened by fear, or maybe just muffled by the thick concrete walls.

"Don't panic; the chairman told us it is safe"—the voice of Usher was just as faint.

"To hell with him. There's a bloody dingo staring at me. It's flapping one of its ears. I don't trust that beast here—it might blow us all up."

"Just get on with the job, will you." Yudu was assured that the plant was safe and sound and that no dingo, whether a phantom or real, could cause any harm.

Gabo Djara assumed that *balanda* could see him, but they kept talking of the dingo, for they were too shy to admit that a man could be scared of a single ant. He suspected that, should the whites reach him, they would prick his abdomen and let the bubble subside, after which he could squeeze through the passage and let the liquid flow through—if there was any liquid left, of course. Behind, the heat grew, and the ant could sense the familiar atmosphere of Namanama—not the scent of pounded dust but a mysterious feeling of rock whirling into a pool of melting earth.

Yudu complained again: "That bloody beast is staring at me. Look, it is going to blow up!" he yelled.

"Have you ever seen a reactor exploding?"

"No, and if I do, I won't be able to tell about it, afterward, will I?" He warned his mate that, whether a phantom or a real beast, the dingo is not to be trusted and that the Red Alert should be given. "There it goes—the world!"

Silence fell again, dark and threatening.

When Gabo Djara next saw the light of day, he was already high in the sky, riding on the edge of an immense mushroom-shaped cloud. Too frightened at first to tell how fast or how high he had traveled, the ant then reflected that Jambawal works in strange ways. It was good that the ancestor had come at last and . . . it certainly did not take him long to do the job, a single sweep of the *larpan* and a huge flash of *maramara*! Such lightning—in a single stroke the whole country was lit by a flaring flash. The earth became a trembling speared fish and then, as though swept by an immense sea, it eddied crazily, before sinking into some immeasurable depth.

The pulsing tide of light spread fast. Gabo Djara watched it roll across the countryside, gulping green paddocks and trim hedges; the edge of a forest pricking the distance became, in a blink, a patch of bare earth strewn with ashes, a lake tucked among hills trembled, and as the land parted with the ugly mouth of a chasm, slid, silvery, into the unknown.

Never before had Gabo Djara seen Jambawal so angry. He had watched the ancestor after every Dry, making his way to Namanama, uprooting trees and splitting boulders with his mighty spear, should they stand in his way. He had roared, making the waves of the sea leap up and lash at the mangrove and pandanus forests along the coast, but however angry he became he had always calmed himself when he reached Ngaliur, and had split the clouds open to empty every drop of rain upon the country. Now, though, half a world away in the white man's country, the ancestor, all fire and dust, seemed driven by a rage such as the ant had never seen.

Borne on the rim of the cloud, Gabo Djara floated somewhere between earth and sky. Though his feelers were laid back to protect them from the storm, the strong scent of Namanama filled the ant's whole being, feeding him the hope that he was on the way to his country. Below, the tide of lightning washed against a cluster of buildings perched on a rise. Gabo Djara anticipated that a pillar of dust would form, similar to those he had seen so often when a willy-willy clawed at the bush, but there was nothing so spectacular to see; the buildings simply crumbled into a pile of debris. From the ruins emerged a large container, molded out of concrete and steel, and, buffeted about by the storm, it tumbled down the slopes. It seemed like a huge box but so enormous, ah . . . the vault! The ant glimpsed the heavy metal door, a human hand with skin and flesh stripped off still clinging to the handle, while the forearm thrashed aimlessly about. The vault hit a derelict bulldozer and the door swung open, disgorging a heap of shining metal bars which tarnished as they emerged. As the tide of light washed over the vault and the machine, the metal—to the last scrap—became a molten mass and oozed to the ground, forming a murky pond.

The molten pool spread across the earth and from this billabong rose, as usual after any storm, a rainbow arching between earth and sky. Gabo Djara watched and waited and . . . yes, they came at last—Specs, Usher, Queen, the pontiff (carrying a small statue of Sister), and the tycoons, all toiling up the rainbow, and behind them came the general, the black man with a bow tie, then a bearded face—it was hard to tell if that was Nobel or one of the early explorers; he was followed by Madame Curie carrying her rose. A human figure in a safety hat also climbed, silhouetted against the sky. As it turned around, Gabo Djara thought the time had come at last to see the white face which had tracked him for so long, but instead of flesh, only an emptiness lay there. The hat jerked as if trying to convey some message as it moved upward, and a briefcase followed it at a distance, with the flexible hose of the anteater poking out as if to sniff the way. As the rainbow began to tremble and then to melt, the machine emerged from the briefcase, rapidly grew into a ball of flame, and though it tried to squeal, the sound was cut short before it could be heard. A moment later only a puff of smoke remained and even that was fast dispersing into the air.

Far beyond the scene on the leaden horizon, Recluse's face was silhouetted. Gabo Djara was going to ask to which world the man belonged, but realized he had known it ever since the first day he saw him on that book.

Far below and scores of skies away Marngit appeared at last, sitting on the dusty ground. His figure contrasted sharply with the green patch that had grown over the burial pit. He held *bilma*, two sticks from the broken pick handle, and while clapping them, he looked into the distance as if seeking to trace the sound of his floating voice. Gabo Djara listened, too, and tried to tell if the chanting was to soothe Jambawal, or to praise the ancestor for coming in anger at last, with his mighty spear.

Glossary

bala—initiated one
balanda—white man
balbak—termite tree
barg—kangaroo
barung—barramundi fish
barura—non-sacred ceremony
bilma—clapping sticks
boberne—mosquito(es)
bogo—spear, with wooden blade barbed on one side
boiweg—gecko
boong—derogatory term for Aborigines
bulg—tufts of wild cotton or feather down used for body decoration
da—stringybark tree (*Eucalyptus tetrodonta*)
dal—magic power
dalangurk—kurrajong tree and nut (*Brachychiton paradoxum*)
damo—three-pronged spear

didjeridu—immense deep-note wind instrument made from up to eight feet of hollow tree
diridiri—pubic hair
djad—digging stick
djalg—waist cover; paperbark tree, piece of paperbark
djalkurk—orchid
djamar—feather headdress
djang—spiritual ancestors, objects, and sites
djeno—forked tongue of serpent
djumala—banksia
djungun—young unmarried woman
dodoro—pigeon
Dreaming—myth of creation
dudji—fire-making sticks
gabo—ant
gad—ceremony, ritual
gadayka—bloodwood tree
gaidba—call invoking spirits
galei—woman, young wife
galgal—white ant, termite
galpar—stone axe
gara—stone spear
gargu—sandpaper fig
goarang—anteater
gugu—yam(s)
gulwiri—palm nut, coconut oil
gunuru—woollybutt (Eucalyptus miniata)
gurg—color fixative obtained from plants
jagnara—pandanus tree and fronds
ja, ja—calls invoking spirits
jamba—tamarind tree
jogu—lily
julunu—purple beech convolvulus (Ipomoea pes-caprae)
jurdu—beehive, honey
larpan—ritual spear carried by Jambawal

lharang—quinine bush (*Petalostigma pubescens*)
lida—ritual objects
lingar—snake vine
magarada—peace-making ceremony
maidja—breast girdle worn by girls
malambi—quail, tribal totem
malnar—red ocher pigments
marain—sacred
maramara—lightning and thunder
marngit—medicine man, healer
mimi—spirit people
minda—mistletoe tree (*Exocarpos latifolius*)
minimbaja—porcupine grass
mogo—crocodile claws
muljurun—ironwood tree
munbi—styptic tree (*Canarium australianum*)
murga—dilly bag, worn around neck
nagigid—sorcerer
Namanama—tribal country
ngadu—damper baked in hot ashes
ngambi—stone blade(s)
ngerdno—dead
ranga—sacred ceremonial object
ubar—hollow log used ritually as drum, sacred ritual
waku—nephew
waran—dingo
wuramu—mortuary pole
wardu—malevolent spirits
wawa—brother
wongar—world of spirits
worki—wattle tree (*Acacia latifolia*)
yudu—child or child in a cot
yuln—tribal man